WITHDRAWN

Why I

—LOATHE—

Sterling Lane

Why I LOATHE Sterling Lane

INGRID PAULSON

Entangled Publishing, LLC
2614 South Timberline Road
Suite 109
Fort Collins, CO 80525

Entangled Teen is an imprint of Entangled Publishing, LLC.

Visit our website at www.entangledpublishing.com.

Edited by Kate Brauning
Cover design by Erin Dameron-Hill
Interior design by Toni Kerr

ISBN: 978-1-63375-700-4
Ebook ISBN: 978-1-63375-701-1

Manufactured in the United States of America

First Edition June 2017

10 9 8 7 6 5 4 3 2 1

For My Ry.
May you never bring home a boy
like Sterling Lane.

REASON 1:

NO ONE, AND I MEAN

NO ONE,

DELAYS THE START OF CLASS.

*P*er Rule 10 and common sense, I arrived at my first class thirty minutes early to secure my usual seat in the middle of the front row. That privileged seat was the best vantage point for taking notes, with the added benefit of showing the teacher exactly how much time I spent preparing for every lecture.

The rest of my classmates wandered in like lost cattle, with less than a minute to spare.

When everyone was finally settled, forty-five seconds after the start of class, the door opened again. I looked up and smiled, determined that Mrs. Stevens would not see how distressed I was by her tardiness. She'd always been my favorite teacher; she was grievously underemployed as a high school history teacher.

But it wasn't Mrs. Stevens. It was a boy. A boy I'd never seen before. A boy who was out of his seat a full fifty-two seconds after the start of class.

Fortunately for him, Mrs. Stevens was detained elsewhere.

He didn't seem to realize his luck. Instead of racing to a desk, he just stood there, looking at us.

Transfers were a rare and exotic animal in our tiny, out-of-the-way boarding school. This unfamiliar face quieted the simian chatter of my classmates. Everyone was silent. Staring. I could imagine all too well how mortifying it must have been, standing there, tardy *and* alone. While I'd never allow myself to be the former, I could write a dissertation on the latter. That's always been the price I pay for my grades—a sacrifice laid at the altar of the Ivy League. A top-notch undergraduate education was the key to getting into a prestigious law school.

Just as I started to feel sorry for the new boy, he cracked a grin that made those few tenuous tentacles of empathy snap back like a rubber band.

It was too brazen, too smug. Like we were all beneath him somehow. It was the type of smile that firmly cemented him in the ranks of the cool, confident students. Of the ilk who had nicknamed me "Harper the Hag" and hurled curdled milk all over my dorm room door when I got the basketball captain suspended from the team right before regional finals. Contrary to popular misconception, I didn't do it to be spiteful. He'd been on the verge of failing three finals and broke down during one of our tutoring sessions.

True to his smile, the new boy sauntered down the aisle slowly, dramatically, without so much as glancing down at the faces he passed. When he reached the last row, he settled noisily in the corner desk, stretching his long limbs out in front of his chair. Head tipped back and eyes closed. Like he was lounging next to a pool and inviting the whole world to take him in.

I twisted all the way around in my seat, ignoring the curious gazes of the few students who weren't doing the same.

The first thing I noticed was his tan. He had the kind of even, flawless glow few people had the dedication—or leisure—to achieve. It came from weeks and weeks of doing nothing at all but relaxing in the sun. You couldn't do a single productive thing, or the UV just didn't hit right. In the bronzed planes of his not-altogether-unpleasant face, I saw weeks on a sailboat and endless afternoons reading in a chaise at the end of a pier.

Sunglasses rested on the top of his head, and the moment he was settled, he slid them onto his nose, completing the sunbathing effect. He was planning to just sleep in class. I was sure of it. Rules 47 and 68 shook their heads in disapproval.

Since second grade, I'd carefully cataloged the behaviors that ensured success and happiness. The first three came from my mother. She died just a few weeks later, but I know she would applaud how unswervingly I'd adhered to her instructions. Just like she said, I always looked out for my brother, my room is cleaned and organized per her specifications, and my grades have always been above reproach. Over the years, the list had grown into 537 Rules that guaranteed I'd never even contemplate sleeping through class.

My careful observation of the new boy was so absorbing that I didn't notice when Mrs. Stevens materialized at the front of the classroom. I glanced at my watch. We were already four minutes and thirty-seven seconds into first period.

"I apologize for the late start." Mrs. Stevens moved across the classroom, distributing stapled packets of paper. "This handout outlines the details of our spring project."

I practically sighed with relief as I slid the handouts into individual plastic sleeves and filed them in my Master

Course Binder. Then Mrs. Stevens picked up the class roster to take attendance. She'd successfully checked off seven names before she hit a stumbling block.

"Sterling Lane," she called out.

The name mowed me down like a runaway semi.

Courtesy of my twin brother, Cole, I'd heard the rumor that Sterling Lane might be transferring to Sablebrook. His name had meant nothing to me, but Cole had filled me in on all the sordid details. Sterling's rap sheet had expulsions from all the big New England boarding schools—Choate, Andover, Exeter—even Proctor couldn't put up with him for more than a semester. Our lacrosse team was ecstatic at the prospect of admitting him, but the administration was nervous at best. So I'd assumed they'd never capitulate. Sterling's father was an admiral, his uncle a senator, and his grandfather had founded some New York investment firm. But even *those* family connections had been taxed past their limit trying to compensate for Sterling's profligate ways. No wonder I'd been immediately wary of him.

Mrs. Stevens looked around the room at each of the familiar faces she'd taught all year, coming to a stop at the chestnut-haired stranger slumbering in the corner.

The guy in front of Sterling nudged him. Sterling jumped. He slid the glasses down the bridge of his nose and peered over the top of them. I glanced at my watch again.

I had fourteen summer internship applications to complete and AP coursework in five subjects, including an independent study in history since the full AP course wasn't offered at Sablebrook. I couldn't afford these juvenile dalliances.

"Pardon me," Sterling said, showcasing his perfect New England diction. It was a stark contrast to the South Carolina twang the rest of us were prone to. "I didn't realize you wanted my attention." He gave Mrs. Stevens an insincere but charming smile. I could hear his political genes activating, pumping liquid lies right into his bloodstream.

"This is ridiculously immature," I snapped. "Can you please just pay attention? The rest of us are here to learn." It was against Rule 85, and therefore my nature, to blurt things out in class. But Sterling's little saga had already dragged on far too long. A few eyes turned my way, including Sterling's. I tapped my watch, reminding everyone that time was ticking past.

"I'll overlook it this once," Mrs. Stevens said. "But it's unacceptable for you to sleep in this classroom."

"Narcolepsy," Sterling said, flashing teeth that any orthodontist would be proud to claim. "Flares up now and again."

I actually rolled my eyes, not caring who saw. We were seven minutes and twenty-seven seconds late starting class.

"Maybe if you removed your sunglasses, the light would help you stay awake." Mrs. Stevens's voice was razor-sharp.

"I'm afraid that's not possible." Somehow, Sterling managed to sound genuinely sorry. "Diagnosed with a rare eye condition. Allergic to halogen lightbulbs." The words unleashed a ripple of nervous fidgeting, like people do when they're fighting hard not to laugh.

"I'm sorry to hear that," Mrs. Stevens replied in a tone that strangled any student giggles threatening to escape. "I had no idea such a condition even existed. But that's an issue you'll have to take up with the headmaster. I'm afraid until he tells me otherwise, I can't permit your eyewear in my class."

"I have a note from my allergist explaining the situation."

Sterling produced a folded, tattered piece of printer paper from his shirt pocket. "I'm the only reported case. Ever. They may name it after me."

"Speak with the headmaster, Mr. Lane," Mrs. Stevens said firmly. "You're excused from class until you do."

My heart performed a little tap dance of victory as I watched Sterling Lane rise slowly and tuck in the tail of his dress shirt, which had become dislodged during his little nap.

With Sterling gone, Mrs. Stevens deftly steered the class back to its proper course. I'd just settled into my usual routine when the classroom door opened with yet another interruption.

"Mrs. Stevens, may I have a word in the hallway?" Headmaster Lowell asked.

From the way Sterling sauntered back to his chair, I knew I wasn't going to like this.

Minutes later, Mrs. Stevens returned, shoulders slumped. I turned and watched the way Sterling aimed his crocodile smile right at her when he positioned those sunglasses back in place.

Mrs. Stevens stared at the roster as she said, "I understand you need someone to take notes for you, Sterling, as a result of your carpal tunnel syndrome."

"Yes, ma'am," he said, smiling bright as the midday sun.

"Quite a litany of ailments for someone so young."

"I appreciate your sympathy." Sterling stretched his long legs out into the aisle and crossed them at the ankles—a veritable picture of ease.

Mrs. Stevens looked so tired. I ached with sympathy. She'd always been my favorite teacher, ever since I'd signed up to help her tutor second graders at the elementary school on Tuesdays. She could balance being kind but firm while being smart and charismatic. It was forever eluding me, but one day I aspired to that kind of balance.

"Fortunately," Sterling continued, "Harper Campbell will be taking notes for me." At the sound of my name, I jumped like my chair had been electrified. Giggles erupted behind me.

When I turned in my seat, he was watching me. One eyebrow shot up. He couldn't have known who I was until the shock and confusion written all over my face gave me away. He must've found out my name ahead of time—and that my notes and study habits were as flawless as my academic record.

He'd done his homework.

I allowed myself a little flash of pride before the tsunami of irritation smothered it. An ambush was not the way to get in my good graces.

I opened my mouth to set the record straight, but the smile Sterling aimed right at me stopped me in my tracks. It was confidence incarnate. Warning sirens wailed inside my brain. *Tread carefully*.

"She'll also type my papers. Which I'll dictate, of course."

"Isn't that generous of her." Mrs. Stevens looked at me like I was now Sterling's accomplice in ruining her month.

I sucked in a lungful of air, ready to unleash a river of denunciations. I was outraged—and not just on my own behalf. He'd just victimized my favorite teacher.

Every face in the room watched me with thinly veiled anticipation, waiting for the show.

I took another deep breath, this time a calming one. If I called Sterling a liar, I'd fall right back into the Harper the Hag trap. I'd give my peers the circus act they so clearly had come to expect from me. I couldn't give them the satisfaction of watching me explode. I'd promised myself and Cole that this semester would be different.

So I bit my tongue. I'd set Sterling straight on my own time, on my own terms.

Sterling Lane had no idea who he was messing with.

REASON 2:

THIS WAS SUPPOSED
TO BE MY YEAR.

NOT HIS.

*S*terling Lane had squandered fifteen minutes and forty-eight seconds of the first day of history class. Fortunately, there were still eighty-nine days of classes in the school year, assuming no cancellations due to inclement weather. I had more than enough time to make up for one ruined morning.

As I headed to European literature, I spotted Cole perched on the broad stone stairs inside the entryway, talking to his friends. Normally, I'd wait for a chance to catch him alone, since I tended to drive his friends away or run my mouth and make things awkward for him. But I hadn't seen him for two weeks. I'd been stuck at home for break while he'd been at school training for lacrosse. We'd talked on the phone, but that wasn't the same. After the morning I'd had, I needed a friendly face more than ever.

So I wandered slowly in his direction, hoping he'd sense how much I needed to see him—and maybe even how much I'd missed him. Cole shifted, enough that I could see another person beside him on the stairs. Sterling. My heart lurched in my chest and I turned, ready to flee.

"Harper," Cole called out. He smiled and patted the spot next to him on the steps. There was no way to walk away without causing a scene for Cole. Plus, I wanted to see him more than I wanted to avoid Sterling Lane. I took a deep breath and walked over.

"What the hell, Cole?" a deep voice grumbled. The movable mountain who played defense on the lacrosse team and was a tireless bully in the school hallways loomed over Cole. "Blowing off practice? *Captain*. Coach was going to make us run sprints until you showed up. Which would have been hours. Where were you?"

I could tell from Cole's strained half-smile that he was uncomfortable, but it wasn't like him to let it show. It also wasn't like him to skip practice—lacrosse was as vital to Cole as oxygen.

"I had some things to take care of," Cole replied, but his voice was off. Something was wrong.

"Like what?" The mountain had no intention of letting the subject drop.

"Why don't you mind your own business," I said, regretting the words as soon as the mountain shifted his focus to me.

"Right back at you, Hag," the mountain replied. The word ripped into me like a bullet and I started to turn away. It was a mistake coming over here in the first place.

Cole shifted next to me, and I knew he was preparing to launch into my defense. And somehow that made it worse, that yet again he'd have to argue with his friends on my behalf.

"That's Cole's sister you just insulted. You know my thoughts on that subject." Sterling leaned back, propping himself on one elbow. I was dumbfounded. What subject? Surely he didn't mean me. The mountain turned to me. His eyes narrowed.

"I'm sorry." He ground the words out. Far from sincere, but I almost stumbled backward in shock anyway. He never backed down from anyone, yet a few cryptic words from Sterling had him apologizing to the school pariah.

"Cole had his reasons for missing practice," Sterling continued. "And if you can't handle a few sprints, time to hit the gym."

Cole shot Sterling a grateful look, and Sterling nodded ever so slightly. There had to be a reason Sterling was ingratiating himself with Cole. And whatever it was, I knew I wouldn't like it.

"Look, I need to talk to Harper," Cole told his friends, and my heart swelled. Of course Cole had read me like an open book. "I had a good reason for missing practice. I already explained it to Coach. I'll catch you guys later."

"That's our cue." Sterling rose. His cell phone chimed, and he glanced at the screen before striding away down the hallway, pressing it to his ear. "I always have time for you." Sterling's instantaneous switch from snappish to gentle was jarring. "I'll be there right after practice—and I'm bringing your favorite." That smooth, soothing tone was probably for some girl he was charming on the other line. "Oh, it is? Then put the nurse on the phone."

Nurse? I strained my ears as curiosity got the better of me.

"Look, my grandmother gets confused sometimes— would it kill you to just play along? I thought that was the whole point of putting her there." The gentle tone of moments ago had evaporated. He was all business. Sterling took a few more steps down the hallway, moving out of range, but I could see his hand gesturing emphatically to the nurse who couldn't see him on the phone. It seemed Sterling couldn't charm his way out of every problem. Still, I felt a little sorry for him as I watched him hang up the phone and sigh before disappearing through a classroom door.

"Was it about the new weight room?" the mountain asked, snapping my focus back to Cole and the matter at hand. The mountain still ignored his dismissal. "You got the funding for it?"

After the headmaster refused Cole's petition to upgrade the weight room, Cole had taken it upon himself to raise the funds—he'd launched an aggressive campaign, asking alumni and parents to contribute. And when they did, and Cole's results surpassed all expectations, the headmaster rerouted the funds to replace the gymnasium's roof instead. It wasn't fair and everyone knew it, but Cole was still determined to find a way to make good on his promise. He'd even thrown together a barbecue fund-raiser, hosted and prepared by the student athletes.

"Of course I got the funding," Cole said. "Did you ever doubt me?" He grinned, but something in his voice was off. Whatever it was, he'd tell me as soon as the others were out of earshot. Fortunately, his friends didn't notice. They were too busy celebrating the weight room news and clapping one another on the shoulder—like boys do to express affection or solidarity. Finally, they dispersed, heading toward class.

"Thanks for the care package," one of his friends called back.

A lump settled in my stomach. His thank-you was for Cole's benefit—they wouldn't have even acknowledged me if he wasn't here.

"That care package was for *you*, not them," I told Cole.

I'd missed him so much that I spent two whole days baking and assembling a box of his favorite desserts. Time I could have devoted to studying—or catching up on my favorite crime dramas. I don't allow myself to watch television when school is in session.

Still, my fervent baking wasn't entirely selfless. There was nothing like the precise movements and measurements of baking to put my thoughts back in order. For years I'd been reluctant to admit to such a domestic hobby, particularly in front of my father, but baking was in many ways a chemistry class. Mismeasure one simple ingredient and your chocolate cake will fall flat.

"Did you really think I wouldn't share? You sent enough to feed an army—either you're trying to fatten me up or you planned for me to share. It was sweet of you. And here's a tip: next time, tell him *you're welcome.*"

"Whatever," I mumbled. Even though I knew he was right. "We should head to class. You have European lit now, too?" Of course I already knew the answer. I always memorized Cole's schedule as well as my own.

He nodded and fell into step beside me. I wanted to tell him about my horrible morning—about Sterling Lane and how he'd ruined my favorite class. But I was trying to listen more to others, since that was on my list of social skills to practice.

"So you did it?" I asked. "You raised the money for the new weight room? I'm impressed."

He stopped walking and grabbed my arm, tugging me out of the stream of people heading to class. Surprised, I turned to face him. The intensity in his gaze made my shoulders tense up.

"I didn't," he whispered. "I came close. I did everything I could."

"Then why did you tell your friends you did?" I asked. "Just have another fund-raiser or something."

"It's too late for that." Cole glanced around nervously, clearly not wanting to be heard. But the hall was empty, meaning class was about to start. We would be late, and tardies could be recorded on our permanent academic records. My hands balled into fists at the thought. But I took one look at Cole's face and forced myself to breathe right through the tight-chested feeling. The panic in his eyes was infinitely more urgent than a broken Rule or two.

"Coach asked me about the money in front of a bunch of the guys, and I couldn't let them down. So I lied. And they all went crazy celebrating, so I couldn't take it back without looking like a total ass. I didn't know Coach would just start ordering things. I mean, I figured he'd ask again or something. But all of a sudden he was handing me this invoice and wanted to reconcile the budget. Since I was the one managing the money."

The pressure behind my eyes was back and building with every word.

"How much?" I asked. "How short are you?" I had nearly a thousand dollars in my savings, and I could get a few hundred more if I cashed in the savings bond our grandmother sent at Christmas.

"I need five thousand by Tuesday."

"Dollars?" I practically shrieked. "Five thousand *dollars*?"

"Shhh." Cole's glance darted up and down the deserted corridor.

"You have to tell them," I said. "Tell them before they spend more money. They'll understand."

"No, they won't," Cole replied. "They'll think I'm a liar. And a failure. My friends trust me. That's why I'm captain.

I'm supposed to be a leader. This will ruin everything I've worked for—you think they'll vote for me next year after this? If this got out, it could ruin my chances of making a professional team."

"Then go to Dad," I said. "He can give you a loan. Just until we figure something else out."

"Tried that," Cole said, shaking his head. "He said no. And gave me that lecture about how easy we have it. Compared to how they struggled when he was a kid."

I nodded. That rant always rankled me. *He'd* chosen to send me to a fancy school. I never asked for it. And still, I work twice as hard as anyone. My life was determined by *his* financial successes and *his* subsequent choices for us. While I admired my father's business acumen, it always seemed unfair that we were criticized for not living up to it when our professional lives hadn't even begun yet.

"Worst part is," Cole continued, "Coach told Dad about the weight room. That I'd come through. Dad called yesterday to say how *proud* he was—that he'd been wrong to doubt me." Cole shook his head. "I can't un-tell this lie."

I'd always figured the word "proud" fell outside Dad's emotional repertoire. Cole was right—he had to find a way to fix this without coming clean.

"Cole, I—"

"I didn't tell you so you'd feel sorry for me," he said. "So don't look at me like that. I told you because you'd understand. I was going crazy being alone in this. Look, I'll figure something out. I have an idea, sort of."

I took in the stubborn set of his jaw and the determination blazing in his green eyes. And I knew Cole well enough to be concerned. "Just promise me you won't do anything crazy," I said. "Give me time to think this through. I'll help you. I promise we'll figure this out."

"It's not your job to rescue me, Harps." His phone chimed and he glanced at it. His eyes doubled in size. "Shit. We are so late. I can't believe you didn't say something. Have you *ever* been tardy before?"

"Sure, lots of times," I lied. I hated seeing the guilt in his eyes, mingling with all his other worries. I followed a half step behind as he started walking toward the closed classroom door. My stomach swan-dived into my intestines at the thought of marching into that room. Me—late. Tardy. Fallen to the ranks of deviants like Sterling Lane.

"Promise me—Cole, seriously," I pressed. "I'm not going in there until you promise me you won't do anything. I'll figure this out. No bank robberies."

He grinned, and the weight of his worry disappeared in an instant. Cole was a ray of pure sunshine when he wanted to be.

"No bank robberies. Pinkie promise." He hooked his little finger around mine, the way we'd done since before I could remember. "Let's go. Given your attendance record, they're probably sending out an Amber Alert."

"Not something to joke about," I told him, opening the door.

"You say that about everything." His words were uttered to the entire class with absolute confidence no one would mock him. Everyone always liked Cole.

Mr. Halpern stopped midlecture and turned to look at us, one eyebrow arched.

"It's my fault," Cole told him. "Little family emergency. I'll take her tardy, too."

"Not a problem, Cole," Mr. Halpern said, smiling. "Just take a seat."

The two remaining desks were at opposite ends of the room, so I shuffled over to the nearest one and pulled out my Master Course Binder. Since I was never late, I was never unprepared to take notes when a lecture began. The thrum in my chest made my fingers shake as I pulled out my pen and frantically copied everything that had been scrawled across the whiteboard in those first few moments we'd missed.

I glanced across the room at Cole. He was staring vacantly at the board. A worry line pressed its way between his eyebrows, and he frowned at nothing and everything.

Knowing Cole, he'd fibbed about having a plan in order to reassure me. He knew all too well how I could worry myself into a panic attack. I glanced down at my notes, struggling to focus on the individual words. The fingers clutching my pen were white-knuckled.

I'd thought history class was horrible that morning, but watching Cole suffer was all-out excruciating. Even if I couldn't care less about lacrosse, the weight room, and the thorny territory of our father's approval, Cole cared passionately about all of them. So of course I would find a way to salvage Cole's situation. After all, I'd been rescuing him since before either of us could remember.

REASON 3:

I INTENDED TO JUST IGNORE HIM,
AND I REALLY DID TRY.

BUT HE SPENDS AN INORDINATE
AMOUNT OF TIME ENSURING THAT'S

IMPOSSIBLE.

*A*fter my regular lunch of carrot sticks and an avocado sandwich, I filed into physics early. Eating was far more efficient without the added burden of dividing my energy between food and conversation. That's why it didn't bother me that I always ate alone.

Since I had time to spare, I pulled out a blank index card and started listing all the money Cole and I could access. Per Rule 15, I was thorough. I'd saved money to buy new books for my second graders, but I'd give it to Cole instead and find a way to get by with what the classroom and library already had. Ultimately, those kids needed attention more than anything else. Yet no matter how I racked my brain, Cole and I were still four thousand dollars short.

I needed to be broader in my thinking instead of just scrambling to scrape together small sums. But how? Cole needed an anonymous benefactor, or else a way to host another fund-raiser without letting the team know why.

Something slammed into my chair. Like an earthquake.

Or like a shark taking an exploratory nibble.

Ink streaked across my note card, ruining my list.

I turned.

Sterling Lane sat in the chair behind me. Examining me with lazy brown eyes that reminded me of the cocker spaniel I'd had as a kid. In all my worry about Cole, I'd completely forgotten Sterling Lane existed. And now more than ever, I did not have time for his shenanigans. I would not be taking notes or typing papers or whatever other acts of servitude he envisioned. I set my pen down and prepared to set that Rulebreaker straight.

"Harper Campbell," he said. "I've been looking forward to actually meeting you. Didn't mean to catch you off guard in history. Cole and I tried to find you at breakfast." He looked so benign in that moment that I had to conjure the image of Mrs. Stevens's stricken face in order to summon the rage I needed to put him in his place.

"Save that slippery smile for the day you run for office," I told him. "Your antics in history class spoke volumes about what lurks behind it." Sterling's eyebrows rose. He glanced around as if wary of having an audience, then shifted closer, until our faces were barely two feet apart. My first instinct was to recoil, but I couldn't risk anything that would be perceived as backing down. Unfortunately, at that proximity, I couldn't help but notice the rich brown of his eyes, or how they were framed by ridiculously long eyelashes. They'd almost look feminine if the line of his jaw and the rest of his features weren't such a clichéd version of handsome. Not that it mattered.

"Easy there, tiger," he said. "Did I do something to offend?"

"I'm not offended, just incredibly busy."

"Right. You look like you're about to disembowel me. Look, the last thing I want to do is alienate Cole's sister, so whatever I did, I apologize."

"Whatever you did?" I repeated, incredulous. As if he'd already forgotten about his behavior in history class. "No need to pretend to be friendly for Cole's sake," I said. "I know you all laugh at me behind his back, and now you expect me play your little secretary? No thank you. But I have no doubt you'll bulldoze someone else into it. Until that time, I ask that you refrain from interrupting class with ridiculous fictional illnesses." I turned back to face the front of the room, but not fast enough to miss the way those hazy eyes perked up with interest. A new wave of exasperation washed over me as I stared at the card. Not only had he ruined my note card by knocking into me, he'd made me lose my train of thought.

"Interrupting class? Is that all it takes to get you this heated up?" he asked.

"No," I said, turning just enough that he could see the scorn on my face. "It was how you did it. You enjoy tormenting others. Lording your power over Mrs. Stevens, and now trying to manipulate me. Cole told me all about you—how you got expelled. And if you step out of line here, rest assured the headmaster will throw the book at you."

"Cole told you about that?"

I nodded. Even though I suddenly wasn't certain what we were talking about.

"Well, that's a first." His eyes narrowed as he surveyed me. "Most people give me a standing ovation for putting that asshole in his place. You're an odd one, Harper Campbell."

I had no idea what he was talking about—Cole had never given me any specific details about Sterling's past. But expulsion was expulsion, and Sterling had most likely deserved it.

"I'm glad you found someone to stroke your already sizable ego. But I think you'll find I'm not susceptible to your games."

"You know, that almost sounds like a challenge." There was a quiet menace in his voice that made the hair on the back of my neck stand on end.

I pulled out my notebook and pretended to be too engrossed in my studies to hear him.

"Harper, Harper, Harper." He sounded almost regretful as he repeated my name. Like he lamented my fate. "It's a strange name for a girl. It almost sounds like a boy's name. Is that why you did *that*?"

I didn't need to turn around to know what he meant. Someone like Sterling would have no trouble intuiting that I'd gone too far the week before when I'd ordered my dad's barber to cut my hair off, until it was shorter than Cole's. It had been an impulse born of practicality. I resented the time I wasted drying it almost as much as I hated going out in the winter with damp hair.

"Lemme guess." An edge crept into his voice, sharpening itself on each and every syllable. "Your parents wished both twins were boys. Decided to pretend you were one anyway. Something you took up a little too willingly. It's a shame. Minus the prune expression, you might make a pretty girl."

I stared at my notes, refusing to subject myself to his mocking scrutiny. But try as I might, I couldn't regain my focus.

"Maybe you should smile more," Sterling prompted. "Like Cole."

Those words were a Molotov cocktail, setting my whole psyche on fire.

Sterling Lane might as well have trespassed in my

father's thoughts and brought a few choice arrows to fling at my unsuspecting back. I had to work twice as hard as Cole to get a fraction of the recognition. I was constantly harangued to smile, to be gracious and gentle, instead of being a "spiny, sharp little sea urchin."

I didn't have time for Sterling Lane and his sadistic games.

"You don't know anything about me," I said, turning to face him. He watched my every move with the careful, calculating gaze of a chess master. My fingers strangled the edges of my desk. Rearranging his perfect face would violate at least five different Rules.

"I know enough. The rest I can infer." His mouth curved up a little as he poured coffee into the little cup of a sleek silver Thermos.

"You flushed when I called you pretty." He grinned like the Cheshire cat. "You liked that."

"I. Did. Not."

"Fine," he said. "I take it back. I was just being polite."

For some reason that stung more than anything else he'd said that day. "That's not what I meant…" I started to say, but the way he crossed his arms across his chest and leaned back in his seat was so malevolently self-satisfied that I swallowed the rest of my words. "Leave me alone." It came out like a plea. One that Sterling gleefully ignored. His arm shot out.

I tried to block him as he reached around my shoulder to grab my notebook off my desk, but he was fast—reflexes that had to have all the coaches adjusting their starting rosters. We scuffled for a moment, both tugging on the pages and collecting the curious stares of our classmates as they wandered in for the start of class. Which distracted me into giving Sterling the upper hand.

He sat back, holding my notes aloft. The pages wrinkled under his careless fingers as he shuffled through them.

"Pre-made notes and an outline?" He smiled like he'd crafted them himself. "I had a feeling you were just the girl I was looking for. Knew it from the way you're perched there all uptight, like you'd just sat on a telephone pole."

"Give me my notes." I managed to keep my tone polite, even if he hardly deserved it.

He released them into my waiting fingers and watched as I smoothed the wrinkles from the pages. He took another sip of his coffee, savoring it.

"If you'll consult section 1.3 of the student handbook, you'll discover that food and beverage are not allowed in class unless specifically provided by the teacher for educational purposes," I informed him. Because he really ought to know. "I have no intention of associating with a Rulebreaker. You can't have my notes. And you can't sit here."

One eyebrow shot up, a solitary sign of life in an otherwise impassive face. "Rulebreaker? Are we in kindergarten?" Then he winked. "Don't look so uptight. I'm not staying. I fly business class." He motioned toward the far corner, to a solitary seat under the open window with an unobstructed view of the football field. Outside, a group of girls were prancing around, rehearsing some sort of gymnastics routine.

Then he produced a money clip with a fat wad of cash. He pulled it right out of the tiny square shirt pocket that was intended for decoration only. He was carrying roughly a grand around like it was change for the parking meter. Money that would make a sizable dent in Cole's problem.

I stared as Sterling peeled off one crisp green bill after another, until I had to look away. Right down at the flash of his yellow shorts. He was dressed like he'd just blown in from a beach in Bermuda.

"Yellow shorts don't comply with the dress code," I pointed out. "And boat shoes are definitely not dress shoes. Either way, shoes require socks." I paused. "And you need a haircut."

He let his eyes search all over me in imitation. "Checking me out?"

"Your infractions are impossible to miss." I hated the flush creeping up my cheeks. "And I think you spend a lot of time making sure of that."

He laughed like I was making a joke. And a good one, at that. He even tipped back all the way in his chair, momentarily off-balance. Then he folded five crisp twenties in half and set them on my desk. They formed a little green pup tent pitched in the middle of the chipped faux-wood surface.

"That should cover it," he said.

I stared at the bills—at this offering from the gods presented by the devil himself. "Cover what?"

"Your time." He was already rising out of his seat. "There's a monthly bonus based on performance. Sliding scale. Double for an A—you can extrapolate the rest. Just learned I've got a literature paper due next week, apologies for the late notice, but I'm sure you're up for the challenge."

Cheat? Me? He assumed I'd jeopardize my entire future for a few paltry pennies, so that he didn't have to work?

Every muscle in my body convulsed in conflicted horror. All at once. I had a Sterling Lane–induced seizure.

I crumpled the bills and shoved them back into his hand.

His mouth curled into a wicked grin that should have warned me this wasn't over yet. "And to think I heard you were an absolute hag. I accept your generous offer of complimentary assistance."

"I'm not offering you anything," I replied. "Except the chance to leave. Right now. Before I take this to the headmaster." I turned, exiting that conversation before things got even worse. But an unmistakable odor demanded all of my attention.

"Is that—that's not just coffee," I stammered, pointing to the Thermos. While I could definitely detect the rich aroma of an expensive Italian roast, there was an undercurrent of something else. Something that had no business being anywhere but the crystal decanter in my father's study.

He looked at the steaming liquid, appraising it. "I take my coffee Irish on a morning like this."

Shock rendered me momentarily speechless. I needed to shift my focus away from this black hole of vice and back to my notes, but he was such a train wreck I couldn't turn away.

"A morning like what? A morning with classes?" The last word turned into a shriek. Curious eyes flickered my way, so I slid lower in my seat.

"How rude of me." He switched back into charming mode. "I'm not the only one who has to sit through this BS. Allow me." He pulled a second insulated silver coffee mug out of his bag and actually started filling it.

All I could manage was a slight shake of the head. There were no words. No words to convey the shock and horror building inside me.

"Oh, right," he said, winking. "You should stay sharp. Knew my grades were safe in your hands. Four-point-oh and all that. I look forward to doing business with you."

"I think I've been more than clear. I want nothing to do with you. I will not help you cheat—now or ever."

Sterling circled me until he stood directly in front of me, then he placed his palms flat on the surface of my desk, leaning down so that he was practically at eye level. "We'll see about that," he said.

"No, we won't. I'm not susceptible to your little games."

"Challenge accepted." He gave me a condescending little smirk that made my temper flare.

"This isn't a challenge," I said. "It's a non-negotiable, unilateral decree."

"Everything is negotiable." He slipped the words out as he strolled away—the exact second class started, like he had it on good authority I never left my chair once class started. It was *that* important to him to secure the last word.

I took out my notebook and documented every detail of Sterling Lane's depravity, even though I'd never forget even the tiniest little tidbit. Not as long as I lived.

Sterling Lane wasn't just an annoyance—he was a public menace. And I had every intention of staying as far away from him as our tiny campus would allow.

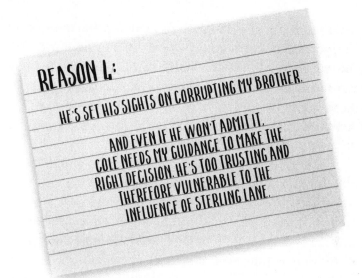

REASON 4:

HE'S SET HIS SIGHTS ON CORRUPTING MY BROTHER.

AND EVEN IF HE WON'T ADMIT IT,
COLE NEEDS MY GUIDANCE TO MAKE THE
RIGHT DECISION. HE'S TOO TRUSTING AND
THEREFORE VULNERABLE TO THE
INFLUENCE OF STERLING LANE.

I spent the afternoon studying, and in between history and physics homework, I slipped into the tiny kitchen on the lower level of the dorm. It had been all but deserted since the new microwave was installed in the upstairs lounge. No one but me did any real cooking—they just microwaved popcorn or heated up canned soup.

The kitchen was only minimally equipped, so I kept my own baking supplies in my closet. Baking was a secret I shared only with Cole.

Whenever life presented an insurmountable obstacle, here I could literally whip a solution together. The kitchen was where I did my best thinking.

I always started by premeasuring all ingredients and arranging them in optimal order—designed for ease of integrating the powders with the liquids and solids. I melted the butter and stirred in the sugar and eggs. With each beat of the whisk as I blended in the cocoa, the tension in my shoulders uncoiled. By the time I put the batch of

Cole's favorite double-fudge brownies in the oven, even the worry line between my eyebrows had smoothed out into nothingness. I'd give half to Cole and take the rest to tomorrow's tutoring session at the elementary school. At the start of the semester, I'd emailed the parents for permission to give the occasional treat. And to inquire about any food-related allergies.

I'd let Sterling provoke me. I'd been mean and let all my flaws come out and hurl themselves right at him. Regardless of what he'd done, Mom would have wanted me to be kind. Cole would, too. Shame made my eyes brim with tears that I angrily blinked away. Because I wouldn't let Sterling get the best of me like that again.

Now all I needed was to see Cole. I didn't have a solution for his problem—not yet. But I had been crafting a story we could tell Dad. Something that would loosen the chokehold on his purse strings. Nothing—not Cole's problems, not Sterling Lane—could shatter my focused, Zen-like concentration.

Tupperware of brownies in hand, I knocked on the door to room 412. A voice that was neither Cole's nor his roommate's called out, "*Entrez.*"

I turned the doorknob slowly. Who other than Cole or his roommate, Aiden, would be in their room greeting visitors?

The door swung open, away from me, taking my stomach with it.

Sterling Lane was lounging in a worn but expensive-looking leather club chair that was definitely not Sablebrook standard issue. And therefore contraband.

A mistake. I'd made a horrible, nightmarish mistake.

I took a step back, grabbing the knob to pull the door closed behind myself, but like Pandora, I was too late to shove that evil back into its box.

"Room service?" Sterling said, shifting in his chair. "Hardly necessary if you want your job back. A simple apology would suffice." The words were coated in a caliber of confidence that made my skin crawl. "Tell you what, I'm feeling generous today. Let's say one-fifty per essay instead." He pulled out his wallet.

I had to get out of there fast or I was seriously in danger of hurling Cole's lacrosse stick right at that smug face. I shook my head and clutched the Tupperware of brownies tighter against my chest. I wouldn't put it past him to somehow convince me they were actually his.

"That's not why I'm here," I said. "I'll never do your schoolwork."

"Oh, did you want something else, then?" He shot me a filthy little smile that startled the air right out of my lungs.

I blinked, once again frozen in place by the implications of his words. There was no way to respond to that. I took another step back, away. He couldn't mean it that way. I was misreading social cues, as always. That was the only logical explanation.

"I don't know what you're talking about." My temples pounded with my racing pulse.

"Oh? That blush tells me otherwise," he replied. "It tells me quite a bit, actually."

He reached behind himself and cracked the window. A thin and very welcome breeze crept through the room, ruffling the loose papers on his desk. He pulled a small silver box out of his pocket. He was wearing a silk smoking jacket, like he'd just time-traveled here from the Roaring Twenties.

"This is Cole's room," I said. "Why are you here?"

But I knew. There was only one reason Sterling would be sitting there, in a chair that was so clearly his. It explained all too well why he knew so much about me. Knowing my gregarious, warmhearted brother, Sterling Lane was probably Cole's new best friend and closest confidant. His new roomie.

"Apparently, I live here." He looked around the room with marked distaste, and I wondered for a minute what his other, fancier boarding schools had been like. Or where he lived the rest of the year. I vaguely remembered Cole saying that Sterling was from New York. My mind flashed from images of posh penthouses overlooking Park Avenue to sprawling mansions in the countryside, an easy commute to the city.

Sterling turned the silver case over in his hands. It was antique, expensive-looking. Then he opened it. I had to be seeing things—a trick of the light. Because from where I stood, it almost looked like a cigarette case. And smoking was against about a dozen school rules.

From inside the box, he produced two thin brown pencils. They were short, like the type of pencil bud used to record golf scores. I exhaled, relieved.

Until he lifted one to his lips and let it dangle there precariously. He looked a little like James Dean, or some other heartthrob from an era when smoking was socially acceptable.

"That's—those are cigarettes," I said.

"You don't miss a thing, do you?" He held out a cigarette, actually offering it to me. I managed to shake my head without letting it spin all the way around.

"Cole already has a roommate." I was clinging to that fact, wrapping it around myself like a blanket.

The second flash of silver was the lighter, produced

from a smaller pocket in the front of his weird silk coat. "Change of plans," Sterling said. Then he did it. He lit that vile death stick.

"You can't smoke in here," I hissed, careful lest anyone in the hallway hear me. After all, the door was wide open. And when it came to smoking, Sablebrook Academy had a guilt-by-association policy.

But the only reply I received was three painfully symmetrical smoke rings. One after another.

"This is Cole's room, too," I said. "And he hates cigarettes."

"Tell you what. I'll only smoke in my half of it." As if to illustrate how absurd his little compromise was, he turned his head toward Cole's unmade bed and blew three more perfect rings.

"Stop," I said. "You can't do that." But I was getting nowhere. "Where's Cole?" I wanted to charge across the room and shove that cigarette down his throat. I recited Rule 14: self-control is a virtue.

"I'm standing right behind you," Cole said, using a spooky ghost voice as he materialized at my back. "What's with the shouting? I could hear you all the way down the hall."

"Don't sneak up on me like that," I snapped. My anger was scrambling for an outlet.

"Chill." Cole reached out and squeezed my shoulder. "Sterling—I was hoping you'd be here when Harper came by. Really wanted the two of you to meet."

"As did I," Sterling replied. "It's a pleasure, Harper."

"I think we both know it's anything but," I told Sterling before turning to Cole. "He's smoking in your room."

"Smoking?" Cole frowned and looked back at Sterling. His forehead furrowed. "In here? It does smell weird."

Sure enough, Sterling's hands were empty. The silver cigarette case was gone, as were all traces of his weird brown cigarette. He lifted both eyebrows, making his eyes all wide and innocent. Then he shrugged and produced a thick candle ensconced in glass from the window ledge behind him.

"Scented." He was so proud of himself. I wanted to strangle him.

"He was smoking a second ago," I said. "He has a cigarette case in his pocket."

Cole laughed like I was making a joke, one that he didn't get and was too polite to ask me to explain. Sterling slid his leg off the chair arm and sat up. He reached into all three of the pockets in his smoking jacket and emptied them, one by one. Pulling the fabric all the way out so that we could see the quality of the silk lining. "See—no cigarettes. You must have been seeing things."

Cole was still watching me, puzzled, so he didn't see the way Sterling was maintaining perfect eye contact with me. Challenging me. And this time, I knew ignoring him simply wouldn't be possible. If he was Cole's roommate, it was now or never. I couldn't back down.

"Hallucinating a cigarette. That sounds just like me. Excellent explanation," I replied. "He's lying."

"Harper, calm down." Normally, Cole's soothing voice might do just that, but we were way beyond the meditation tricks he'd taught me.

"Why are you suddenly living with the Marlboro man?" My voice was getting loud enough to draw outside attention, so I took a deep, calming breath. I was here to help Cole—not to argue with Sterling. "Where's your real roommate? Where's Aiden?"

"He moved," Cole said. "His dad was transferred to

their Buenos Aires office last minute."

"Lucky for me," Sterling said, flashing a sunny smile. It was as out of place on his face as it would have been on that of any other dangerous predator. "I couldn't have asked for a better roommate."

It was too much—picking on Cole when Cole needed help. "I've had enough of your snide comments for one day, thank you," I said.

Cole's jaw clenched. It took a lot to make my brother angry. But I'd just crossed that line. "He wasn't being snide. Seriously, what is *wrong* with you, Harper?"

"He knows what I'm talking about, and that's all that matters."

"No, it's not," Cole said. "Remember our conversation about overreacting?"

I aimed my index finger at Sterling. "He was completely inconsiderate in history. You know how hard I work. You of all people know how important that history AP exam is to me. The entire class had to sit there for fifteen minutes and forty-eight seconds, waiting, while he regaled us with his idiotic health conditions."

Cole's eyes narrowed. "Idiotic health conditions? Empathy, Harper. Fifteen minutes is nothing in the grand scheme of things."

I could feel Cole slipping away from me, just as surely as if he were dangling at the edge of a precipice, with only my spindly arms to haul him back up to safety.

"Save your little treatise on empathy for Mr. Lane," I said. Inexplicably, a lump formed in my throat, turning my voice weak and mealy. "He humiliated me in Mrs. Stevens's class. He claimed I'd take notes for him because of his carpal tunnel syndrome. Just one more ridiculous lie."

Sterling parried with his most sadistic smile yet, white teeth flashing like lightning. But Cole didn't catch it. He was too busy shaking his head in utter disappointment.

"What do you mean *claimed*? Why wouldn't you want to help him? You've got the grades for it. Remember that conversation we had—when you asked me how a person converts an acquaintance into a friend? Well, this is the kind of opportunity I was talking about. And I practically threw it at your feet. Sterling's new. He doesn't have any friends here, either."

Sterling swallowed his chuckle seconds before Cole would have seen. Waves of humiliation washed over me. And hurt—that Cole would bring up our private conversation, baring my insecurities to the boy who was rapidly transitioning from a nuisance to a nemesis. Standing squarely between Cole and me when Cole was desperately in need of my help.

"Ordinarily, I'd consider it," I said. Sure, I tutored my second graders every Tuesday, but that was different. The school was understaffed and those kids needed my help—last month, one of my students told me he'd doubled his scores on mad-minute math tests. And he'd thanked me for it. Me. I'd been the one to figure out that Sabrina needed glasses, and that was why she struggled with reading. My kids depended on me and I'd do anything for them. While Sterling was just trying to fob his homework off on someone. And after my adventures with the basketball captain, there was no way I was getting tangled up with another struggling athlete's academic drama. With my luck, Sterling would rally the team to state and then flunk out of school before a big game, leaving me to blame. My classmates would happily throw me off the roof next time. But that wasn't the point. "He's lying. Just like he lied about smoking. Every time you turn around, he does something provocative that only I manage to see."

At that, Cole whirled around, and Sterling lifted both hands in a shrug.

Rage simmered under my skin, bubbled through my veins. "I was planning to avoid him, like I do everyone else. But now that you're involved, I can't just—"

"I'm really sorry," Cole interrupted me, not even waiting to hear the rest of what I was going to say. A sharp, stabbing pain struck my chest as my darling brother wasted a placating smile on Sterling. "She's not normally like this. Just close your eyes and pretend she's the girl I told you about. The first day of classes gets her all wound up."

"Really?" Sterling said. "Maybe I can help with that."

He winked. Right at me.

Cole glanced at him, for an instant seeming to catch that flash of malice. But he was fooled by the thick layer of innocence Sterling immediately slathered all over his face.

"It's good, I mean, that she's so intense. Her grades are amazing, like I told you," Cole said. "And she's really warmhearted and sensitive, deep down. So let's just start over. Both of you. Tabula rasa. Clean slate."

Cole searched my face, begging me to go along with it. The creases of tension in his forehead I'd noticed earlier that day had deepened. Cole had enough on his plate with the weight-room drama. The last thing he needed was a feud between his sister and his roommate.

And he was right. I did make rash judgments and regret them later. How many times had I wished for a fresh start at school? I had to walk away and let this go. For Cole. I locked my righteous indignation away in a little box inside my brain.

Cole faced me, his eyes pleading. But I looked past him,

at Sterling. I opened my mouth, the word "truce" forming on my tongue.

Sterling's gaze locked onto mine. He lifted his hand to reveal that missing cigarette butt, pinched between index finger and thumb. Then he flicked it out the window and waved at me—a ridiculous beauty pageant wave.

"You're an asshole," I said.

"Harper!" Cole sounded beyond exasperated.

Even though I could sense failure looming, I had to make one more plea to win Cole back over to my side. "You don't understand what you're dealing with here. He didn't just want my help in school. He tried to bribe me to write his papers. To cheat."

"Is that what all this is about? All that shouting?" Cole asked. "I think there's been a misunderstanding." He glanced from me to Sterling, as if searching for consensus. "Sterling needs help with his classes while his hand heals. And he's had a rocky ride at all those other schools. He wants to turn over a new leaf, really try this time. *I* told him you'd help."

"That you did," Sterling drawled, leaning forward in his chair like the show was just getting interesting. "Sang her praises and all that. But I understand her reservations. After all, my own mistakes have put me in this position. Which is why I wanted to compensate her for time spent tutoring me. It's the least I could do." He was a model of contrition as he uttered this bald-faced lie. I narrowed my eyes, ready to pounce. But the way his lips twitched when he took in my expression was revenge enough. That expert liar had almost blown his cover.

"She'll help you—of course she will," Cole said. "You don't need to pay her."

"Like hell I will," I said, shaking Cole's hand off my

arm. Of all the outrageous suggestions. I'd never help that horrible cheater—especially for free. Not when Cole desperately needed money. But ultimately that didn't matter, because I wouldn't help Sterling if he emptied his trust fund and laid it at my feet. I spun toward the door. I needed space. Air. But most of all, I had to get out of there before Sterling Lane took a sledgehammer to the wedge he'd just driven between Cole and me.

Cole had been a starting midfielder on the lacrosse team since freshman year. And for a good reason—he was fast on his feet. He easily blocked my escape. "Sterling's new at this school. He and I have been stuck here for the last two weeks for lacrosse practice. He's a good guy. It's your responsibility as a top student to help him."

"No, he's not, and no, it isn't."

"Do it for me." His voice softened. "I pinkie promise you won't regret it."

He reached out and wrapped his little finger around mine. The moment hung there between us, weighted down by a million memories. I'd do anything for Cole. Anything. But this—Cole had no clue what he was getting us both into.

"No." Cracks spread across my aching heart. "I can't believe you're taken in by that—that libertine." I slammed the brownies down on Cole's desk. "I came here to help you—to talk to you about—about what you told me today." As I said it, Cole's eyes shot to Sterling. He was terrified I'd say more. "And instead Sterling ambushed me. For the third time today. And for the record, he drinks in class. Alcohol. He puts it in his pretentious little coffee Thermos."

Cole just stared at me, eyes wide with disappointment. Or maybe it was shock. I wasn't about to stick around long enough to find out.

"Harper, wait," Cole said, reaching for me.

"I shouldn't be surprised you'd side with him." I had to make Cole see, and I knew somewhere inside me were the words that would make it happen. "Given your other mistake in judgment this week." But as they slipped out, I knew those were the worst ones I could have chosen.

He took a step back. The hand that had reached for me a second ago dropped to his side. I wanted to suck those syllables back down my throat. But it was too late—the shattered look on Cole's face said it all. Once again, my temper had taken things too far. And I'd failed, so quickly, to live up to the rules Mom had given me.

I pushed past him and forced myself to walk away calmly. But as soon as I hit the stairway, I broke into a run, repeating Rule 26 with every thud of my tennis shoes against the polished linoleum.

I do not cry.

Once outside, I looked up at the building and counted seven windows over, figuring out which one belonged to Sterling and Cole. Then I pushed through the low shrub skirting the building and dropped to my knees. I searched from left to right, moving aside leaves and branches until I found it. A half-burned cigarette butt.

I pulled a piece of notebook paper from my bag, folded it into an envelope, labeled it *exhibit one*, and placed the butt inside.

Evidence was evidence, irrefutable and undeniable. And I had every intention of gathering an overwhelming pile of it.

Sterling was up to something—something so nefarious that it involved keeping in Cole's good graces while showing me his wicked side in all its glory.

As much as I wanted to ignore Sterling Lane, his

entanglements with Cole made that impossible, at least for the time being. He needed Cole for something, and I could guarantee it wasn't something good. So I would rescue Cole from his fibs and financial mistakes, and I'd also protect him from Sterling Lane. He'd hurt Cole over my dead body.

REASON 5:

HE'S TURNING
EVERYONE
AGAINST ME.

With exhibit one safely filed away in my Master Course Binder, it was time to focus back on the problem at hand: Cole. I whipped out my phone.

It was time to call in reinforcements.

Even though I told her it was an emergency, it took me almost four minutes to get past his assistant and talk to Dad. By then, I was pacing back and forth, not bothering to acknowledge the people who walked past. Still, my chest felt tight when three girls I'd partnered with for a physics lab shook their heads and looked bewildered after I brushed them off. That behavior was hardly helping me overcome my social issues. Add that to the tally of Sterling's transgressions—distracting me from my goals, both academic and otherwise.

Finally, my father's gravelly voice was on the other line. "Harper."

I could tell he was irritated from the clipped way he said my name. Only Dad could reduce it to one syllable.

"I'm taking an additional SAT prep course—" I said.

"That's not an emergency," he cut in, talking right over me. He sounded far away. I must've been on speakerphone, being broadcast into a room filled with God knows who. "That's an update. This is the third time this month you've called me at work with fake emergencies. Do you need me to explain the difference?"

"No, I don't. But you're not letting me finish," I said. "I need to pay for it."

"Send the invoice—you know I'll handle it."

"The thing is, I'm late to register, so I need you to send money so I can pay today."

"You?" Dad sounded skeptical. "You're never late for anything."

I bit my lip so hard I tasted blood. I'd never lied to my father—not like this. "I didn't know about it until today. I need eight hundred dollars. It's—it's important. Please, Dad."

The genuine panic in my voice must have resonated with him on some level, because his voice softened as he said, "Of course. I'll transfer it into your student account. Is there anything else? How's Cole? He didn't call Sunday."

No doubt Cole didn't want to hear Dad praise him for the fund-raising he'd lied about.

"I'm worried about him." The truth slipped right out, surprising even me. "He has a new roommate—a transfer student."

Dad cleared his throat, paving the way for whatever lecture he was about to unfurl. "Transfer students need roommates, too." The gentle tone of moments ago was gone.

I closed my eyes. "You don't understand. He's horrible. He—"

But Dad was talking again, his voice cutting through

and shredding mine to pieces. "You can't form an opinion of someone in one day. We've talked about these snap judgments, Harper. He's a new student. You should welcome him, not judge him. Cole seems quite fond of him already, so I can't imagine he's that bad."

"Yes, he is." My voice cracked as I tried to summon words potent enough to re-create what I'd witnessed in Cole's room, what had happened to me in class earlier that day.

I pictured my voice drifting down a conference table lined with people. Bored businessmen wishing my dad would keep his private life private and let them close whatever deal they were working on. I should have been embarrassed that strangers were probably listening to this family spat, but I was accustomed to Dad's folksy business practices, tracing all the way back to the days when he was a plain old general contractor who taught us to unclog drains after school. That was before he got his big break — before he started Campbell Construction and attracted the attention of some of the state's biggest developers.

Money was new to our family. As was my fancy private-school education. But Dad's own meteoric success was due to charm and networking, so he focused on charisma as the key to success. I would never, ever measure up on that front.

Dad sighed. "Cole can take care of himself."

"No. No, he can't," I said, struggling to keep my voice calm. "He's too trusting. You're always saying that, too. Sterling Lane cheats and drinks and tried to coerce me into helping him cheat." I held my breath, waiting for my words to settle in Dad's ear and steal back the three-quarters of his attention I'd already lost to whoever was in the room with him.

"That's right. This is the Lane kid? Not a bad connection

for Cole if he wants to take over my business one day. Politics are in the Lane blood, just like stubbornness is in yours." He laughed at his own joke. "And who knows, maybe Cole *can* be a good influence." Dad's attention was gone. Drifting away on the river of blueprints and papers I could hear him shuffling on his desk. "Influence can go both ways, Harper. Influencing people for good or bad. We all deserve a second chance. And Cole has a real way with people. He told me you're trying to make a friend or two this year, and well, maybe this is a good place to start. Listen to Cole. You could learn from him."

The bile rose in my throat. I was so tired of being the defective one. Cole wasn't perfect, either. But I pulled the reins on that thought. I couldn't let anything or anyone come between Cole and me. Not Dad, not Sterling, and not the ugly face of bitter jealousy that had just photobombed my psyche. Cole valued me—he understood me. And I understood him and his patient, forgiving heart. I'd even tried unsuccessfully to emulate it back in junior high, when it became glaringly obvious that Cole made friends just as quickly as I drove them away.

Way with people or not, this time Cole was in over his head. He owed money he didn't have and he was rooming with a boy who'd probably embroil him in some scheme and get him expelled. Whatever reason Sterling had for pretending to be rehabilitated around Cole was unlikely to be a good one.

There was a shuffling of papers and my father barked, "Don't touch that!" at someone in the room. Clearly, his patience was being burned at both ends. I could picture him leaning on his elbow, pressing his forehead into his palm, like he always did when I exasperated him. Something I often achieved by merely existing.

So I was surprised that his voice had softened when he spoke again. "Harper, honey, I know you mean well, but you need to let Cole be. He can take care of himself. Focus on yourself, your grades, and this whole making-friends thing. I was so happy Cole told me about that conversation." Dad paused. "Give Sterling Lane the benefit of the doubt. You know how boys can be. A little friendship with the right person could make a world of difference."

"Right," I said, hoping the acid in my voice could burn right through the phone line and into his ear. "Cole can rehabilitate anyone just by trusting them. And fortunately, he's immune to deceit and manipulation."

"That's the spirit," Dad replied. Apparently my sarcasm didn't transmit over speakerphone. "See? There was no reason to get all emotional," he added. "If you want to be a trial lawyer one day, you'll have to be able to handle boys like that just being boys—without sounding like you're about to burst into tears over it."

"What about girls just being girls?" I asked.

"That's what you just did, honey. Overreacting. Now, be sure to call your grandmother next Tuesday. It's her birthday. And remind Cole. I'll call you this weekend." And with that, I was dismissed.

Boys being boys? Boys like Cole spending money they don't have. Boys like Sterling drinking and lying and trying to coerce me into cheating. *Boys being boys* could have consequences Dad would regret overlooking. I blinked back the moisture in my eyes and shoved my phone into my bag. There was no reason for self-pity, since ultimately the call had been a resounding success. Cole and I were now eight hundred dollars closer to our goal. Better yet, the moment that goal was achieved, I'd find a way to sever all our ties with Sterling Lane before he wrapped Cole up in his web.

REASON 6:

HE'S AMASSING AN
ARMY OF MISCREANTS.

*B*oarding school is like a four-year plane ride. Confined in a cabin with a bunch of grumpy strangers, feeling obligated to be polite or make chitchat simply because you had a common destination. Roommates are the man in the next seat who smells like blue cheese and hogs the armrest. Give them a half-smile or a hello, and there's no going back. Not that I'd ever been paired with a roommate who wanted to be best friends, but I'd still prepared a list of potential disadvantages of that situation, just in case.

When I reached my room that afternoon, I slammed the door behind me and locked it immediately. It was a stroke of outrageous luck that I had my own room that year. Apparently the student who'd been randomly assigned to room with me successfully lobbied the administration for alternate accommodations.

Fortunately, she hadn't been replaced.

My room was small, with two twin beds on opposite walls and two scuffed and scratched desks side by side between the beds. I was particularly fortunate that my room overlooked the quad, affording a view of the entire campus—the brick-and-ivy library was always my favorite, as much for the content as for the stately architecture. I also had a soft spot for the administration building. It was newer than the rest of the historic brick buildings on campus, but its architecture was Greek Revival, helping it blend into the overall ambiance. When I was a freshman, I would weave between the pillars and imagine I was at an ancient font of learning in Athens, drinking in the knowledge of the ages. I still enjoyed reading there, perched behind the pillar on the far right and hidden from the casual observer.

I unpacked my bag and popped open my laptop. Sure enough, the wire from Dad had already hit my account. He had his faults, but he always came through for us when we needed him. The next morning, I could take a bus into town and withdraw the money in cash to avoid any sort of paper trail. The bank could also cash my savings bond.

We still had a considerable sum to raise, but we were moving toward our goal. My phone chimed, reminding me that it was time to review my notes from the day.

A return to my regular routine would mitigate the horrors of that afternoon. There was nothing like a well-organized regimen to restore order and decency to my universe.

Halfway through outlining the physics chapter for the next day's lecture, the door flew open. The handle slammed into the full-length mirror and the door ricocheted back to conceal the intruder. I rose, shocked that someone had a key to my room when the only duplicate was securely locked in the office of campus security.

Kendall Frank blew into the room. She was a little out of breath, and her highlighted bangs were in uncharacteristic disarray. Kendall always looked glossy and airbrushed, like she'd just walked out of a magazine. When we were freshmen, I'd actually pause at times to ponder how she maintained such a perfect exterior. Perfection should always be admired, even in a discipline I didn't prioritize.

Kendall was dragging a suitcase behind her.

My stomach plummeted through the floor.

I could handle mean and overlook spoiled, but it physically pained me to watch a girl play dumb. I'd accidentally seen Kendall's transcript while waiting in the office for a copy of my own. Her grades were quite commendable, even though she was always rolling her eyes in class and complaining that the subjects were too hard. Not only was it disingenuous, in my mind it was far worse than actually failing. Kendall could use the power of her popularity to inspire others. She could be a role model; instead she opted to be an albatross.

There was no logical reason for Kendall to be in my room with a suitcase. She had a room already, and any girl in our grade would give both kidneys for the chance to live with her. Because wherever Kendall was, boys swarmed.

So I wasn't all that surprised to hear a deep voice from the hallway, followed by a boy whose face was concealed by the three quilted pink duffel bags stacked in his arms.

"You've got to be kidding," Kendall hissed, stepping inside and eyeing me like I was a hunk of rotting meat. She was talking to the boy behind her, not me, so I looked away, pretending she'd actually been as discreet as she should have been.

Then the boy took another step forward. Parker. I'd been stuck with him as a lab partner last year and ended up tutoring him against my better judgment. It had just sort of happened. Nothing official. He'd been sweet, in a wide-eyed, earnest kind of way. He won me over when I realized his mediocre grades weren't from lack of effort, but rather lack of ability. And really, there's not much you can do about that.

My opinion of him fell into a downward spiral, though, and could have burrowed its way fifty feet into the ground when I saw him scampering behind Kendall like a bellhop.

"Hey, Harper," Parker said cheerfully before turning to Kendall. "Living here, your GPA will go up a tenth of a point just through osmosis. Mine did."

"Excellent use of vocab," I said, trying to diffuse this ticking time bomb of an awkward situation. Parker grinned—a wide, boyish grin that made Kendall roll her eyes.

"I guess I'll survive for a couple of days," Kendall said, throwing her purse onto the floor in the middle of the room—an area that should be kept free of clutter, per Rules 74 and 84, which dealt with cleanliness and tripping hazards, respectively. "Our room flooded," Kendall said, finally deigning to explain why she was invading my room. "A ruptured pipe. And they didn't even ask me where I wanted to live while they fixed it." She wrinkled her tiny nose, making her look like a Boston terrier. "Personally, I think they should have moved us to a hotel if this was all they had."

"Yes," I said. "That would have been preferable."

"Why don't you have a roommate already?" Kendall asked, her huge green eyes finally settling on me. Her gaze had so carefully avoided mine until that moment that I was beginning to wonder if I had, in fact, disappeared from my own room.

I cringed when she flicked her fingers impatiently and pointed, wordlessly telling Parker where to set her bags. I sat on the edge of my bed, careful not to let my outdoor clothes come in contact with my sheets. I was morbidly curious to see if he'd unpack for her, too, or if his services were limited to manual labor. It wasn't just seldom that I was included in this sort of dormitory drama—it was never.

But Parker set the bags down with surprising haste, given that he was in the inner sanctum of Kendall's boudoir. Then he was halfway across the room a second later.

"Where are you going?" Kendall pouted. "You can't just abandon me here." She said it like she'd be marooned in the middle of the desert.

"I told you already," Parker said, leaning in quick to give her a kiss and confirming he was Kendall's latest acquisition. "I have a lacrosse meeting."

"What do you mean—a meeting?" I asked, glancing at my watch. "Isn't practice over already?"

"This new guy asked us to hold one," he said. "They used to do it at his old school. He's got some ideas. Strategy stuff."

"Of course," I said, from between gritted teeth. "Sterling Lane."

"Yeah." Parker paused at the door and looked back at me. "Cole introduced you?"

"Unfortunately, yes," I replied.

"I know, I know." Parker smiled. "I was a little skeptical, too. Heard he was nuts. Got his team disqualified from a tournament. Launched firecrackers at a referee. Someone else said it was just smoke bombs." He shook his head. "But when you meet him—I mean, really talk to him—he's a good guy."

"No, he's not," I said. I couldn't sit by and listen to Sterling Lane being defended one more time that day. "He lies and drinks and cheats."

"Well, I don't know about all that." Parker laughed nervously, running one hand through his hair. "But that's nothing compared to what everyone was saying before we met him. His parents must have some pretty deep pockets if he only got expelled instead of arrested."

That was a leading statement if I'd ever heard one. He was dying to tell the story but didn't want to be an outright gossip.

Kendall's eyes snapped up at that. "Why?" she asked. Then she looked at me. "He's Cole's roommate, right? Have you met him? Is he cute?" The sweet siren of money had hypnotized Kendall into revealing way too much about the inner workings of her self-centered mind, and I wasn't the only one who'd noticed.

"What do you mean *is he cute*?" Parker asked.

"Just curious." Kendall's eyes cut to him for a fraction of an instant, gauging his reaction. Either she was completely heartless or just trying to make him jealous. Although little as I knew about dating, it seemed to me there wasn't much difference between the two.

Before Kendall delivered the punch line to their joke of a relationship, I asked, "Why?"

But Parker was too distracted to answer. "Exactly," he said. "Why would that matter?"

Did Parker honestly think Kendall thought he was special—that he'd last more than a week with her when no one else could?

"No," I said, "I meant why was he expelled—what did he do?"

"Oh." Parker's focus shifted back to me. Kendall slid forward to perch on the edge of her bed like a puppy anxiously awaiting a treat. She was clearly enamored of either gossip or obnoxious playboys, and most likely both.

"Arson," he said.

"Arson?" I couldn't picture Sterling doing something

as uncivilized or proactive as lighting a fire and running to hide. "From what I've seen, that doesn't seem like Sterling's style. He's so—lazy and spoiled."

"Well, at least he gets things done on the field—when he wants to." There was an edge to Parker's tone. And for the first time I started to hope that I wasn't the only one who saw through Sterling's facade. But the shadow almost immediately passed. Like Cole, Parker thought the best of everyone. "Cole made me swear I wouldn't tell anyone. He said Sterling deserves a fresh start."

The words pelted me. Here was yet another secret Cole wasn't sharing with me. Was that a sign of a new rift between us, thanks to Sterling, or had the distance between us been growing all along?

Parker frowned, clearly deliberating over how much to share. Curiosity threatened to completely consume my internal organs.

"What did he light on fire?" I demanded. "The school? His dorm?"

Parker took a deep breath. "Apparently Sterling had a fight with one of his friends. And it had something to do with Sterling's sister—the guy did something bad. You can draw your own conclusions since that guy was expelled, too."

I felt a little twinge of guilt. Sterling had said that most students had given him a standing ovation for putting an asshole in his place and I'd insinuated that they should have thrown the book at him. I should have had all the facts before I'd spoken. Perhaps Sterling had been correct on that front, if on nothing else. Sometimes you had to go to great lengths to protect family. But the idea of him angry was equally intriguing. One of the things that bothered me most about Sterling was his impassiveness, even when insulted directly to his face. Like nothing and no one could unsettle that knowing smile.

I nodded, urging Parker to continue.

"Anyway, Sterling wanted revenge," Parker continued. "So he lit the kid's room on fire when he was sleeping."

"He what?" Kendall gasped. I wasn't sure if she was impressed or horrified. Knowing the cruel streak she displayed from time to time, it could have gone either direction. Kendall was there the day my nickname Harper the Hag was coined. I'll never forget the way she giggled hysterically as her senior boyfriend eviscerated me in the cafeteria. All because I'd insisted a group project meant he had to contribute, too.

Parker absently stroked Kendall's shoulder. "Not the whole room. He wrapped it up in string, like a spiderweb. Then he set the string on fire. And it lit up like a Christmas tree. The kid woke up to a room full of flames. But it was just string, so it probably couldn't have spread." But Parker didn't sound so convinced. And I liked him better for it.

"That's psychotic," I said. "And dangerous."

Parker shrugged. "Like I said, not likely it would catch. Guess he flooded the floor with water at the same time. Just in case."

"That was thoughtful of him," I said drily.

"People say he wove the word 'Judas' into the string. But I dunno if I believe that. I mean, sounds pretty complicated."

Actually, that part of the plan matched exactly with the Sterling I'd met. A smug flourish to drive his point home. Or perhaps a self-aggrandizing fictional detail he added to the rumors after the fact. The whole thing sounded more like urban legend than a factual account. "He has quite an opinion of himself," I said.

"Who?" Kendall asked.

"Sterling. Judas is a religious reference," I explained. "Judas betrayed Christ." I wished I hadn't sounded so harsh. For once, I was in a conversation with my peers and it wasn't half bad. This was a step closer to a tentative sort of social inclusion. I turned back to Parker. "And then he got expelled?"

"That's everything I know." Parker shrugged and glanced at his watch. "Except that he's one hell of a left attack. Cole would know the rest. They're always hanging out."

My stomach sank. I'd had no idea the situation was so dire.

"Hmmm," Kendall said. I looked up and she was eyeing me curiously from her perch on the opposite bed.

"I've gotta go." Parker gave Kendall's shoulder one more casual squeeze and left, closing the door softly behind him.

As soon as he was gone, Kendall stretched out on her bed, planting her platform sandals right on her flowered pillowcase. I cringed at the violation of basic hygiene, and at the name she sighed as she committed it. "Sterling." She had clearly forgotten whom she was talking to, because her tone was almost conspiratorial. "It's a perfect name. Regal—royal, that's what that means, right?" She paused and rolled up onto her elbow, looking at me. "Is he cute? You never answered."

I thought about it for a second. "A little. But not my type." That was the understatement of the year. On both counts.

"I think you're lying." She fluffed the ends of her hair so they draped artfully behind her shoulders. "He *must* be your type. You perked right up when Parker told that story."

I nearly choked on my own tongue. "Never."

Her eyebrows shot up. "Look, I know we've never been friends. And you probably think I'm just some bubblehead." It was shocking beyond words, the note of self-doubt that slipped into Kendall's voice. Curiosity flashed in her eyes, as if she did actually wonder what I thought of her.

I opened my mouth, contemplating informing her that she did an admirable job of camouflaging her intelligence.

"But I'd like to get along since we have to cohabitate." She chewed her lower lip as her eyes cut to the expanse of floor between us. "I've always felt bad about that time we egged your room. It wasn't my idea. You know how it is when you're young. Older kids can get you to go along with anything. I tried to apologize that time in the cafeteria. But you know, it always seems like you're too busy to talk to anyone."

My tiny twinge of curiosity about Kendall—at what lurked underneath all that lip gloss and haute couture—exploded into nothingness. I'd never known who'd committed that particular act of vandalism, and I wasn't prepared to forgive it. I'd wasted precious hours of study time scrubbing the dried yolk off my door, trying not to let anyone who passed see my red and puffy eyes. Years of being harangued and ostracized couldn't be erased through a halfhearted apology.

"I'd forgotten all about that," I said. "Why are you telling me this?"

"Because if we're going to be living together, we can't be chasing after the same guy."

I blinked. Once. Twice. "I have no idea what you're talking about."

"Sterling," she said, clearly exasperated. "You said he's a little cute, which I'm guessing for you is like saving his photo as your computer wallpaper to ogle daily."

I actually gagged at the mere idea of it. "No. No. No."
I could have repeated that word into infinity.

Her eyes narrowed, like she didn't quite believe me.
But then she smiled. "Perfect. Then I'll have to see if he
lives up to the hype."

"I think you're perfect for each other," I blurted, for
some reason needing to put even more distance between
me and her suggestion that I found that vile sybarite
attractive.

"That's really sweet of you, Harper." Kendall tipped her
head to the side and smiled at me. I observed her cautiously,
waiting for the smile to transform into something sinister, or
for the sarcastic verbal jab that would follow. But as seconds
ticked past, I started to wonder if she'd been sincere.

Then she reached over into the nearest pink duffel bag
and unleashed a hurricane of clothing.

"What about Parker?" I asked, feeling sorry for him
and the puppy-dog way he chased after her.

"What about him? We're just friends." She glanced over
at me. "Oh, stop looking so scandalized. It was *his* idea.
He's the one who said he needs to focus on his lacrosse
career instead of a girlfriend. As if anyone's ever heard of
a professional lacrosse player. He wants to play around?
Fine. So can I."

I didn't have the heart to tell her that professional
lacrosse was very much a reality, and one of Cole's dreams.
Which made it all the more urgent that we preserve his
integrity as captain by concealing his mistake.

"And Parker had the gall to pretend he was jealous,"
Kendall continued. "You know—when I asked if Sterling
was cute. If he really cared about me, he'd commit, not just
act all jealous when I talk about other guys. Am I asking
too much just to have him acknowledge our relationship

outside of his bedroom?"

It was like she'd just switched into Greek. Except if it had been Greek, I would have comprehended more of it.

"Am I?" she demanded. "Is that asking too much?"

"Of course not," I murmured, pretending I had any insight into the inner workings of the male mind.

Kendall applied a generous layer of cherry-red lipstick that made her look like one of those glamorous pinup girls from the twenties. I watched, reluctantly fascinated by how easy it was for her to go from pretty to beautiful.

I glanced down at my nails, chewed to the quick. At the rumpled pleated skirt that made up my daily uniform. There was a splatter of coffee on my blouse I'd never noticed before. I'd never cared about my appearance, living in a male-dominated house. No one taught me about makeup or nail polish or fashion. Yet I could tell from photos that these were all things my mother knew in spades. I'd missed out on so much. Irony of ironies that Kendall Frank's makeup bag made my heart start aching over it for the first time in years.

Kendall used a painful-looking metal clamp to make her eyelashes double in length. The entire production was fascinating in its intricacy and economy. What would it be like to smile and bring a roomful of people to their knees? I'd seen Kendall do that more than once.

"Sterling Lane, get ready, 'cause here I come," Kendall singsonged, sliding into a pair of heels that could double as circus stilts. "Here's to hoping he's not a horrible commitment-phobe like Parker."

What had started as a little inside joke with myself at Kendall's expense suddenly seemed like a decent option: encourage Kendall to chase after Sterling. Not only was it a match made in hell, Kendall was unrealistically high maintenance. She would keep Sterling away from Cole while I found a way to revise their room assignments. It was a long shot, but even if it ultimately didn't work, Kendall would keep Sterling occupied for a day or two, which was all the time I needed to get the money from Dad, cash out my savings bonds, and fix things between me and Cole.

"The important thing is finding the right outfit," Kendall said, prattling on about first impressions and quoting Coco Chanel. And I was nodding along, reluctantly sucked into her alternate dimension.

Tank tops that a newborn could barely squeeze into flew through the air, landing haphazardly on my desk, followed by shiny sequined fabrics that could have been either dresses or distress signals. I watched as one by one the pieces of clothing tumbled onto the floor, floated over a lampshade, or worst of all, landed on the counter, actually brushing against my plastic basket of toiletries, including my toothbrush. Horror and fascination vied for control. This was a new experience for me, sharing a room with someone so utterly uninhibited that she'd hurl bras and underwear across the room, not caring that they were in full view of me and anyone else who might wander in.

"You know, this would look really good on you," Kendall said, flinging a tiny scrap of green fabric at me. "Your short dark hair and huge green eyes—this would make them pop."

"Thank you?" I asked, folding the item and setting it on my desk. Upon closer examination, I determined it was some sort of one-sleeved shirt.

"Wish me luck," she said, slipping off the bed and smoothing her hair with an electric device.

"Good luck," I said. And I meant it.

After all, I hated Sterling and I was less than crazy about Kendall. As far as I was concerned, that was more than enough for the two of them to have in common. Sterling was a liability Cole couldn't afford, and while I was figuring out a way to take Sterling out of commission, I'd let Kendall at least start the process for me.

REASON 7:

HE CAN'T JUST STOP AT BEING BAD.

NO, HE'S DETERMINED TO CORRUPT
EVERYONE ELSE, TOO.

When Kendall left, I sat back and surveyed my room. As she'd unpacked, a tornado of fabric had whirled through the room. So I was surprised that when she finished, her half of the room was tidy and organized. Throw pillows adorned her bed, and she'd taped up an interesting collage of postcards from around the world. Kendall had an eye for colors and textures that hinted at artistic proclivities. All her other faults aside, that talent was something worth pausing to appreciate.

And now that the room was silent again, I did just that, peeking in her closet at the way her clothes were sorted into a spectrum of colors. The Rules nodded appreciatively over that. The few decorative flourishes she'd added—the lamp, the antique clock—exponentially increased the attractiveness of the room.

I texted my dad a hasty thank-you for the money, confirming it was received. My alarm chimed, reminding me it was time to switch to calculus, even though I hadn't even put a dent in my history reading. It wasn't like me to wander so far astray. The pressure behind my eyes started to build, so I sat down and revised my study schedule to reflect the seventy-five minutes that had just slipped between my fingers.

Halfway through my problem set, Parker's words drifted back to me: "team meeting." The fact that it was Sterling's idea made my stomach sink with dread. Sterling wasn't the type of guy who was proactive about anything other than trouble. And as captain, Cole would be front and center at any team meeting—as well as responsible if anything went awry.

It was already getting dark, and the schedule taped to my desk clearly stated that I should be outlining the next day's history lecture. Still, I set down my pencil and calculated that as long as I postponed my independent study work until tomorrow and canceled all bathroom breaks until morning, I could carve out a twenty-minute recess. After all, Cole was on the line.

I pulled on my sweatshirt and ventured out into the night. The gym was nearly a quarter of a mile away, across campus, so I'd have to run both ways in order to keep this mission within its allotted time frame.

When I rounded the side of the gym, I could hear it— the raucous noise of boys cheering the way they do when they're trying to humiliate someone into doing something they don't want to. I approached cautiously, careful not to be seen. The door to the locker room was propped open with a dirty tennis shoe, which meant I'd be fully visible to anyone standing right inside.

I rounded the corner and dashed behind the bushes lining the sidewalk just in time. Sterling Lane's voice floated out of the darkness, followed by the devil himself heading toward the gym. A huge water jug dangled from one hand. But as he moved closer, I got a look at the label. It was a plastic bottle of vodka.

When he reached the door to the locker room, he paused, listening to the tumult inside like it was Mozart before sauntering inside. The boys who had been lingering in the hallway followed.

The shouting inside doubled in intensity ten seconds after Sterling entered.

I shifted closer, hoping I'd be able to overhear what they were doing, but the shouts were distorted, overlapping nonsense by the time they echoed outside to me. From what I could see from the safety of the hedge, most of the noise was coming from behind a bank of lockers. A few stragglers were loitering to the side, leaning against the painted cinder-block wall with a full view of the outside. One of the boys turned and looked straight at me long enough that I was certain I'd been seen, but then he leaned back against the wall, laughing at something that happened out of my line of sight.

It was a close call, but I still didn't pause before I acted. If I had, I probably would have lost my nerve. Sneaking into the boys' locker room was heinously against the school rules. But I had to know if Cole was there—and rescue him if so. He'd be suspended or even expelled if he was caught drinking on campus. His academic record would be ruined, his scholarships would evaporate, and so might his hopes of playing professional lacrosse.

I dashed forward in bursts—around the bushes, across the sidewalk, and in through the door. Something slammed into my stomach, knocking the air from my lungs. I caught the recycling bin I'd crashed into moments before it would have hit the ground.

Fortunately, the clamor in the other room was so loud no one seemed to hear the collision.

Once inside and safely hidden, I took a moment to catch my breath and instantly regretted it. The air tasted like mold and sweat.

I pressed my back against the wall and inched along, peeking around the corner before slipping into the next aisle. And then the next. It was slow going, but I drew closer to the far end of the locker room, where the team had congregated just outside the shower stalls.

I'd taken less than half a step forward when I heard voices behind me—voices that were approaching fast. There was nowhere for me to go. No place to hide. If I ducked down one of the aisles, I'd still be in plain view of any passersby.

My heart hammered in my chest as the voices drew nearer still. I chanced a quick peek around the corner. Two boys were pausing to read the game schedule posted on the bulletin board. There was no escape. But just as I resigned myself to my fate, my eyes landed on the darkened window cut into the wall beside me. Next to it was a door. It had to be the coach's office.

I grabbed the handle, my hand shaking so hard I could barely turn it. And just in time, it gave way under my weight. I shut the door softly behind myself, slipped to the floor, crawled into the corner, and then pulled my knees up to my chest and wrapped my arms around them. The shadows of two sets of feet walked past the bottom of the door.

I crept to the window to peek outside and confirm the coast was clear. Voices headed my way again, this time coming from the direction of Sterling's little party.

"It's in Coach's office," the deep voice shouted. "I'll be right back."

"Shit." The word slipped out, even though I never swear.

I looked around. The room was small and cramped, with a tiny desk littered with food wrappers and used tissues pressed against the wall. A narrow bookshelf sagged under the weight of garish copper trophies. I wedged myself under the desk, behind the chair, just as the door flew open.

The lights flickered on.

Parker reached one long arm out and grabbed one of the trophies off the shelves and shifted like he'd race right out of there. He was chuckling to himself, like he was plotting something. And as he turned back toward the door, his eyes were still glued to the silly shiny man perched on the wooden base. A little sigh of relief escaped me as he reached for the light switch to flick it off.

He looked back at once, and his eyes met mine.

"What the hell?" he murmured.

I pressed one finger against my lips. My eyes begged him to obey.

"What's taking so long?" another voice asked. Someone else was outside, standing at Parker's shoulder. My heart thudded so fast the individual beats blended into a steady hum.

"I'm coming," Parker said, barring the new arrival from the door. He jostled him away, cast one more look over his shoulder at me, and turned off the light.

If it were anyone else, they would have turned me in, but Parker had been friendly ever since I'd tutored him. Perhaps cultivating relationships with other people wasn't always a complete waste of time.

I was just getting up the courage to check if the coast was clear when the door opened. Parker slipped inside, towing someone else behind him.

"What?" Cole asked. "What's the emergency?"

Parker didn't reply. He just pointed at me.

"Harper?" Cole's eyes widened, then he looked back at Parker. "What's she doing here?"

"I have no idea," Parker said. "But I thought you'd want to know. So you can get her out of here."

"I can take care of myself," I told Parker. "Unlike some people."

"Have you completely lost your mind?" Cole asked. "I know you pretend that you don't care what anyone thinks, but seriously, you'll never live this down if they catch you in here. Plus, this must be against some sort of school rule. I'm surprised your head didn't explode or something."

His face was unusually flushed. Then the smell hit me. Cole had been drinking.

"Yes," I said, pushing myself up to my feet. "It's against three different school rules. But that doesn't matter—drinking is against a whole lot more, and it's against the law. We're getting out of here before you get yourself suspended—or worse."

Cole shifted on his feet. I was losing him, so I redoubled my efforts. "You're not like this. You don't drink because it could interfere with sports. If this is about that other pressure you're under—well, I'm finding a way out of that. Some of it, anyway." Cole's eyes widened, like I'd betrayed him by even mentioning it. "Come with me. Now. I'll fix everything. Pinkie promise." I grabbed his hand and squeezed. He squeezed mine back. The twin connection sparked between us. I could feel it—I had him.

There was a flash of guilt in Cole's eyes when he looked at me. Then he looked away, his jaw set. "I was thinking about what you said earlier," he said, pulling his hand free. "And it wasn't okay. All you do is judge and categorize people. You have some box in your mind labeled 'Cole,' and you expect me to fit in it forever. But people change."

"People don't change," I pleaded. "Not like this. Not so suddenly."

"It's not sudden." Cole's voice hardened. "You just ignore things that don't fit your worldview. Or you throw my mistakes back in my face when I least expect it. Like earlier."

"This is Sterling's influence," I said, my voice growing shrill. "He's corrupting you. Stealing you from me."

"No," Cole said quietly. "You don't understand."

"But I do," I said, glancing at Parker. I had to say enough to convince Cole while being vague enough to confuse Parker. "You're under too much pressure. I get that. But the guys pressuring you into drinking are also the ones who pressured you into that. And look where it landed you. You need to start thinking for yourself or you'll end up getting into worse trouble. Or expelled." The thought of being at Sablebrook without Cole slammed into me like a right hook. I couldn't let him get caught. I'd die if we were separated. Die if Cole's entire future was jeopardized over a night of underage drinking and some stupid weight room equipment. "Please. Just come with me before anything else happens."

Cole's lips pressed together in a thin line. His jaw was clenched so tight that my own muscles tensed in sympathy. It was an expression I hadn't seen since we were kids fighting over Legos or the last piece of birthday cake.

"Maybe I'm just an idiot," Cole replied. "For telling you. For thinking you'd actually be there for me like a normal sister. Instead you're using my screwup as a weapon. You're not trying to help me—you're trying to control me. I could write a book about all the things you don't know about me. And you don't even care. You just want me to keep pretending I'm your perfect brother—like we're a pair of fucking bookends. But I'm not, Harper. I'm not perfect like you."

My lungs went rigid with shock; they could no longer effectively suck in air. That was what Cole thought? All this time, Cole had been feeling that horrible, competitive pressure, too? Living with another child the exact same age invariably drew comparisons. That was the one thing we always promised we'd never let come between us.

"Cole," I said, desperate to keep him there, talking to me. "I didn't mean that—you're not an idiot. You just made a mistake."

"And you followed me into the locker room to rub my nose in it," he replied. "Because attacking me in my room wasn't enough. Well, rest assured I went right out and did something even worse."

I winced at those words. I'd been joking earlier about the bank robberies, but knowing Cole's stubborn streak, anything was possible. "What—what did you do?"

He just shook his head. "I love you. You know I do. But you need to let me handle things my way and let me be myself."

Then Cole turned and walked away while I stood there with a visibly uncomfortable Parker. I was pretty sure my heart and all other major organs had ceased to function. Cole's words had crawled under my skin and sliced them all to ribbons.

"That didn't go at all like I planned," I said, slumping against the wall.

"It never does," Parker murmured. He lifted his hand, and for a moment I thought he'd touch my arm. But he didn't. Instead, he let his hand drop back to his side, shoved it into his pocket, and shrugged. "Cole has been stressed out lately. Probably just worried about our game. He snapped at Coach earlier, too." He ran his other hand through his hair. "Look, I'm gonna go back outside, and I'll make sure no one comes this direction so you can get out. Okay?"

I looked at him, amazed that he actually thought I'd leave my vulnerable and distressed brother in this den of vipers.

"Okay?" he repeated.

I nodded to get rid of him, and Parker slipped out the door of the office, casting one last look over his shoulder and shaking his head.

Per Rule 63, I avoid humiliation at all costs, particularly at the hands of my peers, but Rule 9 insisted I couldn't give up. It didn't matter if the whole lacrosse team found out I'd sneaked into the boys' locker room. I wasn't leaving Cole in a situation that could get him thrown out of school. Still, it was with more than a little trepidation that I crawled to the window again and peeked through the blinds. The coast was clear. The hinges creaked as I eased the door open, but the crowd of boys down the hallway drowned it.

I slipped back into the hallway. Whatever those boys were doing, it was getting louder by the second. When I reached the partition of lockers, I stepped on the bench and tried to pull myself up to the top, balancing one foot on the metal shelf dividing an open locker in half.

Someone grabbed my arm. I was too terrified to scream. When I turned around, Parker was standing there.

"What are you doing?" He hissed, "You were supposed to leave."

"No," I whispered back. "Not without Cole."

Parker looked at me. Then he shook his head again. "You're not going to win this fight. At least not tonight."

I turned away and put my foot back on the shelf, trying to scamper up to get a better view of where Cole had gone.

"Here," Parker whispered, putting his hands on my waist. It distracted me, the way his massive palms made me feel so tiny and oddly safe. Was this what drew girls like Kendall in—some sort of need to feel protected?

Parker lifted me up like I was made of air until I could shift my weight onto the locker shelf. And then he stood there, propping me up as I peered over the bank of lockers at the heads of the boys below.

Six inches below me, on the other side of the row of lockers, Sterling Lane was presiding over the lacrosse team, lounging in a leather desk chair that I recognized from the headmaster's office. There were two sawhorses in the middle of the room with a piece of plywood resting on top. A makeshift table.

And on the table were six shot glasses and a now half-empty jug of vodka. As I watched, Sterling lifted the first shot glass and emptied it into his mouth without even wincing. Like it was a refreshing sip of water. Even though I'd never touched alcohol, anyone with a rudimentary grasp of chemistry would know it should burn. I slid my cell phone out of my pocket and snapped a photo as he slammed the shot glass back down on the table.

Then he pointed at someone in the herd of shifting boys.

Cole took an uneasy step forward. I closed my eyes, hoping he'd slipped back to normal, back to the brother who could transcend peer pressure. Instead, he took another step. A hand reached out and clapped him on the back. Cole had always been so focused on excelling at sports that drinking and drugs were never on the table. My heart lurched when his fingers curled around a shot glass and he lifted it to his lips and downed the liquid. Had Cole changed abruptly or had I just been blind for too long—not seeing my brother for who he really was and making him feel judged when he tried to show me? While I wished he wasn't doing this, it didn't change how I felt about him one iota. Even when he smiled victoriously at the rest of the team and reached for the next glass in a line of six.

Parker was right: there was no way Cole was going anywhere with me. But that didn't mean I'd given up on him.

My stomach twisted into a tessellation as I inched my way down from the side of the locker. My foot slipped, and I would have definitely cracked my skull open if Parker hadn't been there to catch me.

"Satisfied?" he asked in a low whisper.

I shook my head, digging my nails into my palm to keep back the tears I could feel struggling to escape. Parker didn't follow me when I turned and ran from the room.

REASON 8:

HE'S A TOTAL SOCIOPATH.

HE THREATENED ME.

Midnight found me lying awake, staring at the ceiling. And not just because Kendall snored. Cole had never pulled away from me like that, even when I'd done something to deserve it.

It would be so much easier if I could blame Sterling for driving a wedge between us, or Cole for misunderstanding my intentions. But my conscience wouldn't let me. I never expected Cole to be perfect, to be my matching bookend. I wanted him to just be himself, and to trust me as much as I trusted him.

And I'd failed, utterly and completely.

After an hour turning in circles, I made up my mind: I'd go to the headmaster. Sure, Rule 54 forbade tattling and similar immature behaviors, but that Rule should yield right of way in the face of a direct danger to Cole. After all, looking out for Cole was Rule 1, the most fundamental Rule of my existence. I'd always been able to live within the confines of all 537 Rules, without exception, but desperate times called for desperate measures.

First thing in the morning, I made my way to Headmaster Lowell's office. His door was shut, which was unusual. He liked to pretend that he was friends with all the students and encouraged casual drop-ins.

"Is Headmaster Lowell in?" I asked the secretary. As usual, she was dressed like she'd time-traveled in from 1952, creepy android hair and all.

She nodded. "He's in with a student, but you can wait here until he's free."

My shoulder blades twitched at the thought of being late to history. "Will I be excused from a tardy?"

"Of course, dear," the secretary said. "Now just have a seat."

Being late to class was against Rule 87, but I'd never specified whether that included excused absences. My palms were sweating at this obvious flaw in Rule 87, but since I was already in over my head, why not plunge in deeper? Sterling Lane would be shipped off to his penthouse on Park Avenue, where he could squander his smiles on all those Upper East Side girls. With him gone, exposed for what he truly was, Cole would be considerably safer. Then we'd sort out the weight room funding and whatever other trouble Cole had stumbled into.

It wasn't equitable that Sterling would get in trouble for something the entire team had done. But life wasn't fair, plus he'd started it.

I glanced at my watch. I was now officially five minutes late to history. Was my usual seat vacant, patiently waiting for me?

"I'm assuming I'll be fully excused for this tardy," I told the secretary. "Or can my time just run out—like a parking meter? Is there a statute of limitations on being excused?"

She looked up at me, rheumy eyes refocusing through the upper half of her bifocals. "Unless you're here just to skip a quiz, I'm sure Headmaster Lowell will excuse you."

"Skip a quiz? Of course not. It's just that I have the utmost respect for Mrs. Stevens. I wouldn't want my absence from class to convey anything otherwise."

She stared at me for a full count of five before returning to the stack of papers she was sorting into red and blue plastic folders. After that unhelpful exchange, I took out my notebook and started to revise my study timeline for that evening. To no avail. I looked at the clock and back at my notes again. Seconds ticked past—seconds that Mrs. Stevens might be using to administer a pop quiz or to give the details of an extra credit opportunity—an opportunity that I would therefore miss. Not to mention all the extra studying I'd have to do that night to ensure I didn't lag behind on preparing for the AP history exam. I tried to take a deep, calming breath, but it turned into little panicked gulps of air.

Headmaster Lowell's office door finally cracked open an inch, then swung open full force. I shot out of my chair.

Cole walked out, head hanging. My throat tightened at the regret that radiated from him.

"Oh, Harper, you're here already," Headmaster Lowell said, as if he was expecting me. "That was fast."

Cole must have come clean himself, told the headmaster about Sterling's terrible transgressions, and had enlisted me to corroborate his tale.

But Cole refused to meet my eyes. His shoulders slumped until he was almost as short as me.

"I'm sorry about what I said last night," he whispered. "You know I didn't mean it, right?"

"I'd hoped you didn't," I replied, sighing. It was the first time I'd been able to take a full breath since last night. "But I'm sorry, too—I wasn't judging you. Or trying to make you feel worse. I wanted to help."

"I know," he said quietly.

Relief washed over me. Everything between Cole and me was going to work out just fine.

"Just, whatever you hear, don't hate me, okay?" he said.

"I could never hate you," I replied, emphatic. "Never. And what happened last night wasn't your fault."

Cole looked at me, really looked me. Then he dropped his gaze. "You'll see," he mumbled.

Headmaster Lowell turned away from his secretary, whom he'd been conferring with quietly. Then he handed her a sheet of paper.

"Bring the rest in, but stagger it," he said. "I'd like to talk to Sterling Lane next. He's your roommate, correct, Cole?"

Cole nodded without looking up.

"Of course you need to talk to him next," I said. "It really doesn't concern anyone else, does it?"

Headmaster Lowell frowned. "Maybe we should move into my office, Harper." He held the door open and motioned me inside.

His office looked like what a Hollywood set designer would imagine a headmaster's office should be. Because Headmaster Lowell didn't recognize the difference between books that were actually important and books he figured people would expect him to have read. Or between real antiques and flea market specials.

Two spindly, cheaply made wooden chairs perched on the rug in front of his broad mahogany desk. Matching bookcases full of outdated leather encyclopedias and second-tier classics lined one wall, while the other was littered with gaudily framed Picasso reprints and a certificate from a weekend seminar on adolescent psychology that hadn't benefited him one bit.

I sat in the chair nearest Headmaster Lowell's desk. I'd been there only a handful of times, and only when I was being given a commendation for my grades or perfect attendance. It was unexpectedly intimidating to be there for any other reason.

Because I was suddenly nervous, I started spilling my story before the headmaster had even settled into his cracked leather desk chair.

"I know Cole technically incriminated himself if he told you all the details of what happened last night. But really, it wasn't his fault. Sterling is a master manipulator. I have firsthand experience with that."

"Sterling?" He looked genuinely taken aback. "Sterling was involved in this? Do you have any proof?"

I'd watched enough crime dramas to know that the cigarette butt was circumstantial at best. And in this age of digital tampering, admitting photos into evidence was always rife with controversy. First, I had to lay a foundation of facts.

"I think we should start with my testimony," I said.

"Then let's hear it."

"Well, it all started yesterday morning." I leaned forward in my chair. My nervousness dissipated. I told Headmaster Lowell all of it, from Sterling's rude interruption of Mrs. Stevens's class to the way he'd tried to bribe me into doing his homework under the auspices of tutoring him. I was just finishing my itemized list of his dress code violations when Headmaster Lowell held up one hand.

"Maybe I should explain why we're here," he said. "While it's clear you and Sterling have had a misunderstanding regarding his tutoring needs, due to his, um, medical conditions, that's relatively minor in light of what happened last night."

"Oh, I know all about that, too," I told him. "I was watching."

"Watching?" His jaw dropped. It was the perfect opportunity to finish my story without any further interruptions.

"Well, after everything Sterling did yesterday, I had a feeling that any alleged lacrosse meeting he arranged was probably suspect," I explained. "I should add that since my own record is above reproach, I'm trusting that you'll overlook this minor indiscretion." I paused to suck in oxygen. "I snuck into the boys' locker room on a hunch they were up to no good. And I was right. I have photo documentation."

Headmaster Lowell's eyes widened, like he couldn't believe his good fortune at having a firsthand witness. But instead of rejoicing at his windfall, the headmaster massaged his forehead with his fingers, just like my father does every time I try to explain something important to him. "Before you tell me anything else that could incriminate *you*," he said, "you need to hear why we're here. Last night someone stole one thousand dollars from a locked box in the athletic department office. Based on security's detail, we know it occurred between midnight and six a.m., and there were no signs of forced entry. Cole and the rest of the team raised that money with their annual barbecue fund-raiser to purchase weight room equipment. The administration intends to launch a full investigation."

I was so caught off guard that my brain couldn't switch tracks and process what he'd just said.

"What does this have to do with me?" I demanded. "Or Cole?"

"Nothing, at least directly." He took off his glasses and

set them on the surface of his mahogany desk. "Whoever did this had a key. Cole was given a key due to his responsibilities as lacrosse captain so that he could have access to the locker room before games."

"Then all the other sports captains have keys, too." I wasn't at all surprised that the headmaster had missed something so obvious. "Not to mention all the staff and teachers. That doesn't mean anything."

"A key was found at the scene of the crime. Which is why I've asked everyone to produce their keys, as proof of their innocence." Headmaster Lowell dropped his voice. "Cole claims he lost his key during practice yesterday. While I want to take his statement at face value, I was told by several members of the faculty, most notably his coach, that Cole has exhibited unusual behaviors the last two weeks. He has been withdrawn and has struggled to complete his assignments. The faculty and I have been discussing the possibility that substances are involved. It's not at all uncommon for these types of incidents to indicate a deeper underlying issue."

"Cole wouldn't do this." But the sinking feeling in my stomach wouldn't let me lie to myself *and* to Headmaster Lowell. I hated that I wasn't certain how far astray Cole's desperation would carry him. Still, it made no sense—why would Cole steal from his own fund-raiser when he was desperate to increase the funds?

"I keep telling myself the same thing," Headmaster Lowell replied. "After knowing him for years, it just doesn't add up. Which is why I wanted to see if he'd said anything to you. Anything that would shed some light on the matter."

It was a crossroads—tell the truth and betray my brother, or throw my lot in with him, knowing that somehow I'd find a way to make this right.

"No," I said. "But you should ask Sterling. I wouldn't put it past him to steal Cole's keys and take that money just for laughs."

Headmaster Lowell sighed. "I was hoping we could keep on topic here, Harper. Sterling is working hard to turn his life around, and I won't have you or anyone else discriminate against him based on his past mistakes. We don't fling mud just to protect our families."

He was defending Sterling *and* criticizing me all in one breath. Worst of all, he seemed determined to blame Cole, no matter how much reasonable doubt I cast upon the situation. My hands wrapped around the seat of my chair, squeezing so hard my fingers ached. But nothing I did was enough to hold it back.

The Sterling Lane fury clawed its way right out of its cage and hurled itself at Headmaster Lowell.

"How is this off topic? I know why he got kicked out of his last school. Arson. And I just told you he tried to bribe me to write his papers, and that he was drinking in class. Does it really seem all that amazing that he'd do something like this?" Somehow, I was on my feet, yelling in the headmaster's face. "On the one hand we have Cole, who's never stepped a toe out of line, and on the other we have an absolute reprobate with unfettered access to Cole's keys."

There was a soft knock on the door. "Everything all right in here?" The secretary peered around the corner of the door. "I heard shouting."

"Everything is fine, thank you," Headmaster Lowell snapped.

His secretary was eyeing me like I was vermin she wanted to chase out of the room with a broom. "Sterling Lane is here," she said. Her voice warmed as it wrapped around his name, like he'd been sitting out there charming those knee-high, flesh-colored nylons right off her. "Such a polite boy. Shall I send him in?"

Headmaster Lowell glanced at me, visibly annoyed, and I assumed I would be dismissed. Given how raw and out of control I was, that would be the safest course of action — even if it meant I'd failed, again, to expose Sterling Lane in all his horrifying glory. I was primed for detonation and Sterling Lane was missile-grade uranium.

Headmaster Lowell examined his glasses, turning them over on the surface of his mahogany desk and adjusting his nose pads. Finally, he nodded. "Yes, send him in."

I started to rise, ready to flee, but Headmaster Lowell extended a hand toward me. "No. Sit for a moment, please, Harper."

Panic consumed me — palms sweating, crippling nausea. I couldn't be trapped in that tiny room with Sterling Lane. But per Rule 305, I couldn't defy the headmaster, or any other teacher. Maybe I could throw up right on the faded beige carpet and get banished to the nurse's office.

Then Sterling Lane sauntered in, dressed to perfection in a starched white shirt and pressed khaki slacks with a crease down the front. I had to admit, he cleaned up well. But it was a trick. He was trying to win Headmaster Lowell over to his side. When he smiled, it was mild and sedate. Every last ounce of viper venom had vaporized.

"Good morning, Harper." Sterling sounded genuinely delighted to see me.

"You're not fooling anyone. We all know your views on the dress code."

Sterling's eyebrows snapped together. Then he cracked a grin and looked down sheepishly. It was an Oscar-worthy performance. "I know," he said, rubbing the back of his head with one hand. "I'm grateful you filled me in. It's hard to learn the ropes at a new school. But you've been so helpful, pointing out everything I'm doing wrong."

Headmaster Lowell missed the sarcasm, and his warning glare was aimed at me and me alone. "Sterling, I'm afraid I have two things to discuss with you this morning rather than one, as I'd intended. Let's start with what I believe will be the easiest to resolve. It has been suggested that you may have been relapsing into some of those behaviors that got you into trouble in the past."

Sterling looked at me, eyes narrowed. But he quickly schooled his face into a novice nun's meekness. "It has been difficult, sir. But I assure you, I've been fighting hard against those old patterns like you encouraged me to do."

"Your father says you've spent a lot of time visiting your grandmother at Crest Haven—I know he's pleased to see you're rising to the occasion since it's one of the reasons you asked to attend this school."

"I've always been close to my grandmother," Sterling replied. "And my father knows it. I'd never let her down."

I glanced at Sterling out of the corner of my eye. Crest Haven was a private residence for Alzheimer's patients, designed to feel like a normal community instead of like a nursing home. It was famous—world-renowned for its innovative approach—and located just a few miles away. Somehow I couldn't picture Sterling playing the diligent grandson, but I'd heard him on the phone with my own two ears, sounding almost sweet. But that wasn't enough to vindicate him from the rest of what he'd done.

"Just be careful, Sterling," Headmaster Lowell drawled. "The human mind longs for patterns, for the familiar. We need to wear down the path of positivity in your brain so that when you face a difficult decision, you naturally choose the right path. The good path that leads to solid grades and a brilliant future. As long as you avoid slipping back into those negative paths, they'll soon become overrun with weeds and dust, and won't call out to you any longer."

"An excellent metaphor, sir." Sterling nodded, all solemn and contrite.

I couldn't help it. I snorted.

"This is very serious, Harper," Headmaster Lowell said. "We're talking about Sterling's future. A future that is full of promise."

"Yeah, the promise of the penal system. He's playing the contrite little sociopath just to keep you off his back. Rest assured he'll return to his room and his snifter of brandy. I can't believe I'm the only one who sees through this crap."

Headmaster Lowell dropped the pen he'd been twirling absently between his fingers. "I've warned you once already, Harper. Sterling's not the only one who needs to work on positivity. I've talked to you before about your temper, and it seems to me you're losing control of it again."

As Headmaster Lowell bent down to retrieve his pen, an invisible force tugged at the corner of Sterling's mouth. He leveled me with a horrible, wicked smile that slipped back undercover just in time to avoid detection.

"He's mocking you," I said. "As soon as you bent over, he cracked into his sadistic little grin."

Sterling put his hands up in the air, eyes wide with innocence.

"Harper, you need to control your outbursts." Headmaster Lowell shook his head at me. "Now as you know, Sterling has an injury to his hand and can't take notes. Given your academic achievement and the little misunderstanding that seems to be at the heart of this, I think it would be a good exercise for you two to work together.

This is an excellent opportunity to help someone who's trying to better himself. What is the point of excelling if not to bring others up with you?"

"To get away from people like him," I said. "That's the point of excelling. To separate the wheat from the chaff. I'm not helping him. He's a deceitful, manipulative psychopath, and one day you'll eat your words. And if you don't believe me, take a look at this." In a fit of impulsive recklessness, I pulled out my phone and flipped through the photos, searching for the right one. "He got the entire lacrosse team drunk in the locker room last night. I took a photo to prove it."

Sterling tried to strangle the laugh, but it exploded in a fit of coughing. He covered his mouth with one hand, fighting it so hard he bit his palm to keep it in check. I hoped to God he really was choking to death like it sounded.

"Water," Sterling coughed out, doubling over.

Headmaster Lowell flew out of his chair and rushed to the office door. I could hear him outside, filling a glass from the cooler.

"Go ahead, choke on my vindication." I crossed my arms across my chest. "I'll dance on your grave wearing tap shoes."

"Sneaking into the boys' locker room?" he murmured. "I feel so violated. Tell me, sweetheart, did you see anything you like?" He flashed a smile so big that every perfectly polished molar came out to contribute. It sent a shiver down my neck, the way his eyes narrowed as he surveyed me. "Tread carefully, little Harper. You don't need another enemy. Especially one like me."

The shuffle of Headmaster Lowell's feet on the thick carpet seemed to bring him back to his senses. He dropped the smile and cleared his throat again, keeping up the choking act.

"Thank you, sir," Sterling said, accepting the glass of water. He turned those hazy brown eyes on me. There was anger there. The kind of anger I was smart enough to pay attention to. Because Sterling Lane wasn't half as stupid and lazy as I wanted him to be.

I held my phone aloft for Headmaster Lowell to examine the photo. Sterling's eyes scanned the image, then he leaned back, crossing his arms across his chest. He was up to something.

"Are team meetings not allowed at Sablebrook?" Sterling asked. "It's a naive question, because yes, I admit to holding one. I didn't know it would be an issue." I looked again at the photo, scrutinizing it with unbiased eyes—eyes of someone who wasn't there to see and hear the raucous cheering. Sure, Sterling was at a table, surrounded by his teammates, but the vodka was nowhere to be seen. Only the thin rim of the shot glass was visible in his grasp. Truly, he could have been holding anything.

"But—I have more," I sputtered. "This is his." I'd gone too far to turn back. I reached into my bag and produced the small brown cigarette butt, secured in its labeled plastic bag. I set it on Headmaster Lowell's desk as he put on his glasses to examine it. He turned the bag over in his hands, a pinched expression on his face. "I'm afraid we're not equipped for DNA testing at Sablebrook," Headmaster Lowell said, glancing up at me.

"I retrieved this from below Sterling and Cole's window," I told them. "He was smoking in his room and flicked it outside. I saw him."

Sterling's eyebrows lifted in surprise. He opened his mouth to speak but then seemed to think better of it.

"Don't look so self-satisfied," I snapped at him. "You know I'm right."

Sterling uncrossed his arms and steepled his fingers. "I think anyone raised within the purview of the United States judicial system would appreciate how paltry this so-called evidence appears. And how desperate your accusations seem. We both know what this is *really* about."

"Of course we do," I said. "It's about Cole."

"Harper, I'd like us to move past this," Sterling replied mildly, switching to a tone I'd never expected from him. It was the way you'd soothe a wounded animal. "I understand you're hurt. And why you're so desperate for revenge."

"I'm not hurt—"

"Harper," Headmaster Lowell interjected. "Please let Sterling finish."

My stomach contracted into a pea-sized ball with the density of Venus. I had no idea where Sterling was going with this, and that terrified me.

"Now, I don't want to make you uncomfortable, sir," Sterling continued. "But the thing is, I'm really not ready for a relationship. And you know how girls get. Hell hath no fury, and all that."

The pressure. The pressure behind my eyes. My head had either exploded or was in the process of doing so, my brains brightening the puke-brown curtains.

There were no words. No words for the unbridled outrage that was bursting the blood from my veins.

Headmaster Lowell flushed pink, whereas I kept on cruising past red into a hearty shade of eggplant. "I don't want to date you," I shrieked. "I hate you."

"Settle down now, Harper," said Headmaster Lowell. "I think you're right, Sterling. I think it's best if I just let the two of you work this out by yourselves."

"But he's *lying*," I shouted.

"I know how difficult this age can be," Headmaster

Lowell said, breaking out one of the lessons from his weekend course in pop psychology. "You know, Dr. Schwartz isn't just a career counselor. He has training in, well, personal issues as well."

It was too much. Too much for me to endure. I couldn't sit through another moment of this horrible, nonsensical farce of my worst nightmare.

"You'll regret this," I said, pushing to my feet so fast my chair toppled over behind me. If I even looked at Sterling, I'd punch him right in his aristocratic nose. "He'll ruin this school and everyone in it. And when he does, I'll serve you your words on a silver platter." I stormed out of the room, but before the *bang* of the slamming door separated us, I heard Headmaster Lowell apologizing to Sterling.

Apologizing.

For *my* behavior.

I hated Sterling Lane with a white-hot rage that set my whole body on fire.

Air. I needed air. I was suffocating in that room. Choking on the hateful words and lies Sterling Lane had shoveled down my throat. I'd yelled at the headmaster— *me*. I couldn't even process how many Rules I'd just broken, and for nothing. Cole was still in danger and now Headmaster Lowell thought I was attracted to a sociopath. My credibility was ruined.

Cole looked up as I ran past, but I couldn't stop. Even when he reached out, trying to grab me. I surged down the hallway and crashed through the front door of the administrative building at full speed.

Desperate lungfuls of air weren't enough to stop the panic. Rules 1 through 20 danced through my mind in backward order. Then forward. And backward again. I started to calm down as the Rules wrapped their reassuring arms around me.

Sterling Lane would pay. And pay. And pay again.

I just needed time to plot and plan and organize. And no matter what, I'd never tip my hand again. It was a mistake showing Sterling the photo and the cigarette butt. A master liar like him would always outmaneuver me in face-to-face situations. It was all too easy for him to antagonize and goad me into making a fool of myself.

I'd played right into his hands. Next time I would wait patiently and strike when he'd never see me coming. I'd strike without mercy.

One glance at my watch told me I'd missed 85 percent of history class, and I'd neglected to get a note to excuse me for being tardy. And then, inexplicably, I didn't care. There was no way I'd give Sterling the satisfaction of seeing me slink back into the office to ask for one.

I leaned against the building, pressing my forehead into the cool brick facade. My breathing returned to normal, and my stomach crawled down out of my throat. I'd just started to feel like myself again when cold fingers curled gently around my elbow and guided me around.

I opened my eyes.

Sterling Lane was standing there. He held out a starched and folded white cloth handkerchief. When I shook my head, he pressed it into my open palm. Tears brimmed in my eyes and a few escaped down my cheeks. I hated him even more for seeing me that way.

"Walk with me," he said, slipping one hand under my elbow.

"No."

"I have a note excusing both of us from Mrs. Stevens's class," he said. The gentle pressure of his hand on my elbow towed me along two steps. "I suggest you come."

I used his pretentious, monogrammed handkerchief to dry my cheeks as I fell into step beside him, chin aloft. I'd never again give him the satisfaction of seeing me vulnerable.

"I'm sorry we started off so badly, Harper," he said.

"No, you're not."

"Actually, I really am. Because contrary to what you think, I'm not a sadistic person. I can't afford to be expelled again."

"Daddy will take away the trust fund?"

"Yes," he answered. "But more importantly, my grandmother needs me. I can't change schools again."

Well, that wasn't fighting fair. Although knowing him, he was just playing that card for sympathy.

"And I'll do whatever it takes to get what I need. It's how I was raised."

"I don't want to hear your excuses," I told him.

"It isn't one," he said. "It's a fact. You see, my father isn't a nice person." We were halfway across the broad, grassy quad that separated the administrative building from the academic ones. I slowed my pace to match his, wanting to get away from him as soon as possible but also knowing that I needed the note he claimed to possess.

"Apple doesn't fall too far from the tree." I was proud I managed to match his apathetic tone despite the tumult raging through my insides. Two could play at that game.

If Sterling heard me, he didn't acknowledge it. "Every year, he drags my brother and me on some commando-style 'men's trip' to keep us from getting too soft. As if you learn to be a man by pissing in a stream and boiling water to brush your teeth."

"So what?" I asked, failing to hide my interest. "Why should I care?"

"Because sweetheart, last year while sweating my ass off in some godforsaken Peruvian jungle, I stumbled upon a pearl of wisdom that you're desperately lacking."

A little shiver ran down my spine when he paused on the sidewalk and looked at me, standing so close I could see the stubble along his jaw. It was oddly out of place in his new, über-groomed appearance. Try as he might, he couldn't quite remove all lingering traces of laziness. He released my arm, sensing instinctually that I was locked in place by my curiosity.

"We went out one night in this rickety canoe, looking for alligators. Because our guide was a lunatic. We paddled right through this tall grass, shining flashlights into the faces of the alligators floating around us, watching us. Their eyes reflected the beam—lit up like a strand of Christmas tree lights on the surface of the water. It was actually a stunning sight." He smiled a little. "Then all of a sudden, the guide reaches down and grabs one. Just grabs the alligator and rips it out of the water. And it's tiny, a baby. But it lashes and snaps and tries to rip our hands off. Which was pretty awe-inspiring when you think about it—that kind of spirit.

"The guide taught us how to hold it behind the jaw so it couldn't bite. Then we started up again, and after about twenty minutes, my ape of a brother reaches down and tries to grab the tail of what looked like a smallish alligator, floating right in the reeds. And the guide sees him and knocks him away, onto the bottom of the canoe just as the head of the biggest fucking alligator I've ever seen surfaces, with teeth like steak knives, and lunges at the side of the boat. It could have eaten my brother whole. Not that I would have cared."

Sterling paused. I cleared my throat, impatient for him to get to the point. It was destabilizing, standing so close to him. When he stopped talking, his proximity was all I could think about. There was nothing to occupy the space between us but his words.

"Then the guide stands up in the canoe all crazy-eyed, waving around a serial-killer machete. And he picks my brother up by the front of his shirt and says, 'Never grab a gator's tail unless you can see the whole of the beast. Because the tip of the tail is the narrowest part. It's deceptive. And the teeth will come crashing round faster than you can blink.'"

Suddenly, it seemed like Sterling was looming over me. Since he never stood up straight, I'd never realized he was so tall and broad-shouldered.

"And now, Harper Campbell, even if you didn't fully understand the ramifications of what you just did, like my idiot brother, you pulled the alligator's tail. Here come the teeth."

We stood there in silence for a beat, just long enough for all 537 of my Rules to roar back in solidarity. Sterling Lane would do anything to win, as he'd just shown. But in that moment, I realized I would, too.

"Is that some sort of threat?" I asked. My joints felt like jelly as I lifted my chin and met his gaze. I would never again let him realize his effect on me. "Because you have no idea who you're messing with. Whatever you do, I'll throw back at you tenfold. And that's a promise."

His brown eyes widened as I took a step closer, just to show him I wouldn't back down. "So tread carefully, Sterling Lane," I added. "You don't need another enemy. Especially one like me."

REASON 9:

I MAY HAVE LOST COLE FOREVER—AND KENDALL.

BUT I WASN'T REALLY SURE ABOUT HER STATUS IN MY LIFE, ANYWAY, SO PERHAPS THAT PART ISN'T ENTIRELY STERLING'S FAULT.

I sat outside the administration building for two hours that afternoon, waiting for Cole to walk past. Few other students appreciated the manifold advantages of that location. From my hiding spot between two pillars, I had a full view of the quad, stretching from the ivy-encrusted library to the modern glass facade of the cafeteria. Nearly everyone, at some point, had to walk past. Because of the sheer girth and spacing of the pillars gracing the entranceway, I was completely hidden from view unless someone was specifically looking for me.

But it wasn't like my peers were flocking to the headmaster's office or loitering on the steps. Gratuitous socializing and jock-boy horseplay were reserved for the steps outside the library, as if they were intentionally trying to distract the students studying just inside the door.

The concrete stairs can be quite cold, so I brought an extra jacket to use as a cushion. Normally I reserved that spot for pleasure reading. I could close my eyes and imagine scholars in ancient Greece pontificating over scrolls on pillared entryways much like this Grecian replica. But today, I had my textbooks arranged neatly around myself so I could study while watching for Cole. It was far less convenient than the desk in my room, or my usual study spot on the second floor of the library behind the reference section. There, it was always silent as a crypt since no one bothered to use encyclopedias anymore.

Cole had vanished after the meeting with the headmaster, and his phone went straight to voicemail. I'd even knocked on his door, despite my fear that doing so would bring me face-to-face with Sterling Lane and his alligator teeth. But no one was there.

Left with no other course of action, I shifted into stakeout mode. I'd nearly finished my physics outline when a shadow fell across my page. Kendall was standing there, watching me. She clutched a square canvas to her chest, but I could only see the wooden frame of the back. Knowing Kendall, it was probably some fashion-related flowchart to help her pick the perfect shade of eye makeup.

"I heard about your brother," she said, leaning back against the pillar like she planned to settle in and prolong this interruption. "Are you okay?"

I narrowed my eyes, waiting for the second blow of what was undoubtedly a two-punch combination. Cole was the one in trouble, not me. I couldn't fathom why she was asking. There was no way she understood the depths of my loyalty to Cole. But as far as I could tell, Kendall simply expected my reply.

"Not really," I said, surprising myself. Ordinarily, I'd never expose my jugular so readily, but exhaustion had settled in my bones, rendering me vulnerable. "I don't know what's going on with him. He's been acting strange for weeks, and now he could actually get expelled, all thanks to Sterling Lane. I almost ripped Sterling's throat out in the headmaster's office. He had the gall to say…" I let my voice trail off. I'd almost told Kendall about Sterling's wild accusation in the headmaster's office. Maybe Cole wasn't the only one who was behaving out of character. I sat up straighter, wrapping Rule 157 around myself: I never drop my guard around those vultures.

"What did he say?" She nudged my leg with her shoe.

"Nothing," I snapped. "It doesn't matter. What matters is Cole. I'm waiting for him so we can get to the bottom of this. You can leave now. You're distracting me."

"He was in the library," Kendall said, not even acknowledging my dismissal. "Just a few minutes ago. He was reading a magazine in those beanbag chairs. I'm sure he's still there."

I pushed to my feet, sending outlines and paper index cards fluttering across the pavement. That was also unlike me. Years ago, I'd developed a foolproof system for packing my study materials away. Kendall bent down to help gather them up, tottering precariously in ridiculous heels that were better suited for soil aeration than human movement. I glanced over at the canvas she'd set down. It was a landscape—Sablebrook reimagined in impressionist style, all in shades of purple and blue.

"What's that?" I asked.

Her cheeks pinkened as she reached over and turned it to face the pillar instead of outward.

"Nothing," she said, handing me a stack of note cards. Her hands were shaking. Was it possible Ms. Popularity had a chink in her perfectly glossy armor?

"Did you do that?" I asked. "Because it's really good."

"Thanks. I've been stacking papers for years," she said

drily. "I know you think I'm a bubblehead, but give me *some* credit."

"No," I said. "The picture."

"I was just goofing around in the studio. It's terrible, isn't it?" The poised and perfect Kendall Frank was visibly shrinking on the spot.

"No, it's wonderful," I said. And I meant it. Sure, Kendall Frank had egged my room. Probably even sketched one of those Harper the Hag cartoons, given her apparent level of artistic skill. But talent was talent, and always something to be revered—and I should know, because I worked like a demon to maintain the illusion of it.

Surprise and a guarded gratitude filled her face. "You're not just saying that?" Then she shook her head. "No. I know you mean it. You don't give a crap about being polite. That's one thing I really like about you."

"Really?" I asked. "Most people ostracize me because of it."

"Well, most people suck." Kendall straightened to her feet.

"You know, I like how you rearranged the room." I stood, too, tucking my papers into my bag. "If you wanted to add…other decorative items, I wouldn't object." I tilted my head toward her picture.

"Oh, I couldn't do that," she said, horrified. "You mean hang that picture? Where people would see it? I don't know—what would they think?"

"That you have talent?" I ventured.

She shook her head. "It's just—it wouldn't fit in with my image."

At the lameness of that response, the thoughts that had been percolating in my mind since Kendall first moved in finally broke loose. "Fine. Shove it in your closet. Toss it in the homecoming bonfire for all I care. Hide it just like you've been hiding your academic proclivities for the last few years. I know you're smart. I saw your transcript. Sort of by accident, but still. What I can't figure out is why you'd hide it. If I were you, I'd be asking myself what kind of jerks I'm trying to impress by playing dumb and hiding a serious artistic talent. Give your friends some credit. They can't all be as bad as they seem."

Her eyes widened in shock. "This—this is why you don't have any friends," Kendall snapped, motioning to the space between us.

"Good. It's also the reason I don't care," I told her. "And if you don't like my opinion, don't ask for it. You're the one who said you appreciate my honesty. It's not my fault if you don't like the truth. And I'll tell you something else: I like the real you—the one who isn't always worrying about impressing her friends. That girl egged my room, an action that nearly crushed me. I cried for hours. But this girl? She actually felt bad about it."

She stood there, just blinking at me, while I watched her, wondering if I'd just brought an end to the tentative truce between us.

"You're such a jerk, Harper," she said at last, but there was no heat behind it. "I don't know why I try talking to you. You know, there's a happy medium between buttering people up and eviscerating them. A simple *Kendall, be true to who you are and people will accept you* would have sufficed."

"Yeah? Well, I don't know if that's true," I replied. "Look at me—I'm not exactly a social role model."

I turned, prepared to march away in search of Cole, but Kendall caught my arm. "Harper, wait. You act so aloof, like you're better than us. That's why most people leave you alone. I didn't know how much it all hurt you.

I'm sorry. I really am."

"Thanks for that," I said. "Now if we're finished with this episode of *Dr. Phil*, I need to go find Cole."

I grabbed my bag and shuffled down the stairs. As I approached the sprawling brick facade of the library, Cole emerged from the double glass doors, backpack thrown over his shoulder.

"Cole!" I shouted, loud enough to wake the dead.

He just kept walking, which wasn't a good sign. I jogged to catch up, then slowed a half step behind him. "This is ridiculous, Cole. You know I'm here. Please stop walking."

"I'm late for practice," he said. "I don't want to screw that up, too." He didn't sound mad, at least not at me, but he also wasn't himself. Not by a long shot.

"Please, Cole," I said. "Just stop and talk for a minute. I called Dad. I told him I was taking an extra SAT pre-course and he gave me this." I shoved an envelope of cash at him.

"What's this?" he asked.

"Eight hundred dollars," I said. "I know it's not enough, but I'll get there, I promise."

"You didn't have to do that," he said. "But thank you. You make it sound like this is your problem to solve. It's not. You should take this money and put it toward a real class." He tried to hand the envelope back to me, but I shook my head.

"Then how will you get the money?" I asked. "What will you do?"

"It's under control," he said.

"This is about what happened in the headmaster's office, isn't it? Are you going to tell me what's going on?"

"No." He stopped and turned to face me. "I can't."

"Why?" I asked. "Why can't you tell me?"

"Because," he said, shrugging.

"God, Cole," I snapped. "You're being so evasive. What

happened to the money? This isn't a joke—you could be expelled."

"You think I don't know that?" He skewered me with his gaze. "You think I don't know how badly I've screwed everything up? That it's not eating me up inside? The last thing I need is to have you look at me like that."

"Like what?" I asked, taken aback by the way his voice broke over those last words.

"Like I'm a complete disappointment. Like I'll never live up to your standards. Look, Harps, I'll find my own way out of this."

"It's Sterling, isn't it? He talked you into doing something crazy."

"Why do you keep trying to drag him into this?" Cole demanded. "It's got nothing to do with him."

"Maybe because he's turned expulsion into an art form. He transfers in, becomes your roommate, and five minutes later you're committing crimes? Do you seriously wonder why I keep bringing him into this?"

Cole shook his head. "This right here is why I can't talk to you. You just don't listen. Sterling is probably the most loyal guy I've ever known—stop making him out to be some sort of criminal. Look, I need to go. I get your need to keep me on the up-and-up so you can stamp *Rule Follower* on my photo and file me away with your index cards. I get that this is wrecking your world. But I'm late for practice, and your needs aren't the only ones that matter."

The way he said it, so matter-of-fact, so calm and collected, made the words sting that much more. If he'd hurled them at me in anger, I could have retorted or defended myself. Instead, I swallowed them whole. And just stood there watching as he slung his bag back over his shoulder and walked away.

REASON 10:

IF HE KNOWS SO MUCH ABOUT THE FRENCH REVOLUTION, WHY IS HE EVEN IN HIGH SCHOOL?

HE SHOULD JUST GO JOIN THE REST OF THE SCHOLARS IN THE CATACOMBS OF LA SORBONNE.

I'd made a conscious decision not to let Sterling Lane affect my emotional control. But in light of the alligator event, I glanced up at him when he wandered into history. As he strutted to his seat, those brown eyes met mine and narrowed.

I wasn't afraid of Sterling Lane, not in the least. But after what he'd said to me yesterday, his direct and determined stare made me drop my favorite pen.

Rule 295 tells me to be strong in the face of blatant intimidation, so I did my best to glare right back, defying his smug little grin. Ignoring the way he lingered at Kendall's desk, the two of them so intent on each other that they might have been unearthing the secret of nuclear fission.

Suddenly I wondered if it was ill-advised to encourage Kendall to pursue Sterling. He was far more dangerous than I'd previously imagined, and if they became an item Sterling would be imminently invading my personal space.

Then there was the fact that Kendall wasn't entirely

horrible, once you got to know her.

I'd been nervous to return to our room after our harsh words outside the administrative building. When I finally went home, Kendall had seemed nervous, too. I'd had the distinct impression she'd been waiting for me. After a few awkward exchanges, we'd spent the rest of the night reorganizing the room. Her contributions had been quite astute, and my Rules had applauded the area rug and the storage bins we'd added to the bookshelves. I'd never imagined that the worlds of fashion and logical efficiency could merge so harmoniously.

That had to be why it rankled me so much to see the two of them locked together in conversation.

After much shuffling and unnecessary rearrangement of his long limbs, Sterling finally settled in the far corner of the back row. I did my best to avoid looking back there. It was harder than anticipated, especially given that he and I were the only two people sitting silently while Mrs. Stevens distributed our graded quizzes. But Sterling didn't seem to mind. In fact, he looked supremely confident as he met my gaze again and stretched his arms behind his head, letting his hands come to rest on the back of his head, elbows out. A classic vacation pose. All the while never breaking eye contact with me.

The challenge, the threat, was plastered all over those chiseled features. For the first time ever, Rule 295 quivered a little in the face of adversity.

I was afraid, even though I'd already made up my mind that no matter what form the alligator's teeth took, I wouldn't flinch—no matter how many times they bit me.

Mrs. Stevens called us to attention and started the lesson. I glanced back at Sterling, waiting for the fireworks to begin, but he was gazing out the window, watching the grounds crew cut back an overgrown shrub. I'd been counting on Mrs. Stevens to make him squirm a little, so it was infuriating to have Sterling sit there so passively, like class wasn't even going on at all.

After ten minutes of dividing my attention between Mrs. Stevens and Sterling's atypical silence, I let Mrs. Stevens win out. But as soon as I surrendered to that day's lecture, noting how skillfully I'd anticipated the important points in my outline, Mrs. Stevens froze.

"Mr. Lane, I'm going to have to ask you to put that away."

A thrill of anticipation shimmied down my spine. My blood pressure claimed twenty more millimeters of mercury as I whipped around, faster than all the rest of the class. But there was no reason to rush. Sterling was settling back in his seat, digging in his heels and preparing for a show.

On his desk was a small tablet, resting next to his aviators. One earbud perched in his ear; the other dangled at his elbow. His eyes were glued to the screen. As we all watched, he laughed out loud. Then he looked up, slowly and deliberately, as if suddenly noticing that the rest of the room was motionless, staring at him.

He smiled at Mrs. Stevens, wide and bright. "Missed this episode last week." He was savoring the moment; I could see it in the set of his jaw, in the way his eyes flashed around the room, greeting each and every member of his audience and basking in their rapt attention.

"And you'll be missing every future episode as well," Mrs. Stevens said, walking down the aisle and confiscating the small electronic device.

"You can't be serious," he said. "I was hardly being disruptive. No one saw what I was doing until you pointed it out."

"*I* saw what you were doing," she said. "And *I* found it disruptive."

"If you'd teach something everyone didn't already know, maybe I'd pay attention. I was keeping one ear open, just in case." He lifted the dangling earbud.

"Everyone already knows this? Okay, Sterling, I'll bite. If you know so much about the French Revolution, you're welcome to come to the front of the room and enlighten us."

I hadn't been this excited since the year I'd won a special achievement award in French. My heart hammered so fast I felt dizzy as I tried to imagine how he'd wiggle out of this one. I held the edges of the desk to keep myself upright when he rose and ambled up to the front of the room. He folded his sunglasses and set them down on my desk as he passed, staking a claim.

Or throwing down the gauntlet.

My hands balled up into fists, itching to crush those stupid shades like a sledgehammer. But I was in the front row. There was no way I'd give my classmates the satisfaction of watching me crack.

"Won't you be needing these?" I asked, holding up the horrible sunglasses. "Your allergy to halogen lightbulbs, I mean. I'd hate for you to go into anaphylactic shock when I'm not armed with an EpiPen to stab into your heart."

"I think you mean my thigh? I hope you're not planning on medical school." His tone was condescension incarnate. "A miraculous recovery," he added. "From those debilitating conditions. But I appreciate your genuine concern as usual, Harper." He resumed his saunter toward the front of the class, arranged himself on the edge of Mrs. Stevens's desk, and looked out over the class, pretending he actually had something to teach us other than drinking games.

And then he did the unexpected. He started talking,

telling us things. Things from the textbook I'd so carefully reviewed last night in anticipation, and things I'd never heard before. About Robespierre and the original libertine, the Marquis de Sade, whom Sterling talked about with a disturbing degree of respect. Then again, I hadn't known de Sade's role in the revolution, or how he'd settled down later in life with an impoverished widow and her child.

It was an incredible blur of facts, details, dates. For a moment, I actually dropped my guard. I pulled out my outline and started revising on the spot, something I rarely did. At that point in my career at Sablebrook, the teachers were perfectly predictable—I always knew the types of things they were likely to highlight for the exam. But this was different. This was just about learning.

Ten minutes in, Mrs. Stevens held up a hand, silencing Sterling. The look on her face was one I'd never seen before. Pride.

"Impressive," she said. "Care to tell me where you learned that?"

Sterling shrugged. "Figured it's common knowledge." Then he looked right at me, eyes flickering to the notes scribbled all over my outline. Proof positive I hadn't known half of the esoteric tidbits he'd just scattered at our feet. It was meant to insult me—all of it. This fantastic display was an alligator tooth.

"Did *you* know that?" the boy behind me whispered, nudging my shoulder with his knuckle.

"Yes, *did* you?" Sterling prodded. I swallowed bile, along with a helping of pure, unadulterated jealously, and pretended not to hear.

"Common knowledge? Hardly." Mrs. Stevens chuckled, actually charmed by his false modesty. "And I counted seven different primary references you must have consulted. It seems we have a true historian in our midst." It might have been my imagination, but I was pretty sure she avoided my eyes when she said it. As if the comparison was that unfavorable—even after years of knowing me, of teaching me herself, I was a disappointment.

"If you could learn some self-control, you might actually surprise everyone with what you can do. Maybe you could be the first one to finally give Harper a run for her money."

Her words sent shock waves of panic rippling down my spine.

"Well now," Sterling said, flashing me a crocodile smile. "That does sound fun."

Our eyes met, and I half expected to hear a roll of apocalyptic thunder. The air crackled with colliding electrons. The oxygen was pressed from my lungs.

"There's always time for a fresh start, Sterling," Mrs. Stevens said, reaching out and patting his arm affectionately as he walked past. "Maybe it's time to show us—and yourself—what you can do. And in that vein, I'd like you all to write an essay, due next week, on the French Revolution. And I must say, Sterling, after what you just showed us, I'll be looking forward to reading yours."

My throat constricted; my thoughts moved sluggishly, bludgeoned into submission by my hammering pulse.

But then Rule 9 came to my rescue just when I needed it most: I do not give up.

I twisted in my seat and craned my neck to get a view of Sterling Lane. It wasn't until he looked up and started laughing that I realized how long I'd been glaring at him. He scrunched his face up tight, like a crabby little old man. Impersonating me.

It was against Rule 284, but screw it. I grabbed his carelessly discarded aviator sunglasses off my desk and hurled them at him. My aim was dead true, thanks to Cole's constant wheedling for batting practice. But Sterling was an athlete, too. He snatched the sunglasses out of the air with one hand, laughter doubling. His straight white teeth flashed so bright they practically blinded me.

There weren't sufficient words in the English language to describe the width and breadth of my feelings for Sterling Lane—hate, loathe, revile, despise. And if I had a thesaurus on hand, I wouldn't use it to refine the list. I'd hurl it right at his head.

REASON 11:

THE RULES. THE RULES!

HE HIJACKED MY RULES.

When I returned to my room that evening, Kendall was sprawled on her bed, wrapped in a fuzzy white blanket, eyes closed. Her shoes weren't on her feet this time, but they were still resting on her pillow. I shuddered at the thought of pressing my face against such contamination. Then I looked at the floor—the empty Tupperware container was the exact size and shape of the one I'd used to store the batch of chocolate-covered madeleines I'd whipped up to celebrate my A on the physics test. Kendall had refused to even taste them before since they weren't on her diet, yet she had devoured the entire batch from the look of it.

"What is that smell?" I asked. "Have you been burning incense or something? You know, that's been linked to serious, long-term respiratory conditions."

She opened her eyes and looked at me, her gaze vacant and strange.

"Are you okay?" I turned to hang my jacket in my closet.

There, on the narrow strip of plaster between our two closets, was her painting. I smiled, an actual warm feeling spreading across my chest that she'd taken my advice.

A low voice drifted out from the darkened corner of the room.

"I've been waiting for you."

I turned and came face-to-face with the devil himself. He was perched on my bed, filthy boat shoes brushing against the edges of my freshly laundered duvet.

"What are you doing here?" I asked. "Haven't you done enough for one day?"

"On the contrary. The night is when I really shine." He smiled. "But you pose an interesting philosophical question. Is there really such a thing as enough? Personally, I've never thought so."

"Get off my bed," I said. When he didn't move, I crossed the room in five quick steps. Three tugs on his arm, leveraging all my weight, and he still hadn't budged.

"What are you doing?" Kendall asked, sitting up. "I'm sorry, Harper. I tried to make him leave. But I'm just so sleepy." She yawned and stretched, curling back up in her bed, eyes at half mast, like she'd been sedated.

"What did you do to my roommate? And get your filthy street clothes off my bed."

"My apologies, Miss Harper," Sterling drawled, perfectly parroting the Southern lilt I'd worked so hard to stamp out of my vowels—the one that returned full-steam every time my temper hit a boil. "I forgot that Rule 405 has such specific requirements for the maintenance of linens. Quite illuminating, those rules of yours."

My body temperature plunged to absolute zero.

"What did you say?" Suddenly I was in his face, inches away. I wasn't sure what my plan was, but it definitely involved remodeling that perfectly straight nose.

"Well, your good friend Kendall and I have been getting acquainted. You see, she wanted to borrow a little something." He inclined his head in her direction. A half-empty bottle of vodka nestled next to her like a puppy. I looked closer and saw a tiny cigarette. A joint. Pinched between her fingers. That explained the catatonic glaze in her eyes as she watched our little scene.

Disgust rolled through me. What kind of malicious monster would exploit Kendall like this? And what kind of two-faced roommate would summon a demon to our room? Just when I'd started to like her.

"And I wanted to borrow a little something, too." He reached into the backpack resting on the floor and pulled out the pink Hello Kitty box Cole gave me for my fifth birthday. It housed all five hundred and thirty-seven of my babies.

"It's really a lot to memorize," he said. "One afternoon wasn't quite enough, so I took the liberty of making copies. Also made a cheat sheet—modeled after your outlines, of course."

I wrenched the file box from his hand so hard and so fast he recoiled. His expression had been all smug amusement, but now something else flashed in his eyes: surprise. And apprehension. He'd probably never seen anyone as furious as I was just then, and he probably never would again. My Rules were practically religious relics, the only thing I had left of my mother.

And he'd desecrated them.

"You've taken this too far," I said. My voice was terrifying. Smooth and soft, the way a serial killer would sound in order to lure a victim into his windowless white van. "Leave. While you still can."

Sterling's eyes widened. One eyebrow arched. It gave

me a wild shot of adrenaline to know he was curious about what I'd do next.

I wasn't the only one who was morbidly reluctant to disembark from this runaway train to hell.

"Leave?" Kendall murmured. "Yes. I told him to, but he wanted to read all your recipes."

The cool, calm voice deserted me as I turned on Kendall. "Recipes?" I choked out. "This has nothing to do with recipes. What he did—what he did is like reading my journal. What kind of roommate are you, letting my enemy invade my privacy? Didn't you see they weren't recipes?"

"I'm sorry, Harper. I really am. How should I know what a recipe looks like?" Kendall whispered against her pillow. "We have a cook." A little puddle of drool had collected underneath her mouth, soaking into her bedspread. She had fallen asleep on her iPhone, and when she lifted her head to look at us, its silhouette was etched in the side of her cheek. I wanted to laugh, to fall in a heap on the floor and laugh until I cried. These things just didn't happen to me. I had no frame of reference for anything other than being ignored, invisible. The most popular girl in school was stoned and passed out in my room, her hair a tangle of blond cotton candy, while a ruthlessly cunning boy had made it his sole purpose to destroy me. And they'd both just violated every last nanometer of my privacy.

Then Sterling actually laughed. I caught the corner of his flashy smile as he turned away, composing himself. "I had a feeling she didn't know what she was doing. Held that joint like she was going to sign her name with it." He shook his head. "Still, you've gotta give it to her. She put up a valiant effort—although for what, I'm not sure. I wouldn't lay a finger on a girl in that state. And I can't stand the smell of these things." He picked up the remains of the joint and flicked it out the open window.

"Yet you smoke?"

"That was theatrics," he replied. "You pissed me off that day in class. Figured it was an easy rule to break, and I know rule-breaking bothers you so much I couldn't resist."

"Yes, it does."

When he turned back to face me, the storm had passed. My anger had been blunted by the weirdness of that moment. I had almost forgotten we were mortal enemies.

"So don't give Kendall smokable substances in the future, please," I said. "I have to live with her."

"Lucky for me," he said. "Look forward to lots of cozy little nights just like this."

"Why are you doing this?" I demanded. Then I sat on my bed and put my head in my hands because suddenly I was just so tired. "I was protecting my brother. You can understand that. It's nothing personal." I wondered whether the arson story was true—whether he'd been expelled while trying to protect his sister.

"Everything is personal," he said. "And of course I understand your motives. But your problems are just that—yours. Just like my problems are mine. And I need to protect my assets."

"What do you mean?" I asked.

"Your little tattling game, which, if memory serves, violates Rules 54 and 467, could have cost me a year's allowance at the very least, and could have meant I got transferred away from my grandmother. Keep your nose out of my business." He walked to the window and pulled up the blinds. "A lesson I'll teach as many times as necessary. So I suggest you leave me alone."

"Leave *you* alone?" I sputtered. "You're the one who sedated my roommate to invade my privacy. You leave *me* alone. And Cole."

He turned back to face me, those brown eyes sharper and clearer than I'd ever imagined they could be. "Given how little you really, truly know about your brother and the current state of his life, you're hardly qualified to make that request. I assure you I'm the lesser of two evils."

"What's that supposed to mean?" I hated how right he was. Hated that his words mirrored what Cole had said to me himself.

"You're a smart girl," he said. "Figure it out."

He slid the window open and perched on the sill. It was late, and if he were caught in our dorm, all our parents would be called. The irony of what everyone would assume if they found us together made me practically gag.

"Your rules are collateral," he said, hitching one leg over the windowsill. Never would I have imagined Sterling Lane would be climbing out my bedroom window and down two stories after curfew. "As long as you behave, they'll be our little secret." His shoulders looked even broader when silhouetted against the streetlight streaming in through the window. And I despised myself for noticing.

"You think you can blackmail me?" I said.

He turned to look me dead in the eye. "I *know* I can."

"Well, you're wrong," I called out to his retreating back. "And before you go, I have a little story of my own. A little pearl of wisdom I'm willing to cast before swine."

He froze, perched precariously on the window ledge, so that one tiny little shove would bring an end to all my problems forever. It was a full count of five before he turned his face back toward me.

"You don't have a monopoly on asshole fathers," I told him. "Every year my dad takes Cole on a fishing trip, and every year I ask if I can go, too. But he always told me it was a men's trip. And part of me agreed—not because I'm a girl, but because I personally don't have a lot of interest in hurting animals."

"I know," Sterling said. When I tipped my head the side, he added, "Rules 304, and, um, 310, I believe. But I'll have to double-check." He smiled like I should be oh-so-impressed by his amazing memory.

But instead I narrowed my eyes. "In his mind, I should be into clothing and makeup, which infuriated me. But I pretended I wanted to fish because I thought a shared interest would bring us closer, like he is with Cole." I had no idea why I'd shared that last part, so I glowered at him, lest he think I wanted his sympathy. Because I thought I caught a glimmer of it.

"Then one year I finally convinced him to let me come along on a trip. I said I should learn to clean and prepare fish—you know, because cooking is girls' work." I paused for dramatic effect, but I didn't need to. Sterling's eyes followed my every move as I paced across the room, buying time so I could make up a new, more interesting story. One that didn't end with me throwing up in the bathroom after my father sliced into the first miserable white-bellied fish.

"That year they were headed to the Florida Keys. While they were out in the water hauling in sailfish, I stayed in our rental house. It was actually pretty interesting—nestled in the mangroves, which have a fascinating natural history. Did you know they reach all the way to the ocean floor, so they can be a hundred feet tall?"

"No, I didn't," Sterling replied. He was trying not to smile at my digression. "Never been there."

"They came home late in the afternoon, dragging the fish they'd caught behind the boat, partially submerged. And while they were tying up the boat, I heard this thrashing in the water behind it. I look, and there's a massive alligator attacking the fish, trying to pull them lose from the boat. And all I can think about is that it's ruining all my brother's hard work *and* my big chance to be part of their bonding thing. So I jumped onto the boat and reached under the seat, where my father kept a handgun."

Sterling's outside foot slipped off the rain gutter, and he shifted to keep from falling out of the window. Wide brown eyes met mine. I had his full attention now.

His hands were wrapped around the windowsill, knuckles white from the effort of suspending himself halfway between inside and out. I thought for a moment he would climb back through the window, but he didn't. In fact, he looked like he didn't want to get any closer. I had to bite my cheek to hold back the smile as I watched my lies work their magic. Rule 76 was wrong about the power of truth prevailing over lies.

I looked Sterling right in the eye and let a tiny, knowing smile tug at my cheek. A little trick I'd picked up in the Sterling Lane School of Intimidation. "You see, I have outstanding aim. Another little tidbit I picked up trying to keep up with the boys. I shot that alligator right between the eyes."

Sterling's eyelids disappeared completely, and seconds ticked past before that smirk was brave enough to parade itself in front of me. That was how I knew I'd gotten under his skin—exactly where I wanted to be.

Then, with a kick of his other leg, he was gone, leaving me in my room with a catatonic Kendall and a ticking time bomb of emotions so complex that not one of my 537 Rules could tell me how to diffuse it.

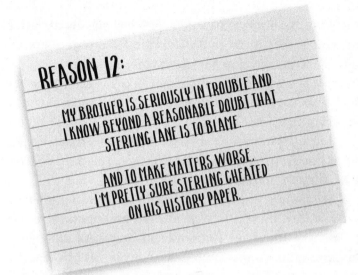

REASON 12:

MY BROTHER IS SERIOUSLY IN TROUBLE AND I KNOW BEYOND A REASONABLE DOUBT THAT STERLING LANE IS TO BLAME.

AND TO MAKE MATTERS WORSE, I'M PRETTY SURE STERLING CHEATED ON HIS HISTORY PAPER.

*T*he next morning, in response to a mysterious summons during dinner the previous night, I arrived at Headmaster Lowell's office bright and early. The administrative building opened at seven thirty, and I didn't want to be late for Mrs. Stevens's class, not with Sterling nipping at my heels. I knew in my gut that his little display of academic prowess the other day was just the first shot in a war that quite possibly had no end.

When I knocked on Headmaster Lowell's door, my stomach was tied in a perfect sailor's knot. After my outburst, which was completely against the Rules and therefore my character, I was pretty sure he was about to deliver another little lecture about my temper. Lately that seemed to be the most pressing issue on everyone's mind, even though this time my explosion was fully justifiable.

"Come in," Headmaster Lowell called out. My hands trembled as I opened the door.

I nearly threw up when I saw my father sitting there

in one of the straight-backed wooden chairs Headmaster Lowell reserved to make certified Rulebreakers as uncomfortable as possible during his inquisition.

It was worse than I imagined it could be. My father had never been summoned to school over my behavior.

"Headmaster Lowell," I said. "I really didn't mean anything yesterday. I had other things on my mind. Really, sir, it wasn't necessary to call my father. You have no idea what kind of pressure I'm under."

My father shot the headmaster a dry smile. "Never amazes me how this one always manages to make everything about her. I'm not even gonna ask what she's talking about. Gonna keep Cole in my sights this time."

I looked at the dark circles under my father's eyes, at the wrinkled suit jacket draped over his shoulders. Whatever had dragged him on the four-hour drive to school by this hour had to be big—Dad only wore suits when he was dealing with bankers.

"Even though Cole returned the money, there is still the matter of the disciplinary committee hearing," Headmaster Lowell said.

"Returned the money? When did this happen? Cole did it himself?" That would be the same as confessing, and I had no idea how the school would respond. Would he be off the hook for taking responsibility for his transgressions, or punished severely like any other criminal?

"Not exactly." Headmaster Lowell cleared his throat. "It was found in the lockbox this morning."

"But how?" It made no sense. "You said you confiscated all the keys—so how did they get in?"

"Cole never produced his key," Headmaster Lowell replied, leaning back in his chair. "Recall that he claimed it was lost."

I shook my head, ready to spring out of my seat. "In the U.S. we require evidence to condemn someone. And if the money is back, why does it even matter? There are a million possible explanations. Maybe there was no crime here at all. Maybe someone just misplaced it temporarily or something. Or miscounted? Maybe the door was unlocked and anyone could have done this. When I sneaked into the boys' locker room, the coach's door was unlocked."

"You did *what*?" my father interrupted.

Headmaster Lowell held up his hand, mercifully cutting my dad off pre-rant. "Harper and I have already discussed this, Cal. She meant well. She was worried about Cole. But you do raise a point that someone else could have done this earlier in the evening. You, for instance—since you were there."

"Me?" I sputtered. "I didn't even know the money in the lockbox existed. I bet most of the school didn't unless they were directly involved in that stupid fund-raiser." But Cole would have. I swallowed hard, praying my dad and Headmaster Lowell weren't thinking the very same thing.

"What did you do when you left the boys' locker room?" Headmaster Lowell asked.

"Well, um, I went back to my room," I said slowly. "I was already behind on my schedule for the night, so I did my homework."

"Did you talk to anyone when you got home?"

"Am I in trouble here?" I demanded. "Are you trying to corroborate my alibi or something? Because I don't have one. Kendall Frank came home from the art studio at around ten and went right to sleep. And honestly, with the way that girl snores, I could have conducted a chain saw convention and no one would have heard me."

"You're not in trouble, Harper," Dad said. "But you and

Cole have always been close. If you know what's going on, you can tell us. We'll help and you won't be in any trouble if you've covered up for him."

"What about Cole?" I asked. Sweat slicked my palms, so I rubbed them dry against the harsh wool of my skirt.

My dad and Headmaster Lowell made eye contact. That was confirmation enough. I could save myself by tattling, but Cole would be toast. And my dad actually thought I'd go along with that.

"Cole is fine," I lied. "Other than the stress of being falsely accused." I crossed my arms over my chest and glared at both of them. "So the sooner you straighten this out, the better."

My dad studied my face carefully. "If I find out you're lying right now, heads will roll." Dad had always been an expert in ferreting out my secrets, but this time, somehow I passed the test. His gaze shifted back to Headmaster Lowell.

"If you don't mind," Dad said. "I'd like to speak with Cole again. Alone."

"Of course," Headmaster Lowell replied. "But you understand that I'll have to move forward with this from a disciplinary perspective, regardless of how you handle it within your family."

"There's no way Cole would do this," I told them, desperation entering my voice. "He organized that fundraiser himself to buy some ridiculous weight-lifting apparatus." But that was incriminating, too. He would have known about the money. He would have known where the lockbox was located. That fact alone put him on a whittled-down list of suspects.

"Harper, honey, this is serious stuff." Dad was using his condescending voice, the one he usually reserved for his overpriced hunting dogs. "It's best if you let me handle this."

My temper rattled the bars of its cage, but Dad was already focused back on Headmaster Lowell. "I'd appreciate it if you'd take your time scheduling your disciplinary committee meeting. I think we can all agree a confession is the best way to salvage this situation for the culprit, to demonstrate that they've learned from and regret their mistakes. And to ensure the school doesn't jump the gun and expel an innocent student. That sort of action might get a headmaster into hot water."

This was one of those moments when my father made me proud. He'd delivered that threat so politely it almost sounded like a kindly intended piece of professional advice.

"Well now, I suppose we could give the matter a little time," Headmaster Lowell said. "Give the boy a chance to own up to his mistakes."

"Excuse me," I said, louder this time. "Cole did not do this. Need I remind you that Sterling Lane has a history of illegal activities? Most notably arson. And he would easily be in a position to steal Cole's keys."

My father looked at me, finally seeing me as something more than a piece of furniture. He frowned before turning back to face the headmaster. "Is that true? An arsonist?" A shrewd look entered his eyes. "Are the trustees aware of this? From a liability standpoint, that's quite a risk to take."

The headmaster held up one hand again, this time trying to placate my dad. "That was a long time ago, Cal, and Sterling has been to counseling since. I don't believe he was involved in this incident. What would his motive possibly be?"

"Motive?" My father's voice was soft, but I could sense the storm brewing. "And what do you propose Cole's motive was? This is my son's future you're talking about here, and you're going to assume that some touchy-feely counselor cured a boy like that? A boy who lit someone else's property on fire?"

I felt a little pang of guilt that I was letting my dad make false assumptions about Sterling's motives. Yes, arson was a serious offense, but it sounded like his motives might excuse at least a small sliver of that crime.

"Let's keep calm here, Cal," Headmaster Lowell said, smiling. The tremor in his lip confirmed my father had the upper hand. "Cole doesn't have a motive, per se, but I wouldn't be the first to notice a shift in his behavior. And we've caught some inconsistencies in his account of what happened that night. His whereabouts."

"Maybe he's lying to protect his roommate," I volunteered. "Cole's like that. He believes the best of everyone." My father looked at me; there was a flash of solidarity and gratitude in his eyes. I'd crafted his argument for him. The hotter Dad's temper got, the more inarticulate he became. Like the Incredible Hulk. A part of me could begrudgingly relate to that.

"You won't mind if I talk to the boys myself?" my father asked. "Give Cole a little time to think this through. Just one week. He'll see reason once I talk to him."

I sincerely doubted that was the case, but no matter what, a little time wouldn't hurt anyone. And even though a week wasn't very long, maybe, just maybe, I'd be able to get through to Cole.

Headmaster Lowell eyed my father warily. "On one condition," he said. "If you get the truth out of Cole, you have to share it with me. Even if it's Cole's confession."

My father nodded and reached out his hand to shake on it. In the Campbell world, a handshake was an ironclad contract. I knew my father would give the headmaster everything he found. Honor was a big thing to him, even if it would condemn one of his own.

I knew what I had to do next. There was only one way to make sure Cole wasn't entangled in this disaster—even if he was guilty, there was someone who was guilty of far more. And no doubt any crimes Cole committed were directly attributable to that boy.

After I left Headmaster Lowell's office, I had ten minutes before class started. My peers were slowly trickling through the hallway, looking groggy and confused, like so many cattle. More than a few of them, I'm sure, hadn't bothered to eat a proper breakfast before first period. My standard breakfast of a hard-boiled egg and dry toast always powered me through to lunch. Studies showed that a balanced breakfast, including protein, improved focus and concentration.

Sorting through the details of my plan preoccupied me as I entered history, so it took me a moment to realize that my usual seat in the front row was occupied. Sterling Lane slouched in my chair. He looked like the cat who'd swallowed the canary and washed it down with a parrot or two.

He smiled when I stopped walking. When I stood still as a statue right in front of my desk.

"Cutting it kinda close, aren't we?" he asked. "A mere ten minutes before class begins? I, for one, have been here since eight o'clock sharp. Can't wait to show Mrs. Stevens this." He tapped a tidy pile of printer paper at least a quarter-inch thick.

"What is that?" I asked.

"My essay."

"I don't care," I lied, even though I couldn't stop staring

at that formidable stack of creamy white pages. "Get out of my chair. Class starts in nine minutes and I need to review my outline."

"I'm quite fond of history. May even major in it one day. Why should you always get the best seat in the house?" He was all feigned outrage. So smug and sarcastic. "Give someone else a turn."

"Because I've always had that seat," I snapped.

"That's my point. It's time you learn to share."

"It's time *you* learn to shut up."

"You can do better than that," he said. "'Shut up' expired in third grade."

The clock was ticking down. My hands started to shake. Sterling tipped his head to the side, waiting to see what I'd do next. Only I really wasn't sure. I had half a mind to tip his chair right over, sending him hurtling onto the floor. If he didn't have such a sizable height and weight advantage, I would have attempted it.

Mrs. Stevens walked into the room and started riffling through the papers on her desk. The other seats were filling up and still I stood there in front of my desk, refusing to surrender.

"Is something wrong, Harper?" Mrs. Stevens asked. "You're just standing there."

"Sterling took my seat," I said lamely. My voice broke, letting the whole class know I was prepared to cry over it.

"We don't have assigned seats in this class, Harper. Just pick another one."

My eyes must have looked as wild as I felt, because Sterling chuckled softly to himself. Then he stood and slipped into the seat directly behind mine. I exhaled one long, exhausting breath. My palms were slick with liquid panic as I touched the surface of the desk and slid into my chair.

"That was very thoughtful of you, Sterling," Mrs. Stevens

said. Then she gave me a quick glance out of the corner of her eye, once again drawing an unfavorable comparison between the two of us. Instead of being flattered that I needed to be so close to her, Mrs. Stevens was annoyed with me.

"I certainly didn't mean to distress Harper," Sterling said. "But I was so excited to turn this in that I grabbed the first chair I saw." He picked up the stapled stack of printer paper and extended it toward Mrs. Stevens.

Her eyes perused the page, slowly. Then she looked up. "This isn't due until next week."

"I know," he replied. "But I was so fired up by your words of encouragement that I stayed up all night to finish it. I just had to double-check the citations. It was all stuff I already knew." He pushed his desk forward until it knocked into mine.

"All stuff you already knew?" Her eyes widened as they returned to the pages. She flipped through Sterling's paper for what felt like an eternity. "This has seventeen references."

I didn't need to turn around to know that Sterling was nodding vigorously, eagerly. "Yes, ma'am. I was even thinking of taking the AP history exam with Harper—independent study. A little healthy competition, like you said. History has always been a hobby of mine."

By now the entire class was listening. He had to know history was *my* subject—my absolute favorite—even if I'd never uttered those words out loud. The AP test was mine and mine alone. I'd lobbied the school for special permission to take it even though the full course wasn't offered.

"And cheating is your other little hobby," I said. "I don't think you wrote that paper. What about your carpal tunnel syndrome? Your first day you said you couldn't even type."

Sterling pulled out a laminated sheet and glanced at it.

"Per Rule 85, I don't believe you can speak unless called upon. Class has officially started." So that was his infamous cheat sheet of my rules. I wanted to jump out of my seat and light that list on fire.

"Maybe I found a lovely little tutor who enthusiastically took my dictation. Need I remind you, if you accuse me without evidence, well." He lifted the cheat sheet again. "That's against Rule 245."

"Don't you dare throw my Rules back at me." I dropped my voice to a whisper even though everyone could have heard a mouse sneeze in that room full of silent, watchful faces. "You promised you wouldn't tell anyone about them." I turned around in my seat to face him.

"Rule 85." Sterling was sadistically savoring every minute of this as he waggled his index finger in my face. "You broke our deal by sticking your nose in my business. Rule 85, Harper."

My fingers itched to wrap themselves around his neck and squeeze.

Mrs. Stevens raised one hand, restoring order. "Both of you, stop this right now." She had summoned her firm voice, the one no one would dare to contradict.

Except Sterling.

As Mrs. Stevens walked to the board to begin her lesson, Sterling shifted forward in his chair, leaning closer until his lips were so close to my ear that if I turned to the side, our faces would collide.

"Who's the Rulebreaker now?" he whispered. The chair creaked as he settled back. Out of the corner of my eye, I watched his shoes inch along the floor as he spread those long limbs out in front of his desk until his legs were practically wrapped around my chair, like an octopus strangling its prey.

REASON 13:

HE'S TURNING ME AGAINST MYSELF.

I shot out of my chair like a bolt of lightning the moment class ended. I barely spared a glance behind me, where Sterling was suddenly surrounded by my classmates. Usually, playing a goody-goody wasn't the way to win the admiration of your peers, but apparently it could be if you did it while being thoroughly obnoxious.

But I didn't have time to anguish over not having any friends at school. I had some serious business to attend to.

During lunch, I made my way across the quad toward Cole's dorm. I glanced around as I walked, trying to look casual but also making sure I wasn't seen. It was perfectly within the school rules to return to your room to retrieve forgotten items. But I wasn't the sort to misplace my provisions, thanks to my comprehensive daily checklists, so any deviation from my routine could potentially attract notice.

Fortunately, everyone appeared far more interested in eating and socializing. The few students I passed paid me no special attention, but I still flipped up the collar of my coat, hiding my face from view.

The lobby of the boys' dorm was deserted, so I slipped through to the side staircase unseen. This less-frequented staircase would bring me to the end of the hall closest to Cole's room. His keys jingled loudly in my pocket. I took them out and once again counted all twelve shiny pieces of metal. I couldn't fathom what doors they unlocked—what secret other life Cole must be living in order to have uses for them all.

It had been all too easy to lift them out of his backpack in the library, proving that Sterling Lane could just as easily have *borrowed* a key. But if I was honest with myself, I doubted that was the case. The more I processed the various details of the theft, the more I started to fear that Cole was guilty—but that was no reason not to rescue him. Sterling Lane had furnished alcohol for the entire lacrosse team just last week. That alone would have gotten him expelled. With any luck, I'd find a way to simply correct the path of justice.

It was wrong—so wrong. Against not just my Rules, but the rules of any civilized society. I knew it was wrong, and I did it anyway. Because Cole was on the line.

I unlocked the door and slipped inside. Cole and Sterling's room was surprisingly tidy. When left to his own devices, Cole tended to slip into chaos, leaving shoes and clothing sprawled across his floor. But under Sterling's questionable influence, their room resembled some sort of gentlemanly study from the turn of the last century. Sterling's brown leather chair sat empty, an iPad balancing on the arm of it. There was an orchid on the windowsill, and three actual framed paintings adorned the wall. Kendall would have approved—even if her own work was far superior.

Sterling's desk was the first place I searched. I slid the drawers open, but they were empty, as was the wastebasket beside it. What kind of history prodigy didn't take notes? I glanced at the two dressers. Was I prepared to go to those lengths? Not quite yet. Instead, I moved my search to Cole's desk, where I found receipts from the local grocery store and at least a year's supply of gum wrappers. Nothing incriminating there.

I glanced inside his wastebasket and saw what looked like a receipt from the bank in town. My eyes nearly popped out of my head when I saw the sum along the bottom—five thousand dollars in cash had been withdrawn yesterday. Where on earth had Cole obtained that kind of money?

But when I rescued the slip from its papery grave, I saw Sterling Lane's name printed along the top. He had withdrawn the money yesterday, right before the missing cash was returned. It was incredibly convenient timing— convenient and incriminating.

I pulled a pen from Cole's drawer and circled the date on the receipt. Then I carefully placed it in an envelope and stored it in my backpack. I'd anonymously place it in Headmaster Lowell's mailbox. He'd be able to connect such obvious dots—and he'd be far more likely to place his faith in this evidence if I had nothing to do with it.

Emboldened by my findings, I turned to face Sterling's closet. The door was slightly ajar, so I stepped closer, peering in without touching anything. For some reason, searching inside felt more intrusive than rummaging through his desk. Maybe it was the way his clothing hung there, approximating his size and shape, as if he were in the room watching me. A messy tumble of mismatched shoes lined the floor. His clothes were a fascinating mix of perfectly pressed shirts and ones so rumpled it looked like he'd balled them up first on purpose. A stack of tattered paperbacks rested in the corner. I inched closer, nudging the closet door open with my shoe, and reached down to flip the top book over so I could see the cover. *Great American Poems: An Anthology* — completely unexpected. Sterling didn't seem like the kind of guy who'd read poetry for fun.

A door slammed in the hallway. I jumped and ducked into Sterling's closet. His shirts surrounded me, brushing against my skin and swathing me in lingering traces of his cologne.

Footsteps echoed down the hallway. Running footsteps. Heading right toward this room. I held my breath. I waited.

The footsteps cruised past the door, reverberating off the linoleum. Another door slammed. The dorm descended back into silence.

I stepped out and closed Sterling's closet door three-quarters of the way, just like I found it. Cautiously and oh-so-slowly, I opened the door to the hallway and peered outside. The coast was clear. I slipped out the door, locked it behind myself, and walked briskly down the hallway.

There was nothing wrong with what I was about to do. Clearly Sterling Lane was up to something with all that money, and before Cole was summarily condemned based on circumstantial evidence, the reasons behind Sterling Lane's sizable withdrawal needed to be examined.

The road to justice was never easy and was rarely direct. And apparently on this particular occasion, it came at the price of petty larceny.

The Rules would forgive me, just this once.

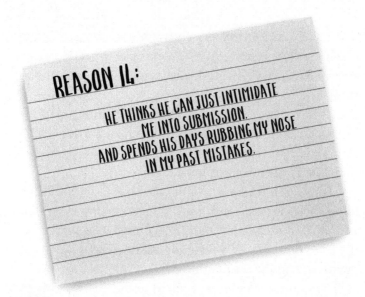

REASON 14:

HE THINKS HE CAN JUST INTIMIDATE
ME INTO SUBMISSION,
AND SPENDS HIS DAYS RUBBING MY NOSE
IN MY PAST MISTAKES.

*T*he next morning, thirty-seven minutes into history class, Headmaster Lowell appeared in the doorway.

"Sterling, a word, please." There was something in the set of his jaw, and in the fact that he'd come to the room himself instead of sending his secretary, that told me something major was afoot. Which could only mean my little piece of evidence had worked.

Butterflies in my stomach erupted into flight.

"And bring your things, please," the headmaster added.

Sterling's eyebrows snapped together. Given his wealth of experience with being in trouble, he grasped the significance of this little visit. It took only a moment for his eyes to find me, and when they did, I lifted my hand and wiggled my fingers. *Bye-bye, Sterling Lane.*

I felt a surge of exultation when in front of the whole class, loud and clear, he said, "We'll see about that." The words were intended for me and me alone, even though the rest of the class looked around, confused.

Sterling had stopped wearing his sunglasses in class ever since he'd become Mrs. Stevens's new pet. He picked the aviators up off his desk and perched them on the top of his head.

Mrs. Stevens could have made a better effort not to look so downtrodden as Sterling disappeared through the door. We'd been fine before he transferred there, and we'd be fine long after he was gone.

Sterling didn't return to history that day, and I didn't catch sight of him again until physics, when he walked through the door and paused. His brown eyes pierced me like a bayonet. He held my gaze until I was forced to look away. I was in the wrong this time.

The chair behind me creaked under his weight, and I felt his proximity as he leaned forward. I knew he was about to say something scathing, words that would cut to the bone. So I held my breath.

But nothing happened. He didn't speak. He just lurked there behind me, a threat even more unnerving because I wasn't sure exactly when it would be realized. I cowered for the rest of the period, bracing for the blow that never came. I started to wonder if that was his game—torturing me with anticipation so I could never quite drop my guard.

For the rest of the day, Sterling's eyes tracked me the way a hungry lion trails after a gazelle. He lurked and lingered and was impossible to avoid. Even at lunch, I heard his voice everywhere. I couldn't escape his laughter as it drifted through the cafeteria and chased me down the hallway.

By the end of the day, I was a nervous wreck, harassed into submission by guilt as much as by the impending threat of whatever Sterling Lane was plotting. Over and over again I reminded myself that I'd done it all for Cole, that I'd do it again. I'd been watching for Cole all day, praying for a chance to set things right between us. But while Sterling was everywhere, it seemed like Cole had disappeared into thin air.

So it was a stroke of unbelievable luck that I saw Cole when I headed to the library. He was walking briskly across the quad toward the parking lot that separated the school from the main road through town. It was close to dinnertime, so I was surprised he wasn't camped out on the grass outside the cafeteria, begging for food like most of the athletes did after practice. I sped up, because Cole was cruising like a missile. It took a half-run for me to maintain the distance between us, much less catch up.

He walked right through the parking lot to the street beyond. There was something guilty and sneaky about the way he moved, shoulders hunched, hood pulled up over his head. When he reached the road he turned and looked around, like he sensed I was there. I jumped behind a pickup truck just in time. I wasn't really sure why I was hiding, since I'd been hoping to talk to him, but something in his behavior was off enough to pique my curiosity.

Cole scanned the entire parking lot. When satisfied that he was alone, he approached a rusty blue station wagon idling on the curb and leaned down to stick his head through the window. There were two people in the car, one in the front and one seeming to occupy the entire backseat. Cole stood like that for almost a full minute, talking and gesturing vehemently. I couldn't hear what they were saying, but I knew my brother. Cole was far from pleased.

I pulled out my notebook and jotted down the license plate.

Cole backed away, shaking his head.

Then the person in the back seat opened the door and stepped out. The man was massive—the way you'd expect an NFl player to look. Cole stopped backing away. He muttered something under his breath and reluctantly climbed into the passenger seat.

There was no way I was letting Cole go anywhere with that man. I'd never dealt with intimidating brutes, but it was clear to me that's exactly what the guy in the backseat had been. I looked around for a way to follow them. A bicycle was loosely chained to a nearby fence post. I produced my phone, my heart hammering so hard my fingers shook as I keyed in 911 and kept my finger poised over the send button.

But that wasn't enough; even if I called for help, they'd never arrive on time. It was up to me to stop whatever was about to happen to Cole.

I strolled toward the street, not heading toward the parked car but not heading away from it, either, doing my best to look nonchalant even as sweat beaded my forehead. I was steps away from a shrub that would conceal me when the passenger door flew open and Cole exploded out.

The driver's-side door opened at practically the same time, and the second guy climbed out. He was tall and thin, with blond hair and dark-rimmed glasses that accentuated his pallor.

"We'll be waiting, Cole," he called out. "But we'll only wait so long." It was an undeniable threat, but my brother kept walking, storming back toward the school.

The boy watched Cole's retreating back. I'd never seen him before, but I memorized every detail of his face, each and every freckle. Whatever had happened in the car was the key to understanding whatever mess Cole was in.

I snapped a photo with my phone, just as the mystery

boy climbed back into the car with his sidekick.

By then, Cole was already halfway across the quad. I broke into a run in order to intercept him before he got inside to his friends, where I'd never catch him alone.

"I've been looking for you everywhere," I said. "Did you know Dad's here?"

Cole eyed me warily. "Of course I do." He kicked at a clump of dirt with the toe of his tennis shoes. "I spent most of the day getting chewed out."

"Did you do it?" I asked. "The truth. I need to know. Was this your plan to finance the new weight room? Because it seems to me that stealing money from yourself doesn't solve much."

He studied me like I was a stranger. "It's crazy we can look so much alike, be raised by the same parent, and still be so different."

"What do you mean?" I braced myself for another of his onslaughts about how I'm stubborn and judgmental and would never understand.

"You were right. You're always right."

"I don't understand—tell me. I can help."

"It's better that you don't," he replied, glancing over my shoulder toward where the lacrosse guys were loitering. I followed his gaze. Sterling Lane was leaning against the wall, watching us. This time it wasn't with malice, but rather expectation. He'd been waiting for Cole.

"Does this have something to do with Sterling Lane?"

"I guess you could say that," Cole said, starting to walk away. "I'd be walking with a limp if he hadn't given me that loan."

"What loan?" I demanded, even as my stomach started slowly sinking into the earth. "What were you going to do with that money, Cole? What the hell is going on? Is it—is it drugs?" I was at an utter loss. Cole's obsession with sports and his vicious competitive streak had always kept him clean. That's why the episode of drinking I'd observed had shocked me to the core. But maybe this had to do with his competitive streak. Would Cole take steroids?

"No—not that. Never." He shook his head adamantly, and I believed him. "I made a mistake," he said quietly. "But it's handled. Over. An error in judgment because I'm every bit as gullible as you always say. I'm an idiot."

I opened my mouth to defend him, because no one, not even Cole himself, got to talk like that about my brother. But he held up a hand. The utter somberness of his expression silenced me. "Please, Harper, no lectures. I learned my lesson. Go crow your victory somewhere else." He turned to leave.

I ached that he thought I'd make him feel worse. Was I really that kind of sister—full of bitter recriminations and judgments when my brother was clearly one step away from breaking?

"Is this about those guys? That thug in the blue car?" I demanded. Cole had said he'd be walking with a limp if Sterling hadn't helped him. What exactly was my brother dabbling in? "Were they threatening you?"

His stunned silence was all the answer I needed. I grabbed his arm, not about to let him leave like that.

"You need to tell Headmaster Lowell," I pressed. "Or Dad, or the police. I don't care who, but tell someone. Tell them what's going on. Or you could get expelled. Or in more trouble. I don't know. Just come clean."

"That's the irony," Cole said. "Tell any of them and I'll definitely get expelled. They'll probably lock me up and throw away the key. I'll take my chances with ambiguity."

"But—"

"It's over, Harper." He spoke right over me. "I'll face the consequences, and you'll be the golden one, just like you always wanted." The way he said it, without bitterness or resentment, shattered my heart into a million pieces. It was the first time I'd seen myself through Cole's eyes, and I didn't much like the rendering. And yet he'd always accepted me, always supported me, even when my words and actions apparently cut him to the quick.

My heart was in my throat as I watched my brother walk away. This person I was born with, who'd been beside me since we were cells suspended in space, had been hiding something he'd had to face alone. Something he'd pay for alone.

While I'd been organizing my life into Rules and regulations, he'd needed my help and I'd been as blind to his needs as he'd always been aware of mine.

It was the worst moment of my entire life.

Topped off with a cherry when Sterling Lane materialized at my shoulder, drawn to human suffering like a dog to a butcher store dumpster.

"Illuminating little chat?" he asked. "Sad part is, I was just getting used to him. I'll cry myself to sleep in my lonely private room."

The comment sparked a powder keg inside me. "Is that what this is all about?" I snarled. "You got him into some big mess just so you'd get to live alone? I wouldn't put it past you."

"You would be wise not to put anything past me," Sterling said. "You, however, have everyone fooled. You play the uptight little goody-goody, and then you turn around and perform one of the larger acts of dishonesty I've seen in years. And believe me, sweetheart, I fraternize with some pretty despicable characters."

"I took that page from your playbook, Sterling," I said. "After all, you're pretty much a professional liar. Figured I'd add to your portfolio."

"I might drift from the truth sometimes, and maybe I don't err on the side of full disclosure, but who does?" His arched eyebrow dredged up memories of all the lies I'd told since we'd first met. "Oh, that's right. You. The funny thing is, you're honest with everyone except yourself. Because while you claim the moral high ground, what you did is far worse than anything I've done. That was malicious, outright slander."

"Worse than what you did?" I said, my thoughts scrambling backward through time. To all of the outrageous things he'd said. "Hardly. You've done your share of slander—like how you claimed I want to date you."

"Interesting that's the first incident that pops into your mind when every time I turn around you're accusing me of lying about something." His smile dangled in the air between us like a noose. "Interesting, and definitely worth exploring," he added with a wink. "I said I wasn't ready for a relationship. You drew your own inferences."

He stopped talking and suddenly it seemed like we'd been standing there since the dawn of time staring at each other. I needed a snappy response, something that would wipe that smile right off his perfect face. Or I should leave— walk away. But I couldn't stand leaving him with the last word.

Sterling finally looked away, toward the door as Kendall entered, prettier than I'd ever seen her. She was wearing a black dress that swirled around her knees when she walked. And her hair was up, twisted into a slick knot.

"It seems I have dinner plans. But you wouldn't know about that, would you?" Sterling's gaze met mine. "Harper

Campbell always eats alone. By choice?" He leaned one shoulder against the wall, studying me. "I'll be appearing before the disciplinary committee alongside your darling brother. Because you framed me. Remember this moment, Harper. I repay my debts in kind."

"Fine," I snapped. "Do whatever you want to me. Just tell me what's going on with Cole. Tell me how I can help him."

"I've got Cole's situation under control," Sterling said, dismissing me. "Loyalty is everything, Harper, and he's earned mine. Expulsion is the least of his worries. But yes, the school is one more loose end to tidy up. I'll find a way to weasel us both out of that, no thanks to you."

"Excuse my lack of faith in your expulsion-weaseling abilities, but your success rate is relatively low."

"Not when you deal in the volumes I do."

Kendall grabbed Sterling's elbow with one hand, claiming his undivided attention.

"What time is our reservation?" Kendall asked. They were going off-campus. It was the only explanation for her spectacular appearance, even though Sterling wore a rumpled dress shirt, his trademark scuffed boat shoes, and battered khaki slacks that were fraying at the bottom.

"I'll leave you to your misery," Sterling said, like he was granting me some elaborate favor. "Unfortunately, I can't say you don't deserve it. You're willfully undereducated when it comes to people, at the end of the day. That's as much a part of being smart as all those facts and dates you accumulate."

"No, it's not," I sputtered, choking on the bitter knowledge that he was right.

"Whatever," Kendall said, rolling her eyes. "Being smart is just like being pretty."

"Yes, *just* like it," I snapped.

"No," Kendall said, meeting my gaze. "I meant, what's the point of being either if there's no one there to admire you for it?"

"Well said." Sterling smiled at her like she'd just invented the steam engine. "Dinner's on me."

"I thought it was anyways," Kendall said as they walked away. "Isn't that the point of a date?"

"I don't date," Sterling said.

Kendall stumbled in her heels. I'd never seen her do that before. She deserved better treatment than that, even if her going to dinner with Sterling Lane was a betrayal of sorts.

"Not a date? Then what is this?" she asked, crossing her arms over her chest and putting an additional foot of space between the two of them.

"Reconnaissance," he said, shooting me a cryptic look. "Seems the Campbell family is in need of some professional help."

Kendall nodded. "Like a psychiatrist?"

"Yes, that too," Sterling said.

As they walked away, I strained my ears to catch the tail end of this conversation, far more curious than I'd care to admit.

"What other sort of professional help?" Kendall asked.

"Mine."

It didn't bother me at all that Sterling and Kendall looked like they were in a modeling shot as they walked away, on their perfect little "not date." Kendall was glamorous in a way I could never be, even if I took it upon myself to try. And Sterling had the confidence to make his tattered preppy gear look like formal wear. Physically, they were a perfect match, even if Kendall did deserve a boy with some semblance of a moral compass.

What bothered me, as I sat down to dinner with my history textbook, was that Cole had confided in Sterling while acting like I was both judge and executioner. I had to show Cole he was wrong and that I supported him, no matter what.

I pulled out my laptop and started searching. Between the license plate and the photo I'd snapped, there had to be a way to track down Cole's uninvited guests.

A simple online search revealed that the license plate was likely stolen—it didn't match the make or model of the car, which meant it was little help in identifying Cole's friends. Then I searched for cars similar to the model I'd seen. I hadn't recognized it at first sight, but the more I Googled, the more I narrowed it down to the make and year. If it had stolen plates, it was a safe bet that the vehicle itself had been stolen, too. I placed a call to the local police department, and after being shunted around five times, finally spoke with a junior detective who promised to look into the matter and get back to me.

I pulled up the photo I'd taken of the blond-haired boy. If he had a stolen car and stolen plates, there was a good chance this wasn't his first crime. Even though it meant spending funds earmarked to help Cole finance the weight room, pursuing the thugs in the car seemed a far more expeditious way to solve Cole's problems. I needed someone with access to a police database who could search for the blond boy.

A private investigator—that's what I needed. I'd get to the bottom of this myself, whether Cole wanted me to or not.

REASON 15:

UNLESS KENDALL IS EXAGGERATING,
HIS SUPPOSED RULES ABOUT DATING
ARE TOTALLY DISGUSTING.

IT'S AN INSULT THAT HE REFERS TO THEM
AS RULES AT ALL.

*P*rivate investigators cost a small fortune, so I spent the evening scouring photos of local events, looking for Cole's friends. To no avail. Finally, I found a local agency that specialized in accident investigation and charged only twenty dollars an hour. I left a voicemail, inquiring whether they would negotiate a special fee for a local search.

Kendall crashed into our room at eight o'clock that night wearing a frown as wide as Nebraska.

I looked up. "How was dinner?" Ordinarily, I would have pretended I didn't care, but after my encounter with Sterling earlier that day, I'd been obsessing over what he'd meant about Cole and my needing assistance and exactly what form his *help* would take.

Plus, I was curious.

There was something unsettling about the idea of Sterling dating Kendall. Sure, it had been my idea at first, but that was before I really thought it through. I couldn't stand the idea of him loitering around our room like he lived there. Plus, there were basic differences in their temperaments that made them incompatible. Kendall would have to suffer through Sterling's vindictive streak, while he needed someone who could match him blow for blow. She deserved a boy who would take care of her and listen to her endless prattle. Someone like Parker.

"The food was great," she said. "The company was miserable."

That was unexpected.

"You ate?" I couldn't count on both hands the number of times I'd watched her stare longingly at my evening study snack and then complain about being fat, like it was my job to contradict her and force my food down her throat. In fact, she had not a single physical imperfection, which I'd tried to tell her without sounding creepy.

She gave me a narrow-eyed glare.

"Sorry," I said. "What happened, though? You and Sterling seemed chummy enough when you left."

"Chummy," she said. "Yeah, as in friends. He has rules."

"Rules?" A little shiver of dread wiggled its way down my spine as I imagined him discussing my Rules with Kendall—he'd threatened to make them public unless I stayed out of his business. And framing him for theft was pretty much the opposite of staying out of his business. "What Rules?" I asked.

"They were weird." She wrinkled her nose. "Most of them were boring—stuff about his family and how to plot revenge. Until he got to the ones about dating."

"Rules about revenge?" I couldn't keep the curiosity out of my voice. "And dating?"

"He doesn't do it," Kendall said. "Dating, that is. Or, I mean, only once. No second dates. I thought we'd, you know, go out a few times, get to know each other like normal people. But he told me he doesn't do second dates so anything I wanted from him had to happen that night. You get one shot—his words, not mine."

"What would you want from him?" I asked as the pieces slid into place in my mind. "You mean like—" I made an awkward hand gesture that didn't really mean anything at all. But Kendall understood. She nodded. Her nose scrunched up even smaller, until I thought it would disappear altogether.

"In other words, he doesn't want to be my boyfriend."

"Well, that's okay, right?"

"You don't understand," she said. "Everyone wants to be my boyfriend. I'm never alone."

"I think it's for the best that your little theory was debunked before you make an ass of yourself one day, Kendall," I said. "Because clearly it isn't true. Besides, being alone isn't that bad. In fact, it's healthy. Look at me."

She did, and the pity in her eyes made me want to hurl my highlighter at her face. But a little part of me knew I deserved her pity. Being alone wasn't bad if it was intermittent, but my stretch of solitude was borderline monastic. "If you're really this upset, you could always patch things up with Parker."

"No," she said emphatically. "He's playing this weird limbo game that I'm honestly getting sick of. I'm giving him an ultimatum."

"I'm guessing Parker won't be happy if he hears about this little date with Sterling."

She shook her head slowly.

"So you were using Sterling? That's why you met him in front of the entire school and walked off together, dressed to kill? Parker probably saw the whole thing."

"Well, that makes it seem so cold," she muttered. "I

gave Sterling a chance—I was open to the possibility. But it did occur to me that if Parker got jealous, maybe he'd stop taking me for granted." She threw herself across her bed and kicked off her shoes, narrowly missing my head with one of them.

"Watch it," I said. My head hurt trying to untangle this angst-ridden scheming. Even though he probably deserved it, I was bothered by this game she was playing—toying with Sterling's feelings. Maybe because I'd been on the receiving end of it so many times, tormented by these social games I never seemed able to grasp. But Sterling wouldn't have that problem. He could more than take care of himself.

"You're so confusing," she said, sitting up. "I mean, one second you're nice and we're having a perfectly normal conversation, then suddenly you snarl at me. And I don't mean that in a good way, like what Sterling said about you."

It felt like my skin sprouted an entirely new layer of nerve endings. Every inch of me was tingling to hear what she would say next. I gave her two seconds to elaborate before I snapped.

"What did he say about me?" I demanded. "And why would you think I cared?"

Kendall's eyes opened wide. Really wide. Her eyelashes splayed out like butterfly wings. "Oh," she said. "I can't believe I didn't see it sooner."

"Tell me what he said," I growled. "Even though I don't care."

"I don't think I should." She bit her lower lip and smiled at me strangely, almost the same way she smiled at cute boys. "You're getting awfully upset about it. You have such a crush on him."

"What a disturbing accusation." But that just made her grin stretch from ear to ear.

"I think he kinda likes you, too."

"That would be even more disturbing," I said, even though the shiver that ran down my spine was hardly one of revulsion. "He's a sociopath. I certainly don't want his attention directed at me."

"He said something sweet about you tonight." Kendall was bouncing on her bed like a four-year-old who had to pee. "He told me that your unstable temper is your best quality." She glowed, like she'd just handed me an Emmy.

Once again, Sterling revealed his ability to convey so much through a very few words. Yes, I had an unstable temper, but I certainly hoped that failing wasn't the only noteworthy thing about me. "That hardly sounds like a compliment."

"Yeah, maybe not," she conceded, looking down. "But in context it sounded better. But he asked about you—your habits."

To me that sounded more like Sterling was scheduling his revenge.

"He also kept talking to the waiter about sports. Told him he plays lacrosse, that their game is a sure bet this week, on and on about Vegas and gambling and fantasy football. When I finally asked him if he'd like to invite the waiter to join us, he told me he was helping you." She paused, her expression so blank I almost wondered if she'd suffered a stroke. "Are you into gambling?"

"Or course not." But the wheels were now spinning in my mind. I'd never known Cole to gamble. But I'd also never known him to be in financial trouble.

The expectant look in Kendall's eyes made my skin crawl. She was waiting for me to unburden myself to her, one of those mythical girl-bonding moments that I wasn't willing to concede actually existed.

I stared at my book, but five minutes passed and I still hadn't read a single line.

"Kendall?" I looked over toward her bed, where she was frantically texting someone. Her long, lacquered nails clicked against the surface of the phone with each letter. "Where did you go for dinner?"

"Café Bastille," she said. "I thought it was an odd choice. But then he got all weird about our waiter, even asked to be moved so we'd be in his section."

Sterling was up to something, that much was certain. But for once, the insidious angle wasn't obvious. Where was the personal benefit? Why was he grilling the waiter about sports when he could be making sure Kendall maximized her one shot at him?

My entire stomach seized up at the arrogance of his proclamation, at the disgusting, hedonistic way he had about him. It was fitting that the Marquis de Sade had been the subject of his little soliloquy in history class. He was both disturbed and disturbing.

It almost erased my guilt over framing him. Almost. But my thoughts kept circling back to the other thing he'd said to Kendall—he was helping me. There was nothing I could possibly need from him—at least, nothing that didn't hinge on Cole.

Sterling knew what Cole was hiding. He'd lent Cole money to help him, and I'd repaid him in the coldest, cruelest way possible.

The alarm on my desk beeped, indicating it was time to switch subjects. And I wasn't even halfway through my history outline for the next day. At this rate, I'd be up at least two hours later than I should be. But try as I might,

I couldn't regain my focus—Cole was in trouble and the one person who seemed able to save him had also sworn revenge on me. Was Sterling truly helping Cole, or was it all just another alligator tooth? Something told me whatever Sterling's reasons were for latching on to Cole and me, I wouldn't have to wait long to find out.

REASON 16:

WHILE HE DID WARN ME OF IMMINENT RETALIATION WITH HIS CHARMING LITTLE ALLIGATOR FABLE, IT WAS TOTALLY DISPROPORTIONATE TO MY CRIME.

AND IT TOOK ME A WEEK TO SCRUB THE OIL STAINS OUT OF THE CARPET.

*M*y phone started ringing during class, which never happens since my father and Cole are the only people who call me and they're aware of the school's hours. However, when I checked my voicemail after class, it was from the private investigator I'd contacted. He told me to send the photo of Cole's buddy and he'd see what he could do. It was a long shot, but since I couldn't exactly go knocking door to door with the photo, it was the best chance I had.

Kendall fell into step beside me as I crossed the quad toward our room. I looked up, trying to hide my surprise. No one ever walked across campus with me like that, locked in casual conversation. Red and blue paint flecks littered her cheeks like freckles. It appeared Kendall's little hobby wasn't a secret any longer.

"I've decided to patch things up with Parker," she said. "We're going out this weekend and I'm going to just put it all out there—tell him I like him, that I want this to be more than just fooling around. I want the strings attached, and if he can't do that, I'm walking away."

"Good for you," I said, wondering why she was confiding in me. There were at least two dozen girls at Sablebrook more qualified to give relationship advice. And infinitely more interested in doing so. Even as we walked, I spotted three of her friends standing in front of the library in a cozy little cluster. "You have to ask for what you want," I told her. "Be honest with him and with yourself. And if he doesn't go along with it, then he's not worth your time, anyway. You deserve someone who'll appreciate you."

Kendall smiled at me. "Oh, good, I like it when you're Honey Harper. Heartless Harper has her uses too—like if you really want to know whether your jeans make you look fat."

"You don't need Heartless Harper for that." Her little nicknames made me smile. They were infinitely better than Harper the Hag. "And jeans can't make you look fat. You either are or aren't, and it doesn't matter anyway."

"Oh, so now we have Honest Harper. I like that even more."

When we reached our door, Kendall fished her keys out of her pocket and unlocked the door.

"Oh my God," she said. Just standing there, staring into the room.

"What's wrong?" I asked, peering around her shoulder. My jaw fell open all the way.

There was a car in our room, dominating the space between our beds.

A car.

And not just any car.

Headmaster Lowell's minuscule Mini Cooper. The antique Mini he'd had shipped from London with the steering wheel where the passenger should sit. As if sitting on the wrong side of that death trap would make him cultured. Headmaster Lowell had always aspired to be affected in the most inconvenient and unimaginative ways.

"What's it doing here?" Kendall asked, making a slow circle around the car and then adjusting the side mirror.

"I have no idea," I said, pulling the door shut behind myself. Then I looked out the window and saw the flashing lights in the parking lot. Headmaster Lowell stood in his empty parking space, talking to a uniformed police officer.

I was going to throw up.

"This is fantastic!" Kendall giggled as she crawled inside and honked the horn. "I was just thinking we should redecorate."

"What the hell are you doing?" I grabbed her arm and tried to wrench her back out of it, but she'd moved on to testing the hazard lights. She flipped the key in the ignition and the windshield wipers went wild.

"You realize how much trouble we'll be in if we're caught with this?" I hissed. "We'll get expelled."

"Nonsense. They'll know there was no way two girls carried this thing up the stairs. Someone did this for us. As an offering."

"An offering?" I seriously considered throwing Kendall out the window.

That is, until I looked at the small rectangle of paper she kept thrusting at me.

It was a postcard. On the front was an alligator, jaws wide open.

"Sterling." It felt like all the blood drained from my body all at once. "He did this."

"How do you know?" Kendall asked, sounding not even the smallest bit skeptical.

"The teeth," I murmured. "These are the teeth."

His smug little smile flashed behind my eyes. *I repay my debts in kind.*

He was planning to send me to the disciplinary committee right along with him. I grabbed the edge of my desk to keep upright as the world wobbled uncertainly around me.

"You okay?"

"No," I said. "We have to get this car out of here. Now. This is his revenge. You can bet this is the first strike of a two-punch combination, and the second involves getting me expelled."

"Well, we can't move this," Kendall said. "Not by ourselves."

"Just give me a minute to think."

"Parker," she said. "He'd know how to fix this."

Of course she'd think a boy could fix everything when we were just as able to handle it ourselves.

"Let's not involve anyone else," I said. But Kendall was already frantically texting.

"Parker is on his way. Don't look so mad, seriously. We need some muscle here. Plus, he won't believe this unless he sees it." She giggled like it was Christmas morning, even though a misunderstanding like this could compromise our entire academic futures. I wanted to scream. Pressure built behind my eyes as panic ratcheted my heart into overdrive.

But I looked at Kendall, at her smile of delight, and a tiny bit of it infected me. The rage slowly started to subside. No, it wasn't funny, but it was the smallest bit amazing—Sterling Lane could simultaneously exact revenge on me and humiliate Headmaster Lowell. I sat on my bed and forced my breathing to slow, praying for Rules 1 through 10 to guide me. While they'd been cornerstone Rules in the past, even the most thorough guidance on keeping my room clean wouldn't address removing an automobile from it. This problem transcended even the most sage of my Rules.

I pulled out my phone and started searching. Slowly, a plan began to form.

"Come in," Kendall sang out, thumping toward the door in her platform sandals.

"Why can't you get rid of a cat on your own?" Parker asked, pushing his massive shoulders through the door. Then he froze and stared at the metal monstrosity in the middle of our room.

"Car. You meant a car." He raked one hand through his hair. "I heard this was missing. How'd it get here?"

"Sterling Lane," I said.

Parker shook his head, looking at me with so much indignant outrage I could have kissed him. "How did he get it in here?" he asked.

"If we knew that, we'd know how to get it back out," I said. "But if he can figure it out, *I* can figure it out. He must have pulled it apart enough to squeeze it through the door. Probably the tires? We'll need tools."

We sent Parker off to raid the groundskeeper's shed while Kendall and I composed step-by-step instructions to dismantle the Mini Cooper. Or rather, Kendall sat on the floor painting her toenails hot pink, which she claimed helped her think, while I did all the documenting.

"Nice work, Harper," Parker said when our measurements confirmed that without wheels and the convertible top, the car could be turned on its side and would just barely fit through the door. "But we need more help," Parker added. "I mean, you're handy with a power drill, Harper, but you and I can't lift a car. And Kendall is useless. She won't break a nail even if it's to save her own ass." There was a bitterness clearly born of jealousy in his words.

Kendall's eyes misted over and my whole world turned red.

"You are *way* out of line," I said. "No jock-boy gets to come in here and push Kendall around. Not on my watch. The world needs beauty queens, too."

Parker's eyes widened. Kendall rewarded me with a dry smile, gratitude mixed with surprise. "A backhanded compliment, but I'll take it," she said. "Snarky Harper."

"Still," I said. "You may be right about needing more help." Even though things were hardly perfect between us, Cole would never let me down in a crisis. I sent him a text: *Emergency in my room. Come immediately.*

"There's a freight elevator down the hall," Kendall said. "And a dolly near the loading dock."

"We need a code for that," I said.

"Yes, but I know the code." Her voice dropped to a whisper. "You know that cute security guard?"

I shook my head, utterly at a loss. "Ick, Kendall. I don't check out older men."

"Whatever. He's like twenty or something." She grinned. "Last week I was trying to switch our chair with a better one from the lobby." At that, I glanced across the room. I hadn't noticed the change, but the gray wingback was a definite improvement over the lumpy brown monstrosity that had been there before. "So he offered to help me. I watched him key in the code. I can totally get us in the elevator."

"Fantastic," I said. Without Kendall's contribution, we'd be carrying the headmaster's Mini Cooper down three flights of stairs. There'd be virtually no way we wouldn't be seen.

Ten minutes later, someone banged on the door loudly

and abruptly enough that we all jumped. For one horrible moment, I was positive it was the police. With a warrant. I wouldn't put that past Sterling.

"Harper? You okay?" I was touched by the concern in Cole's voice.

"Is anyone with you?"

"No."

I opened the door a crack and dragged him inside. Then slammed it shut. "What's wro—"The question disintegrated as his eyes landed on the car. He started to laugh.

"That's not the reaction I was hoping for," I said. "Especially since it proves I was right about Sterling Lane."

"No," Cole said. "It proves *I* was right. I told you not to mess with him. I don't know what you did to him, but he's in our room getting drunk as we speak. He asked a few times if I'd talked to you. Guess now I know why." Then Cole paused. "I overheard him on the phone earlier. His father froze his accounts. Does that have anything to do with this?"

That revelation should have given me a surge of exultation. Of victory.

Instead I felt terrible. Truly terrible. Not that I thought Sterling Lane needed to be one ounce more indulged, but this time, it wasn't his fault. This time he was getting in trouble for help he rendered to Cole. I tried to comfort myself with the certain knowledge that he'd definitely gotten away with something far worse in the past, and that this was just delayed justice. But even that argument didn't sit quite right with my conscience. Especially because staying here for his grandmother actually was a pretty good reason. I had a horrible, sinking revelation that I needed to fix the disaster I'd created for Sterling.

"Yes," I said. "But I'll find a way to fix that, too."

I could never live with myself if I didn't. Just like I couldn't let Cole be expelled for whatever mess he'd gotten himself into. I'd seen the regret burning in his eyes the other day—and he didn't deserve to be expelled and have his life ruined when he had clearly learned his lesson.

Now I needed to get two boys off the hook for a crime only one committed.

REASON 17:

JUST WHEN I THINK WE'VE REACHED
THE BOTTOM OF THE DARK HOLE
OF DEPRAVITY THAT IS HIS HEART,
HE DIGS DOWN EVEN DEEPER.

*A*fter we smuggled the car out of the dorm, we hid it among the construction equipment on the far side of the gymnasium. It was surprisingly light—antique British Mini Coopers were more like go-karts, a far cry from today's more substantial American models.

The school was installing the new gymnasium roof that had swallowed Cole's first fund-raising efforts. Wooden crates of tools and a yellow Caterpillar excavator were poised for action the next morning. It wasn't likely anyone would venture into the roped-off area until the construction team arrived at dawn. That gave us ample time and space to reattach the side-view mirrors and inflate the tires.

Finally, the last teacher waddled across the parking lot to their car. The only vehicles remaining were those owned by the handful of students with permission to keep them on campus.

"I'll park the Mini in the back of the lot," Cole said. "You guys go to my room, so you won't be implicated if I'm caught."

"Why would you think we'd do that?" I asked. "I'm not saddling you with my problems."

"I'm already in deep shit," he said. "There's not much that'll get me off the hook anyway. It makes the most sense for me to take the risk."

"No," I pressed. "This is my problem. Let me handle it."

"Nothing's just your problem," Cole said. "I know I've been a bad brother lately. I've said some pretty harsh things. Just let me do this."

"You haven't been a bad brother." His words sent my heart soaring through the stratosphere. I'd been lonely; I'd missed him. And I couldn't believe he was finally back. "And I *will* get you off the hook if it's the last thing I do. I won't let you get expelled."

"Fine." He smiled triumphantly. "I didn't want to play this card, but the fact of the matter is you can't drive stick. We're way more likely to get caught if you lurch your way into the parking lot, stalling every five feet, or if you come with me and we're piling out of this piece of junk like it's a clown car."

As much as I hated to admit it, Cole had won. Rule 1 grumbled a little—it was my job to protect Cole, not the other way around.

"Just give us five minutes to get into position," Parker said. "Harper and I can watch from my room and text Kendall to run interference in case anyone comes across the quad. If we call you, it means abort the mission."

Cole nodded.

It took Parker and me less than five minutes to reach his room. I had to practically jog to keep up with his long-legged pace.

And once inside his room, I sincerely wished I was anyplace but. It was an absolute mess.

"You collect these?" I asked, picking up one of the protein bar wrappers littering the surface of his desk. A pile of laundry was rapidly decomposing next to his open closet door.

I picked my way across the room and watched from the window as Cole drove the car slowly along the road skirting the school. Every time he disappeared behind a tree or shrub, my pulse ratcheted into overdrive. But the plan went off without a hitch. No one saw the tiny car zoom into the parking lot, buzzing happily like a fly, and the coast was clear as it slipped into a narrow spot where it would be hidden from view by a massive pickup truck.

Cole climbed out and strolled back toward us like he didn't have a care in the world. When he reached the edge of the quad, Kendall fell into place beside him. They actually stopped to talk to some guys who'd emerged from the library. It wasn't an altogether horrible idea for him to get an alibi. As we waited, trying to look nonchalant, Parker turned to me.

"You know, you're full of surprises," he said.

"I am the most predictable person in the world, actually," I said. "And I like it that way."

"Doesn't seem like that to me." He looked down at his shoes. "What did you do to get on Sterling's hit list? It must have been amazing."

"Nothing," I said. "Nothing worth repeating, at least."

Parker wasn't perceptive enough to pick up on the shame in my tone; he kept right on going. "I mean, you realize you just dismantled a Mini Cooper?"

"Actually, I just took the wheels off," I said. "Why are you staring at me like that?" I turned away, ready to rendezvous with Cole and Kendall.

Parker placed his hand on my back—my *lower* back.

"I think it was pretty awesome—what you did."

It was such a new situation, standing there alone in a room with a boy, that I didn't know what to do. His palm practically spanned the width of me.

I had to be misreading the situation—this was a language I'd never learned to interpret. Plus, Parker was with Kendall. There was no way a boy would expect me to follow that act. Someone with his academic limitations and social calendar could never think of me...that way. So I tried to dismiss it as nothing when the hand on my back turned into an arm wrapped around me, turning me toward him.

Despite of the seventy-eight million reasons it didn't make sense he was touching me, a part of me was curious, wondering where this was headed.

But that curiosity vaporized when he leaned in and tried to kiss me.

With his lips.

I put one hand on his chest to keep him at bay. But I'd never touched a boy before, at least not like this, so I paused for a moment to take it all in: the way he felt solid and warm, the beating of his heart underneath my palm, and the illogical little thrill the human contact gave me even though it was far from welcome.

Clearly he misread my hesitation, because instead of backing off, he pressed his lips against mine. I went rigid with shock. He pulled back for a moment, his lips parted with anticipation of more—which made me laugh out loud. His eyes flew open.

"I'm sorry," I said, putting my hand over my mouth to muffle the laughter. "But you looked like a fish."

Fortunately, Parker backed away, halfway across the room. His entire face was red with mortification. That was the only thing that stopped me from raining fire and brimstone that he'd just grab me like that.

"God, I'm sorry," he said, rubbing one hand over his face. "I totally misread that, didn't I?"

"Yeah. You did." His cheeks were red. He was visibly mortified. So I tried a different tactic, one that allowed him to save face. "What about Kendall?"

"What about her?" he said. "She's totally cheating on me with Sterling. Wait—not cheating. We're not even together." Parker sounded every bit as sulky about that fact as Kendall did. I was no relationship expert, but it seemed to me those two needed to sit down and come clean with each other.

"No, she's not." I was surprised by how adamant I sounded. Kendall wanted to be with Parker, and for some perverse reason, I was invested in that outcome.

"They had dinner together once," I said, taking a step back and sitting in Parker's desk chair. "She's not interested in him; she was just doing it to make you jealous. You and Kendall really need to sit down and talk. Be honest with each other. Nothing happened between them, and it won't. Sterling has these rules. He doesn't go on second dates. You have to get what you want from him on the first date, which in Kendall's case was nothing."

Parker's eyes widened. "Does that actually work— Sterling's rules?"

"I have no idea. Sterling Lane isn't exactly sharing his deepest secrets with me. Besides, even if it did, would you really want to play those games?" I didn't add that he wouldn't be able to pull it off. There was something about Sterling Lane's confidence and persistence that was alluring to some girls. Or so I imagined. It seemed like Sterling was able to accomplish just about anything he set his sights on.

"Right. 'Course I wouldn't." Parker wasn't very convincing.

Thankfully, his phone interrupted our now extremely awkward conversation. "It's Kendall," he said, glancing at the caller ID. "Who didn't get what she wanted from Sterling and now thinks she can snap her fingers and get me back. Not exactly a thrilling offer."

"It's not like that," I said. "She really cares about you—and I know you care about her, too." When Parker scowled, my newfound Kendall protectiveness flared. "If you and Kendall get back together, you better do whatever it takes to deserve her. You're no saint, Parker, trying to kiss me just now." I rose and poked him in the sternum with my index finger, hard.

There was a knock on the door just as the words left my lips. And pretty much simultaneously, the door flew open.

Sterling leaned his shoulder against the frame, one ankle kicked over the other like he'd been lingering there for hours. "Sounds like I missed the best part." His words slurred around the edges, reminding me of what Cole had said: Sterling had spent the afternoon draining his supply of scotch.

His bare feet had striped tan lines from flip-flops. I seriously wondered if he got pedicures or if the Lane family DNA defied calluses.

"I didn't mean to interrupt," he said, scalding me with that smile. "Came to see if anyone has need of my services." His eyes flickered from my oil-stained hands to the smudge of tire dirt spanning my forehead. I saw the streak in the mirror on the far wall just as his eyes found it.

"Nope," I said, displaying my very best impersonation of his smug little smile. "I think this room is all filled up on assholes at the moment."

Sterling's eyes flashed to Parker, and I caught a sliver of a smile—a twitch of his lips. "Glad to hear it." He straightened, shifting his weight like he was about to walk away. "And thanks for the history outlines. You got them back, right?"

"What history outlines?"

"The ones I borrowed from your room," he said. "Drove them back myself in a charming little car. I borrowed that, too. Now, let's see." He tapped a finger against the edge of his jaw like he was thinking really hard. "I could have sworn I left them in the glove compartment, right where you were sure to find them."

Never underestimate your enemy—especially when he's Sterling Lane. Fortunately, the car hadn't been found yet. I still had time to save myself, and to dodge the second blow in this two-punch combo.

"Now, if you were truly ruthless," I said, "you wouldn't have told me that. Rest assured, Sterling, that when I exact my revenge, there will be no such courtesy."

"I look forward to it," Sterling replied.

"Out of my way." I lost my balance when I crashed right into him, and I hated him even more for the way he caught my elbow, righting me.

"Better bring a bobby pin, sweetheart," Sterling called after me. "It's locked."

"War. This means war. Sterling and his stupid alligator teeth," I muttered as I tore down the stairs past Cole and Kendall, who stared after me, bewildered. I didn't have time to stop and explain. There was no telling how long it would be until someone discovered the headmaster's missing car—and my notes stashed in the glove compartment, incriminating me.

By the time I reached the parking lot, I was panting like

a dog. Cole had no idea how prescient he'd been to leave the car half-concealed behind the pickup truck. And he'd left it unlocked. The keys were on the passenger seat, so I tried each one on the glove compartment lock, but none of them were small enough. There was clearly another separate tiny key I needed to find.

I scrambled around frantically, searching the pockets and nooks and crannies, but I came up empty-handed. There was no choice: I pulled the screwdriver we'd used to reassemble the Mini out of my pocket and wedged it into the crack. It took four tries and two deep gouges in the soft leather console. Headmaster Lowell would have an absolute fit when he saw the damage.

I snatched up my notes and was about to make a break for it when something moved in the cab of the pickup truck. It was a sophomore boy, one who I knew just well enough to recognize that the girl with him was not his girlfriend. And they were both staring at me.

What was it with boys and cheating today?

I rapped firmly on the window, right in his face. He jumped back as if my knuckle would smash right through the glass. "Don't just sit there staring like a goldfish. Go tell Headmaster Lowell that his car is here. Hurry. This is a stolen vehicle. There may still be evidence inside."

He opened the door slowly, the way you would if there was a wild animal prowling outside.

"I don't have time," I added. "Grades like mine don't grow on trees."

Then I turned and walked calmly away, reflecting on the day's manifold victories.

At this rate, I'd soon be leaping buildings in a single bound. I'd never known what I was capable of outside of academics because I'd never had the chance to try. But here I was—winning on every front. My history notes were safely back in my hands, I'd removed a stolen Mini Cooper from my room, and Kendall would soon be back in the arms of the boy she loved, fickle though that title might be. Plus, Cole and I were back to normal.

It was enough to tempt anyone to simply rest on their laurels. But I still had to get Cole out of his mess, and while I did, exonerate Sterling. His predicament was entirely attributable to actions I now regretted—they were born of utter desperation to protect Cole. But that didn't mean I'd let Sterling off the hook for what he'd just done.

Whether I'd brought the Mini Cooper incident on myself didn't matter. I had to show Sterling that I could hold my own—even when playing by his rules. This time I wouldn't resort to tattling or involve the administration. My revenge would be swift and sudden. Sterling wasn't the only alligator in this jungle and certainly not the most cunning.

REASON 18:

HE FRAMED ME.
SO WHAT IF I DID IT FIRST?
MY ACTIONS STEMMED FROM A
HIGHER MORAL AUTHORITY: ME.

*H*eadmaster Lowell pulled me out of history class the next morning.

Me.

I'd never been removed from class before, other than when my grandmother died in eighth grade and our father pulled us out of school to tell us. It felt like every single one of my nerve endings was exposed as I followed the headmaster into his office.

"Do you know why you're here?" he asked.

My hands started to shake. I had no idea how to answer. If I assumed it was about Cole and the money, he might think I knew something that could implicate Cole. But if I said anything about his car, he'd question my involvement, which was the last thing in the world I needed.

"No," I choked out.

"I wanted to thank you for finding my car."

"Oh, that," I said, my loud exhale broadcasting my relief.

"Yes," he said. "Very serendipitous that you stumbled

across it. May I ask how it happened?"

"It was no big deal." I searched for a plausible story. "I was walking home and saw it sitting there. And well, I'd heard about what happened, so I moved in closer to make sure it was yours."

"That was good thinking," he said. "That's why Mr. Evans told me you were looking in my glove compartment when he saw you?"

"Right," I said slowly.

"Makes sense," he said, nodding sagely. "But it doesn't explain how your wallet got in the trunk."

Panic blindsided me, tumbling me in its clutches. It was a primal sort of fear, the heart-exploding, wide-eyed terror of a wild hare with hounds snapping at its haunches.

I thought about turning and running, partaking in the wild hare's solution. Out the door and into the woods behind campus, where I could live on berries, acorns, and the nontoxic plants we'd identified in freshman biology.

I took a deep breath, steeling myself. I'd underestimated the extent of Sterling's carefully executed plan, but that ended now. He probably expected me to tattle, but I'd never make that mistake again. Instead, I'd do whatever it took to slide out of this situation, and I'd live on to fight another day.

"Of course it does." I drew my words out, scrambling through my brain in search of an excuse, any excuse. "I wanted to make sure it really was your car. I know how rare that model is, but still, it seemed so lucky that your car would just be sitting there after you'd lost it. So I searched for any identifying factors. I had to set down my wallet and sunglasses. I realized I was being silly—the registration was in the glove compartment. But at about that time, I remembered that your car was technically a crime scene, and I sort of panicked that I was tampering with evidence." I paused and looked him square in the eye. I'd read once that was the key to effective lying. "That's a felony, you know."

"I'm well aware of that," Headmaster Lowell said, pressing his hands together in front of him, then separating them until just the fingertips touched. He was being painfully slow and deliberate as he searched for his next words—pretending he was capable of deep thought when he was really just savoring his misplaced headmaster authority before declaring his unilateral victory.

"It all seems very convenient, Harper," he said. "While I'm grateful that you found my car, I can't help wondering if this incident has anything to do with Sterling Lane."

It was so deliciously unexpected that I couldn't speak. Finally, someone had seen through Sterling's shiny exterior into the rotten core concealed underneath. Still, I'd never admit it—would never turn Sterling in to the headmaster. *I* would be the one to teach Sterling Lane his lesson.

But that pause gave Headmaster Lowell the opportunity he needed to finish his thought. "And I want you to understand that while we took a chance on Sterling despite his history of acting out, we have a zero tolerance policy at Sablebrook Academy." His eyes stabbed me right in the heart. "I also understand you might feel, well…adrift given Sterling's sudden academic success, and that it might be a bit threatening to you, particularly in Mrs. Stevens's class. But a truly great mind will embrace the success of others. It's a stepping-stone for bettering all of society. There's room at the top for other students."

"But—" I watched the rescue boat drift past.

"I believe this was an isolated incident, Harper." He slid his glasses back in place and lifted a stack of papers awaiting his perusal. "So I've decided not to pursue this any further. Don't make me regret it. You may return to class."

Just like that, I was dismissed. I sat there for a minute, head spinning from the twists and turns of Sterling's latest move. I had to reluctantly applaud his chess move, his carefully plotted and perfectly executed little prank. I'd warned Sterling that I'd fight fire with fire, and now I was poised on the precipice, prepared to jump in after him.

And I wouldn't want it any other way.

REASON 19:

HE THINKS HE CAN FRAME ME — THAT HE'S SOME SORT OF PRANK GURU WHOSE ANTICS SHAMED ME INTO SUBMISSION.

BUT HE'S GOING TO LEARN NOT EVEN A SEDITIOUS, SELF-RIGHTEOUS RULEBREAKER LIKE HIM CAN CRACK ME.

For three days, my outlines languished in neglect while I divided my time between plotting ways to get the best of Sterling Lane and keeping Cole from being expelled.

Thanks to the distractions, I stayed up into the wee hours of the morning almost every night, trying to keep on top of my schoolwork. I spent an afternoon researching high school pranks—infuriatingly, Sterling Lane's escapades were chronicled on pretty much every single website. Apparently, he was a legend in some circles. I begrudgingly had to admit that he was clever. But I was clever, too, and I knew I'd find a way to prove it that would eclipse anything Sterling had ever done.

It wasn't until I ran into Cole at breakfast the next morning that a solution presented itself so tidily it almost seemed like divine intervention.

"Where's your roommate?" I glared over Cole's shoulder so that my frown was certain to be the first thing Sterling saw when he approached.

Cole rolled his eyes. "Don't tell me you're still mad about the car thing. It was just a joke."

"Of course I'm mad," I told him. "If I'd been caught, I could have been expelled."

"Actually, I don't think anyone would believe you put it in your own room. What would be the point? If anything, it would have cast blame on Sterling. Everyone knows how he is. And that you hate each other. He took a stupid risk that you wouldn't tell." He wrapped an arm around my neck. "And I'm proud of you for not doing it. You're lightening up in your old age."

"We're the same age."

"Stop peering around like that," Cole said. "You won't see him down here for breakfast. He sets the alarm for five minutes before class."

"That would explain his hair," I said.

"Don't tell anyone this," Cole said. "It would destroy his image. But Sterling has trouble sleeping the night before games. He takes sleeping pills."

"Really?"

Sterling Lane, completely incapacitated by a pharmaceutical haze—that thought warranted further contemplation. I glanced up in time to see Parker and Kendall enter the room, holding hands. I wasn't in the mood to endure the wet and sloppy side effects of their reunion, so I wrapped my breakfast in a paper napkin and headed to class.

As I made my way across the quad, watching bleary-eyed students wandering around, the pieces fell into place. It was a simple prank, one I'd read about in a blog post rife with typos. No one would be expelled or get injured. Except for a certain someone's pride, of course.

Fortunately, pride was one attribute Sterling Lane had in abundance. It would take me a lifetime to exact enough damage to even put a dent in it. And that would be one thing I'd devote eternity to achieving.

I just had to convince Cole and Parker to play along.

"Why would I want to risk getting in trouble?" Parker asked.

"Because Sterling Lane took your girlfriend out on a date," I'd replied. "And he'll do it again."

Parker raised an eyebrow.

"Maybe not to you," I explained. "But to someone else—unless we stand up to him now and let him know that's not how we do things here at Sablebrook."

Just like that, Parker was on board—which was important, given that there was no way I could move a massive piece of furniture without his help, much less carry it across campus in the dead of night.

The hardest part would be drugging Sterling Lane. Fortunately, thanks to Cole's reveal earlier that day, Sterling would take care of that little detail himself.

REASON 20:
EVEN WHEN YOU THINK YOU'VE GOT HIM ON THE ROPES, ALL BLOODIED UP, HE HAS A THREE-PUNCH COMBINATION LYING IN WAIT.

*I*t took two days for me to get my plan in place. Per Rule 15, I was thorough and exacting in my preparations. During that time, my thoughts were divided between my impending revenge and my burning need to exonerate Cole. We hadn't heard a word from the headmaster about the disciplinary committee meeting or whether the school would press charges. I'd left five messages with the police detective who was supposedly investigating the stolen car I'd seen Cole climb out of, to no avail. I'd finally moved on to his supervisor, who was similarly impossible to reach. The private investigator had turned up little as well.

Whenever I spent time with Cole, I tried to steer the conversation toward the weight room and whether he needed money. But he just as quickly steered the conversation back into more neutral waters. So more and more, we talked about his lacrosse or my goals for summer internships and the AP history exam. While this was normal fodder for discussion, it was weird to not acknowledge the uncertainty that loomed over us, threatening to tear us apart.

At times, it felt like Cole was back, acting normal. But other times, he'd lapse into a strange, sulky silence. Yet when I told him my plan, his eyes lit up.

"I'm glad you guys are finally getting along," he said. "I had a feeling you would."

"I'd hardly call it that," I replied. But Cole just grinned at me and changed the subject.

On the big night, I was edgy with anticipation. I told myself it was because I was greasing the wheels of justice, but in truth, it was more than that. Rule 398 shuddered as the realization dawned on me that this was fun—pranks were fun. Especially when people were in on it with me. And ever since I pitched my plan, I'd been the opposite of lonely. I was overwhelmed. Even Kendall delayed her return to her repaired and repainted room to be closer to the action.

Cole confirmed that Sterling took a sleeping pill as scheduled and texted me fifteen minutes after Sterling went to sleep. I'd read online that it takes an average of thirty minutes for that particular medication to take effect.

It was no easy feat to sneak out of the dorm at midnight. The dorm hallway was dark and deserted, and the thick soles of Kendall's platforms thumped noisily behind me. I gave her a dirty look and her footsteps coalesced into one long, sandpaper shuffle.

The cool night air almost awakened me to my senses, to the idiocy of what I was about to do. But then I pictured the sheepish smile of surrender on Sterling's face when he realized I had the upper hand again. The public aspect of my little prank would up the ante tenfold—just like I promised. Sterling would have to dredge the bottom of his bag of tricks to one-up me next time.

I knocked softly on Cole's door and it opened immediately. Cole and Parker stood there, dressed all in black.

"This is as far as I go," Cole said, motioning with one hand toward Sterling's bed. "I'm not getting in the middle of your little feud."

"You already did," I reminded him. "You helped me get that car out of my bedroom. I'd say you've already picked sides. Besides, we can't do this without you. And I'm your sister."

"Fine," Cole said. "But from here on out, I'm muscle only. If he asks, I'll deny all of it."

Sterling was sprawled out in his bed, his tan, muscled shoulders visible over the top of his blanket. I'd never seen him vulnerable before. I had the oddest urge to touch him, trail my fingers along his exposed skin, just to make sure he was real. It had to be the sleep deprivation from the planning process, because never in a million years would I do something that disturbing.

My mind was playing the cruelest kind of tricks on me. Yes, he was at my mercy for the moment. But he played rough, and he could handle me playing rough right back.

"Let's go." I took position at one corner of the bed. "And don't forget, if you're caught, just leave it there and run. The genius of this is that even if we only get ten percent done, he'll be humiliated."

"Hardly," Cole said. "You can't embarrass a person who has zero inhibitions."

I ignored him. This retaliation was more about asserting myself than it was about winning. Or at least, that's how I wished I felt.

The service elevator creaked and groaned under our weight like it was operated by a team of elephants and a gigantic pulley hidden somewhere in the bowels of the dorm.

The sidewalk leading to the main academic building was lined with lamps that cast broad, overlapping circles of light over the sidewalk. I used to love that the campus was well-lit and that I felt safe wandering back from the library late at night, but when you're trying to drag a sedated boy across campus, public safety precautions are a serious liability.

When a light flickered on in our dorm monitor's window, my heart started to hammer. We'd been caught. I took a step to the side, preparing to dive for the shadows lining the path, before Rule 298 reminded me to be brave and to take ownership of my decisions. If anyone was getting caught, it would be me. I'd create a diversion and let the others get away first.

The light switched back off. We stood there for seventeen seconds, waiting to make sure the coast really was clear.

The instant we started lifting the bed again, Sterling murmured something in his sleep. He rolled until he was perched precariously on the edge of his mattress. One tiny nudge would send him sprawling across the sidewalk. Cole and Parker startled and backed up, like they were about to shift into a run.

There was only one way to salvage the situation.

I took a deep breath and wrapped my fingers around Sterling's shoulders. His skin was warm and smooth, exactly how it looked like it would feel. He shifted again. I used his momentum to roll him over onto the middle of the bed. Without a word, the others fell back into place, lifting the bed and continuing across the quad.

When we made it safely into the academic buildings,

we deposited our little delivery in the middle of the first-floor hallway.

"Leave, you guys," I said. "I have one more little surprise, and I definitely don't want you involved in case I'm caught. It's a big one."

Cole looked at me, tipping his head to the side.

"Don't even think about arguing with me, Cole Campbell," I said. "I'll be ten minutes behind you, max."

As soon as the others disappeared into the darkness of the grassy quad, I walked out to the white van that was waiting for me. This last little surprise was the cherry on top, and I leaned into the darkened van, inspecting the locks on the massive cage nestled within.

*T*he rest of the night I tossed and turned, worrying my plan would fail. That Sterling would somehow wiggle free from my trap. That he'd wake up and be waiting outside the door for me, all starched and pressed and hankering for sweet vengeance.

But the next morning, exhausted and bleary-eyed, I was up and moving, prepared to be at class thirty minutes early per Rule 10. Plus, there was no way I was going to miss this if my plan worked.

The marble stairs in front of the academic building were slick with drizzle and utterly deserted when I arrived. The rest of the student body was at breakfast. While usually I would have at least dashed through the cafeteria to grab a hard-boiled egg and toast, that morning I was too nervous to even contemplate eating.

I tugged on the front door so hard it slammed open,

sending a reverberating *thud* through the empty hallways, and my tennis shoes pounded like timpani as I sneaked down a side corridor. I was way too nervous to venture into the main hallway to see the aftermath of my handiwork.

But as I turned the corner, headed straight for the history room, I nearly bumped right into two girls who were doubled over giggling. While there were a million possible explanations for their silliness, I knew—the way you can just *know*—that they were laughing at Sterling Lane. I hid behind a corner, where one crane of my neck would give me an unobstructed view of the main hallway. But I was too nervous to look. Instead, I watched the people who had passed through already. Everyone kept turning to look behind them, like there was something fascinating back there.

Then I heard the sound I had been waiting for—an eruption of laughter. And I did it: I peeked. A crowd had gathered in the main foyer, growing by the second as students opened the double doors of the school, thinking they were headed to class but instead getting caught up in the spectacle unfolding.

Sterling stretched his arms out, above his head. Then he sat up in bed—a bed that had been magically transported to the middle of the busiest school hallway. The sheets fell away to reveal his bare shoulders, followed by the rest of his chest. I'm sure I wasn't the only one who noticed that his even tan wasn't limited to the parts of him that were visible under ordinary clothing.

His eyes widened. He looked around quickly, his gaze darting over every face gathered around him. I savored the moment as he struggled to decide what to do next, the flash of uncertainty that was gone so quickly I was probably the only one to recognize it for what it was: he was racking his brain for how to save face. And he opted for the usual. His lips quirked into a dry smile. With an impressive display of bravado, he kicked the covers back all the way. The trick had come off even better than I imagined. Sterling Lane had fallen asleep in nothing but a pair of boxers, and he was now trapped, half-naked, in the middle of the hallway with the whole school watching. The only downside was how attractive he looked first thing in the morning. The whole scene came off just one notch shy of a professional underwear commercial.

Rule 67 told me not to gloat, but it was too late. I stepped around the corner, striding through the fringes of the crowd that was now shifting, making way for Sterling to pass.

His eyes met mine as he straightened up to his full height. He just stood there, staring. Or maybe he was waiting for me to make the first move.

The crowd parted like the Red Sea, leaving Sterling and me at opposite shores. I felt everyone's gaze drift from my face to his and back again.

"Thanks for the lift." Sterling smiled. My stomach flopped; he was probably just getting warmed up. I shook my head, filled with begrudging admiration. Sterling Lane was absolutely unflappable. Just like Cole had warned, there was no way to embarrass someone so utterly uninhibited.

Then he pulled the quilt off his bed, and I noticed for the first time how lovely it was. Hand-sewn, a painstakingly perfect hodgepodge of expensive-looking cotton prints. The kind of trinket you picked up for a grand at an Amish craft fair. In Sterling's world, it was just something you'd find in the minor guest room of a Hamptons estate.

He wrapped it around his shoulders, letting it slide down just a little, giving us all an unobstructed view of the excruciatingly chiseled definition in his shoulders none of us had had the opportunity to appreciate before.

He draped his right arm over the shoulder of a cute blond girl I often saw practicing cello on the quad. She looked a little startled at first, but few girls wouldn't find themselves leaning in a little closer when a guy like Sterling Lane wrapped his arm around them.

"Two hundred bucks for a pair of shorts," he called over his shoulder. "Fifty for a shirt. Screw the shoes."

And he walked right toward me, never breaking eye contact. "Who knew?"

"Who knew what?" I demanded, bracing for the onslaught.

He came to a dead stop and looked down at me, smiling in a gently playful way that made all my joints go loose and wobbly in their sockets.

"That we'd be friends." He grinned.

"We're not."

"Au contraire, sweetheart." He started to walk away with the sophomore girl tucked under his arm like a football. "We have far too much in common."

A freshman boy scampered up to him with a bundle of cotton. Shorts. My bark of laughter startled me and the other students nearby. Those vultures had probably never even seen me smile.

Sterling Lane might have a point. I'd enjoyed every minute of that morning, each excruciating, tantalizing moment I'd anticipated watching him squirm. The adrenaline coursing through my veins was probably what had led him to his life of crime in the first place—the sweet siren song of superiority and triumph. It had sucked me under years ago, and only now had I realized it contained more than one melody.

I hummed it softly to myself as I watched him stroll toward Mrs. Stevens's room just as Kendall reached it and opened the door, slipping inside steps ahead of him. That wasn't part of the plan. Kendall screamed. She streaked out of the room, followed by an explosion of Sablebrook school colors. I probably should have warned her about the second aspect of our surprise. It hadn't occurred to me she'd enter the room first.

A piglet the size of a terrier streaked down the hallway with Sterling Lane's lacrosse number emblazoned across his back—in food-safe paints, of course.

The science teacher joined forces with the janitor to corral the unfortunate swine. But it was tame enough not to be afraid and was easily bribed with a candy bar. We'd left a note with the pig's contact information taped to Sterling's sheets, since no prank was worth driving a chubby pink pig into homelessness.

Sterling turned just enough for his gaze to find mine again. He smiled—a smile that I felt in my toes because there was genuine warmth in it. Friends.

Was I *friends* with Sterling Lane?

*T*he next afternoon, Sterling strolled over to my usual table in the lunchroom and perched on the edge of it, right next to me. He put one scuffed loafer up on the chair. My heart started to pound for reasons I didn't want to examine too closely. I'd spent most of the night wondering exactly what he'd meant when he said we were now friends.

Somehow I couldn't imagine us swapping secrets or going out for ice cream cones.

"Your smelly shoe is ruining my appetite." I glared at his foot until he lowered it back to the ground where it belonged. Then he plopped down into the chair instead. Was he planning to sit here? With me? Panic filled my chest and started rising right up my throat. I had no idea what to discuss with him; we'd never had a conversation that wasn't a series of barbs and verbal blows.

"Seat taken?" he asked. "Oh wait, of course not. Unless you're saving it for the invisible man you dine with daily."

Kendall and Parker had moved back to the lacrosse

team table now that our little plot had ended. They'd extended an admirably sincere-sounding invitation for me to join them, but I'd let them off the hook and politely declined. Besides, I had so many neglected outlines to update, I simply couldn't spare the time. Fortunately, after just a few days of companionship, it wasn't that hard for me to slip back into my usual solitary routine.

"Actually, it is taken," I said.

When he raised one eyebrow, I looked away. I kept my eyes averted as he rose, but instead of walking away, he just stood there watching me.

"Well?" He motioned to the chair.

I didn't know what else to do, so I set my book there and finally looked up into that smug, smiling face. "It's infinitely better company than you."

"Then you can bring it on Friday night." He walked around the table and sat in the chair directly opposite me. "I'm not a huge fan of small talk, either."

"What's Friday night?" I asked.

"The last school night of the week," he said. "I'll meet you after the lacrosse game."

"Why on earth would you do that?" I demanded, realizing too late that I'd raised my voice in my panic. A few curious eyes met mine before retreating when they saw the look on my face. "Or think that I would agree?"

"Because Cole needs our help," he replied mildly. "I'm hoping you'll be reasonable for once."

"I'm always reasonable."

"That point isn't worth debating because you are, in fact, uniformly unreasonable. It's one of your more fascinating qualities. Still, Cole is up shit creek with two broken paddles."

"Speak normally," I said. "What are you talking about?

Is this about the disciplinary committee?"

"Worse," he said. "If I'm right, Cole owed money and paid his debt, but there's still something they're holding over him. Something big. As his sister, it's your job to step up to the plate and find out what's going on." He pulled out his dreaded laminated cheat sheet. "Rule 25 demands you take action."

"It's gambling, isn't it?" I hadn't yet worked up the courage to confront Cole.

A flicker of surprise crossed his face, and he nodded. "I'm pretty sure Cole was scammed. We need to break that influence before they suck him down even further."

"Why do you care what happens to Cole?" I asked, genuinely curious. "How is it your problem?"

"Two fair questions, for once." He fired a smile right at me. "I never said I did, and it's not."

"Clearly that's not true," I said. "Because you're sitting here."

"Those are two possible motives out of a field of thousands." He glanced at his watch. "And lunch is over. You can speculate on your own time."

"Wait."

Sterling paused and turned back to face me.

"I hired a private detective," I said. "I saw Cole getting out of a suspicious car, so I wrote down the plate and had it traced. It turns out it was stolen from another vehicle. The vehicle itself was likely stolen, too. The detective is working off a photo I took—to find the guy, I mean. That's why you went to Café Bastille, isn't it? He's there."

"Smart girl." Sterling smiled. "He works this Friday. Dinner shift. I'll see you then. After my game."

I wasn't ready for this—to sit at a table opposite Sterling Lane, pretending we could get along. Even if I was doing it for Cole, being alone with Sterling terrified me.

"For the record, we're not going to dinner together. We'll just eat at the same place, at the same table," I said.

"An important but absurd distinction," Sterling said drily.

"I don't trust you."

"And you shouldn't." He flashed a wicked smile that unleashed a river of adrenaline into my veins. "But we're even now." He paused. "Fun as it's been, we're too well-matched. We can't keep hammering at each other like this. We're likely to just pull each other apart, and the school with us." I was taken aback by the gentler tone in his voice. Who knew Sterling had a serious side?

"That's a disturbingly practical thing for you to say, Sterling. And apparently I'm not uniformly unreasonable, because I agree." My heart did a little leap—half joy, half terror. "I'll see you Friday."

"Outstanding," he said, pushing himself to his feet. "Oh, and try to look like a girl. Got my reputation to protect and all that. Plus, I'm curious to see how it would turn out."

Heat flooded my cheeks. My hands balled into fists. I wanted to punch him—or kick him. Or both. Instead I picked up my napkin, crumpled it up, and hit him in the face with it. His eyes widened in surprise.

"There's no specific way a girl has to look or act," I said. "And with a dad like yours, you should know how it feels to have someone try to cram you into a preconceived little box."

He leaned forward, placing his palms flat against the table. Inviting me to continue.

"I *am* a girl," I said. "A perfectly attractive girl. Cropped hair and all. That's how it *does* turn out. Daily."

"I'm well aware," he said quietly. "Right now, particularly."

Then he straightened and walked away. I sat there, breathing in and out. Watching his retreating back. Sarcasm—it had to be sarcasm. Why would he insult me and then do a complete one-eighty moments later unless it was to provoke me and keep me guessing? Or maybe it wasn't sarcasm at all. Maybe Sterling was enjoying this power struggle as much as I was starting to.

The more I turned his words over in my mind, the more I kept grabbing on to that last possibility above all others. Even the memory of the quiet, intimate quality in his voice as he murmured his cryptic comment sent a surge of anticipation down my spine. Sterling was a roller coaster. As frustrating and confusing as our games were becoming, I knew I'd stay on this ride until the bitter end.

REASON 22:

HE PAID FOR DINNER JUST TO MAKE ME UNCOMFORTABLE.

I arrived during the third quarter of the lacrosse game and watched long enough to observe that Sterling lived up to his athletic reputation. I even caught myself cheering along with the crowd a few times. Cole played well, but I could tell he was distracted.

I was hardly going to give Sterling the satisfaction of seeing me wait around for him after the game. Instead, I caught Cole as he was leaving the field.

"Great game," I told him.

"Thanks," he replied. "I thought Friday nights were for pleasure reading. You never come to these games."

"Well, maybe that's going to change," I said, again aching at the thought that this could be one of his final lacrosse games at Sablebrook if I didn't get him exonerated soon. "I miss watching you play—spending time with you."

"Me, too," he said. "I was just thinking—wanna get lunch tomorrow? Catch up?"

"I'd love that. Text me a time?" Cole headed off toward

the locker room, leaving me alone. So I wandered back toward the bleachers and settled on the steps leading up to them.

But I couldn't focus. Butterflies nose-dived inside my stomach as I waited for my date with the devil. Even though I heard Sterling approaching long before he arrived, I refused to look up. I ignored the people who passed him, congratulated him on the game, or asked what he was doing that night. Pretended I didn't hear the way he hesitated before he told them that he had dinner plans, and the fact that he never said with whom or where even when they asked. His silence gave the whole thing a sordid air, exactly as he intended.

Finally, Sterling reached me. Even when he stood in front of me on the stairs, his dirty boat shoes two steps from mine, I pretended I was so intent on my book that the rest of the world had disappeared.

"I know you see me, Harper," he said. "This is juvenile."

When I finally looked up, he was grinning.

He was dressed like we were going digging for clams in Cape Cod for a lifestyle magazine photo shoot. His button-down shirt was rolled up at the sleeves and hanging untucked over battered khaki slacks. Both were slightly frayed in that casual, entitled way preppy boys have of making broken-in clothes look expensive.

"Ready? Or do you wanna wait around until the rest of the team comes out of the locker room? They're going for pizza and were insanely curious about why I said no. If you stall long enough, they'll find out."

I was on my feet so fast he took a step back, startled. I pitched forward, almost losing my balance. Sterling put one hand on my forearm, laughing. His fingers trailed down along my wrist almost languidly before coming to a stop.

Never in my life had a boy done something like that to me, a lingering touch. Nerves along my arm I didn't even know I had exploded with delight. And it confounded me to know that my body could betray me so completely.

"Let's get one thing straight about all this touching." I jerked my hand away. "Kendall told me all about your despicable dating rules, and there's not one single thing I want from you tonight or any other night. So you just keep your hands to yourself."

"Dating?" He smiled viciously. "This is all business, sweetheart. And if you know all about my dating rules, you know that sanity is a requirement. Ergo, this is not a date."

"You're one to talk, sociopath."

He kept walking, not even breaking his stride.

"I said you're one to talk," I repeated, louder this time. I waited another five seconds before I added, "It's rude to ignore people, you know."

"I heard you," he called over his shoulder. "Just waiting for you to get all fired up. The rabid Chihuahua act is my favorite."

That shut me up. There was no way I was saying one more thing to Sterling Lane for the rest of the evening. I wasn't there to entertain him. My stomach tied into knots all over again as I replayed our conversation in my mind.

I kept a half step behind him as we walked. From there, I wouldn't be assaulted by that smug little smile every time I glanced up at him. I could focus my gaze on those dirty boat shoes and the way his button-down fit so perfectly it must have been tailored.

We'd walked about two blocks before he slowed, waiting for me.

"What are you, a servant or something? Stop walking behind me."

"We don't have servants, so I didn't realize the implication." But even as I said it, my pulse picked up at the teasing tone in his voice. Was it possible I enjoyed arguing with him?

"Neither do we," he said. "It was a reference to feudal times—that servile, silent thing you're doing. Either way, walk next to me."

Moments passed in silence.

"Are you mad?" he asked. "I was teasing you, Harper. Don't be so touchy."

"Fine," I said. When he started walking again, I reluctantly took a step forward so that we were side by side. Then I kept plowing forward, forcing him to walk faster to keep up with me.

"I thought we'd moved past this," he said. "Called a truce, but you're extra snappish—like you get when you're backed into a corner." He stopped walking and turned to face me. "Do I make you nervous?" His careful scrutiny of my face made my skin feel too small.

"Don't flatter yourself," I replied, pushing past him and carrying on walking. I hated him for being right. My heart was thumping, and my knees had a coltish feeling.

"Is there a reason I should perceive that as a good thing?" There was a playful edge in his voice as his long strides carried him back to my side. It was a fair question, since presumably he was no longer trying to intimidate me. But I didn't have an answer I was prepared to share.

We lapsed back into merciful silence, but I felt him glance at me from time to time as if considering something. My jitters grew jitters of their own.

"This is it," Sterling said, holding the door open for me. "Let me do all the talking."

"A night of listening to you nonstop?" I asked. "This *is* the seventh circle."

"I mean when we find him."

"Do you see him?" I demanded, scanning every corner of the restaurant.

"Shhh," Sterling murmured. "Subtlety is paramount."

"I refuse to believe all this secrecy is necessary. You act like you're starring in a spy movie." I poked his shoulder with my index finger. "Maybe that's your motive for helping Cole—plain old spoiled, rich-boy boredom?"

He pressed his index finger against my lips. Shushing me. Once again my body waged a full-blown mutiny, capillaries dilating, blood racing to warm my skin. Blushing like an idiot.

His eyes skimmed over my face. There was no way he missed the effect he'd just had on me, but for once he didn't say anything.

"Why did you drag me here in the first place if I'm supposed to just play sidekick?"

But he was already at the hostess station, issuing orders like he owned the place. I had to admit there was something admirable about the way he took control of the situation. Rule 244 reluctantly approved.

The hostess led us to a small table in the back, right next to a couple who looked like they were five minutes away from bolting for the bedroom. The woman was leaning forward so far her chest was practically pressed against the tablecloth—the universal signal of attraction.

I made a big show of rolling my eyes impatiently as Sterling pointed to a different table instead. A table for four in the corner, positioned so that two adjacent seats against the wall had unobstructed views of the dining room. Then he pulled my chair out for me and pushed it in as soon as I hovered over it—sweeping me off my feet, and not in a good way. As he settled in the seat next to me, his knee brushed mine. I scooted over an inch or two to ensure it wouldn't happen again.

Sterling's eyes roamed all over the restaurant like he was hunting for hidden treasure. Finally, he visibly relaxed and leaned forward, close enough to whisper and be heard above the chatter in the restaurant. I leaned in closer and flushed red as I recalled the couple we'd just seen sitting with very similar postures.

"Since you're about as subtle as a cattle prod, I'll do the talking," he whispered as his eyes roamed over my face. "I know it's killing you to take the backseat, but just this once can you concede, temporarily, that I might be better suited to sweet talk than you? Let Rule 204 guide you. I'll let you berate me the whole way home just to even the score. I won't even fight back."

"That doesn't sound like any fun." The words slipped out before I could stop them.

Sterling barked with laughter. "You don't normally look so startled when the truth sneaks out of those lips." He dropped his gaze to my lips, lingering uncomfortably long.

"Which reminds me," Sterling said, flashing the smile that always warned me to brace for impact. "The lip gloss. Nice touch. You know, you're not nearly as plain as you'd like to be."

Warmth crept up my neck and spread across my cheeks. He was watching me so intently, I couldn't swallow. Couldn't find an appropriate place to rest my hands.

Leave it to Sterling to level a backhanded compliment that tied me into knots. Which part did he mean—if any? I didn't want to be plain, but I also did and didn't want him to notice I'd actually *tried* to look nice. Well, notice it, but not acknowledge it.

"May I take your order?" An unfamiliar voice shattered

the awkward silence that had settled between us.

I looked up into the face of the blond guy Cole had argued with in the blue station wagon outside the main school parking lot. The guy I'd been looking for.

He glanced at Sterling. "You're back."

Sterling slipped into the fakest smile I'd ever seen. "I thought about what you said—about having connections in town. Thought perhaps we could place that wager. Off the record, of course."

The waiter glanced around, making sure none of his other tables were clamoring for his attention. He must have been reassured by what he saw, because his eyes shifted back to Sterling and his shoulders relaxed.

"Who's your friend?" His eyes raked my face, like he recognized me but couldn't figure out why. "What happened to the girl from last week?" I wasn't surprised that he frowned at the unfavorable comparison between Kendall and me. Sterling had clearly downgraded.

"I have lots of friends," Sterling said, unleashing a wicked smile. "One for every occasion. Including undercover operations."

The waiter's smile faltered as he glanced over at me again. Like me, he was wondering about the true meaning behind Sterling's double entendre.

"But Harper here is my favorite," he said. "She's a twin."

The waiter's eyes opened wide.

Sterling laughed. "Oh no, nothing like that. What a dirty mind you've got today, Gilbert. No, Harper's a fraternal twin. Her brother is Cole Campbell. Know him? Of course you do—with your prodigious record you've probably bet on a game or two of his?"

The waiter set his pen and notepad on the table and took a step back, curling his lip. Discreetly, I slid the pen under the table, tucking it away in the little ziplock evidence bags I'd packed, just in case.

Just as quickly, he glanced around the room, remembering where he was, trimming his wide eyes and slack jaw back into a more controlled expression. A bland expression. "Never heard of him."

Yes, I'd agreed to take a backseat to Sterling in this conversation, but I couldn't just sit there and listen to that little weasel lie.

"Liar. You know him," I said. Sterling kicked me under the table. I ignored him and pressed on. "I saw you arguing with him in the school parking lot. I'd say you know him well."

Hidden by the tablecloth, Sterling's hand found my knee and squeezed. But it would take more than that to stop me.

"What are you holding over him? He paid you off, but that wasn't enough, was it?" I could feel people starting to stare, but I didn't care. Sterling's hand left my knee and slid upward, skimming along my thigh. White light exploded behind my eyes.

"Stop," I gasped. I was so shocked I couldn't form another syllable if my life depended on it. From the vicious turn Sterling's smile had taken, that was his intention.

The waiter was using the distraction to slip away—and you could bet we'd never see him again if he did.

I was such an idiot, completely unable to control my mouth.

"You don't want to leave quite yet, Gilbert." Sterling's tone was razor-sharp. Gilbert paused and looked back, his weak little brain susceptible to Sterling's Jedi mind tricks.

"Don't be offended by Harper," Sterling said, leaning back in his seat and stretching his arms out over the table, a picture of ease. "She accuses me of lying at least a dozen times daily. I can set my watch by it. But this time she may have a point. We know you've been threatening her brother, and we're here to tell you the game, literally and figuratively, is over."

Another waiter passed behind Gilbert, nudging him with his elbow—a clear sign the staff had noted this interaction and it was time for Gilbert to move on. "Would you like to start with something to drink?" He practically spat the words at us.

"Scotch. Neat." Sterling glanced at me. "And a Shirley Temple for the lady."

"Hilarious. If you don't mind, I've got work to do. Tell Cole next time he sends his sister to do his dirty work, I send Victor to do mine."

"Victor? Is that your thuggish friend, because—" I was prepared to tell Gilbert exactly what type of reception Victor would receive, but Sterling silenced me with a finger tapping my knee, rhythmic and steady as a metronome.

"Of course," Sterling said, shifting his focus back to Gilbert. "We wouldn't want to interrupt your gainful employment since the less-than-gainful portion of your income is about to be severed."

Gilbert's eyes narrowed.

"My uncle, Senator Lane from the great state of New York, called me just last week. He has a particular bee in his bonnet about illegal gambling—something about it fueling petty crime and violence in the city. I, of course, sat down afterward and thought to myself: How could I, one helpless high school student, make a dent in a problem so massive?"

I glanced sideways at Sterling's shrewd brown eyes tracking Gilbert's every move. At the long, tan fingers he steepled together on the surface of the table, a gesture that on anyone else would seem cheesy and pretentious, but on Sterling transformed him into a conniving megalomaniac who could give 007 a run for his money. Sterling would crush poor Gilbert and he'd enjoy it. And because Cole was on the line, I decided to throw all my weight behind him.

"I remember when fire ants invaded my grandfather's home," I said. "Amazing how much fear those tiny insects can inspire in fully grown men. Especially when they crawled all over Cole and we thought he'd need an epinephrine shot to counteract their venom. Well, being a student of science, I researched and researched for hours. One solution was a slow-release poison that one member of the hive would unknowingly carry back to the others. It's an elegant solution—using one tiny, insignificant bug to root out the entire hive. Cole liked that idea, too." I paused, hoping my meaning was penetrating the irritated glare in Gilbert's eyes. "And it worked. But that's not to say I didn't spend my days tracking down and annihilating any stray fire ants that wandered my way. I have a vengeful streak eight miles wide when it comes to my brother."

Next to me, Sterling smiled. It was a subtle uptick in one corner of his mouth. Never did I imagine a moment of solidarity with that viper, but when our eyes met, it was there—an exploding burst of connection, clapping and rolling like thunder.

"An excellent metaphor, Harper," Sterling all but purred. "I was so intrigued by the gambling conundrum that I called Uncle Howard. He's not my real uncle, just a close family friend. And the attorney general. He told me the best way to root out petty crime is to find one specific criminal and prosecute them to the fullest extent of the law. He said it really doesn't matter who you prosecute, as long as you crush them completely."

I listened to Sterling in rapt attention—that family friend sounded exactly like the kind of career mentor I needed.

"You can't prove anything," Gilbert snapped. Without another word, he turned and left our table. He was rattled—that much was clear from the too-quick steps he took across the room toward the kitchen.

"I thought I told you to keep quiet," Sterling said. "It's a very fragile line we're walking, trying to intimidate him into confessing but not into running. Not when Cole's fate still hangs in the balance."

He was right. I replayed my words in my mind. "Well, you could have cut me off if it was that out of line—like you did last time."

"You enjoyed that?" He leaned closer, propping one elbow on the table right next to me. My entire body lit up at the memory of his hand sliding up my thigh. It was probably the only thing that could have shut me up when I got going—which I didn't care to contemplate under the undivided scrutiny of the boy who missed nothing.

"No, of course not," I said. "If we'd agreed to a structured strategy beforehand, other than me keeping quiet, maybe I wouldn't have started blurting things out to keep you on course."

"I don't think anything could induce you to control yourself." He met my eyes. "Please don't mistake that for a criticism. The ant story was a masterful touch."

"A page from your book," I said. "Not that your ego needs any more fattening up."

He laughed. "Actually, your steady diet of insults has put it back into fighting shape."

I was still deciding if that was sarcasm when a waitress returned with two Shirley Temples and set them down in front of us. Sterling frowned and turned his glass slowly on the table, examining it like you would a poisonous elixir.

"Is that true about your uncle?" I asked. "Attorney general?"

Sterling nodded. "You have another crime to prosecute?"

I shook my head.

"What is it?" he asked. "You look uncomfortable again."

"It's just—impressive," I said. "Sometimes I think that's the job I'd like to have one day." I tried to make it sound casual so I didn't give Sterling ammunition to mock me. But when I looked up, his gaze was thoughtful.

"Given your rules and the rest of what I've seen—how you tap-dance around them?" He tipped his head to the side, studying me. I braced myself for the bite, but he simply nodded. "I think you'd be quite good at that."

The waitress appeared, interrupting what might have turned into an actual conversation between the two of us. "Are you ready to order dinner?"

"Yes," Sterling said. "You're doing a fantastic job, but we'd like a few more words with your colleague, Gilbert." He slid a folded bill across the table in her direction.

The waitress blinked and looked back over her shoulder.

"He asked me to trade," she said quietly. "But I'll see what I can do."

"Excellent," Sterling said. "We'd like two hanger steaks. Well done—and I mean burned to a crisp. That should take at least twelve minutes for grilling alone, right?"

The waitress nodded. "Two steaks, well done." She headed back toward the kitchen.

"Is that why you have your rules?" Sterling asked, the moment she'd disappeared. "They're like the laws you'll get to uphold and prosecute one day as an attorney? Because maybe legislation would be more your forte—you could create an entire nation of obedient Harpers."

His tone was light, but that didn't fool me. His hawkish gaze observed my every movement. "What are your Rules about? I've been dying to know ever since I set eyes on them."

"I've never told anyone that." How could I, when they'd started with one of my last memories of Mom?

"Your secret is safe with me," he replied.

"Says the boy who threatened to publish my Rules if I didn't do what he said."

"That bluff was called ages ago, Harper." He said my name softly, like a secret. "Really think about it—other than the Mini Cooper, have I done anything all that bad?"

He was right. All the chaos and confusion of the last few weeks really amounted to the two of us just grappling for the upper hand. I took a deep breath.

"When Cole was little, he was really wild, climbing on things, jumping off the monkey bars. It drove my mom crazy. So she told me that it was my responsibility to look after Cole—that it was Rule Number 1. Since I was always the practical one. All the Rules followed after that."

"Well, that explains Rule 1, and why you'd hit me with a car to stop Cole from stubbing his toe. What about the rest? Your rules contain some astonishingly specific instructions for living."

"Rule 1 wasn't enough," I said. The words just tumbled out, as if they'd been waiting to escape for eight hundred years. I had to make this boy understand, even if it cost me. "Two days after she died, Cole fell out of a tree and broke his arm. Because my dad didn't realize that tree houses were also subject to building codes." I could have lost them both in the same week. Cole could have broken his neck instead of his arm.

"Ah, I get it now," Sterling replied. "The tree house rule did catch my eye." He leaned forward across the table. "I'm sorry about your mother. I get it now—the Rules. Why you needed them. But—" His voice trailed off and he looked away. I waited for him to finish, but seconds ticked past in silence. "I get it," he said. "My dad puts pressure on me. To perform. To achieve. So I do exactly what he wouldn't want. That's probably as self-defeating as hiding from life behind those rules. The two of us, Harper, maybe we need to meet somewhere in the middle."

He finally looked at me again as he uttered those last words. A shiver scuttled down my spine when our eyes met. He knew what it felt like, the relentless simmering of parental disappointment. What would it be like to meet Sterling halfway—to let my Rules slip away? I'd be free, but also unmoored, drifting out to sea. Where anything could happen.

I sucked in air, just to make sure I still could. My fingers clutched the seat of my chair.

"I'll stick with my Rules, thank you," I said briskly. Sterling blinked and leaned back in his seat, crossing his arms across his chest.

The spell that had been cast between us shattered. But I wouldn't let myself regret it.

"And I need to focus back on Rule 1. Where is Gilbert?" I asked, shifting in my seat to put some distance between Sterling and me, and so that I could better watch for Gilbert to emerge. "I know what it's like to be on the receiving end of your barbs. He won't last much longer. And I can't believe how gleeful I sound about that. Never thought I'd find someone even more my enemy than you are."

"Now why would you say that?" Sterling asked.

I rolled my eyes, realizing how stupid it was to drop

my guard with him even for a second.

"I'm not your enemy, Harper," he said. "Would I be here if I was?"

"Yes. You've made it more than clear you do nothing without a motive, including playing nice. Maybe all this is just to get me to drop my guard, Mr. Alligator."

"Well, that last part may be true." He leaned back in his chair. "But yes, you're quite correct. I'm never nice without a motive."

"Oh," I said, as the pieces slid into place. I'd just told him my deepest secret and all the while he'd been plotting something. How could I be so stupid? "You want something in return for your help. This is just a little show of force—make me realize how powerful you are, how you could help me as long as I help you first."

"It sounds so vulgar when you put it that way."

"I defy you to find a way to put it that isn't vulgar. Because it is, down to the core."

"Hear me out before you pass judgment."

"Lemme guess," I said. "You want my outlines. And a free paper or two."

"Oh, we're way past that," he replied. "And this school isn't quite as unpalatable as the others. I've got my academics under control." His forehead creased in exaggerated concentration. Then he held up a finger like he'd just had an epiphany. "I need a favor from you, Harper. You know, an exchange of assistance between friends? And I want you to know I'm the kind of person who repays favors sometimes even in advance of services rendered."

I hated myself for blushing a little at his choice of wording. "What kind of favor?"

"I can't tell you that," he said. "Not yet. But one day soon I'll come to you, and I'll ask a favor. And you'll comply."

"What is this, *The Godfather*?" I was trying hard not to laugh, especially because Sterling seemed so serious while saying these ridiculous things. It was the first shadow of an imperfection in his ultracool facade. "You almost had me for a minute, pretending we're friends. You know what you're after or we wouldn't be here. Just tell me, and then I'll decide if this is worth it."

"Or you turn around and see it *is* worth it."

"No," I told him. "I decline."

"No?" Something akin to surprise flashed through his eyes.

"Exactly what value have you added? I had Gilbert's license plate. My PI would have tracked him down eventually. *I* told the ant story that rattled Gilbert into leaving. All you've done is tag along and try to make me take a backseat. Tell me, Sterling, what have you done that I couldn't have done on my own?"

He leaned forward across the table and motioned for me to do the same. I did. We were tipped together, practically brushing foreheads, our body language perfectly mirroring the amorous couple across the room. Once we were close, very close, Sterling whispered, "I arranged safe transport home."

He inclined his face toward the window, where a hulking figure stood just outside the door. I couldn't be sure without seeing his face, but the massive, burly shoulders looked like they belonged to Victor, the brawn to Gilbert's questionable brains. He hadn't been there when we walked in, which meant Gilbert might have called him in response to our interrogation. I slipped down lower in my seat, as if that would hide me from pending violent intimidation.

"You don't think—you don't think he's here for us? Because we're asking questions?" My eyes felt like they were going to pop right out of my head.

Sterling shrugged. Was he prepared to leave me here to face some thug unless I capitulated to his absurd favor?

"This is extortion. Crass, even for you."

"Relax, sweetheart," Sterling said, reaching over and giving my hand a slight squeeze. "Of course I'll deposit you safely at your door regardless of what you decide. Not that this is a date or anything."

I twitched in my chair at the mention of that word, and he smiled mercilessly.

"I've given you the extended preview of my services. Now's the time to pay or get the hell out of the theater. Do you accept my terms? I know you're good for your word." He pulled out a folded piece of paper and I immediately recognized the horrible cheat sheet of my Rules. He made an exaggerated show of skimming through it. "I count at least twenty-five rules that address the importance of follow-through and honesty. Even if you've been flying a little fast and loose with them of late."

His smile was saccharine and sickening.

I nodded. I never would have anticipated the perils of confronting Gilbert. I needed someone in my corner who understood the inner workings of the criminal mind. Someone like Sterling.

"Fine," I said. "But just to be clear, these are the terms: not only will you tell me what you know, you're going to help me fix this. Cole will be completely exonerated."

"Even though he did it?"

"Yes."

A waitress appeared and placed two blackened steaks in front of us. "Can I get you anything else? Some ketchup?"

"On steak?" Sterling frowned at me before smirking up at her. "How charmingly proletarian."

The waitress either had a world-class poker face or had no idea what that meant. Her smile didn't falter. Not one bit. "Is that a yes?"

"That's a *no thank you*."

"I'd love some," I told her. "Thank you."

"No reason to suffer those lengths just to irritate me," he said. Then he pulled out his phone and set it on the table. It was open to the *New York Times*. "Good thing you brought your book. It appears this installment of Cole's debacle is over."

It's not like I wanted to talk to him, but it was just plain rude to ignore me like that. The waitress set the ketchup on the table in front of me and I left it sitting there. Of course I'd asked for it just to annoy him, but having him recognize that fact had taken all the fun out of it.

"You wanna tell me the rest of what you know?" I asked. I'd eaten the vegetables off the plate, but my steak was untouched.

"Trade?" he asked. He hadn't eaten one bite of his veggies, and he lifted his plate toward me. The least I could do was let the meat on my own plate go to use. But instead of digging in like Cole would have, Sterling put his elbow on the table and propped his chin up on one hand. He watched as I took a bite of grilled cauliflower. I ate slowly so I wouldn't drip butter on my chin or do something else horribly uncouth.

"How much do you know about illegal gambling?" he asked.

I shook my head. "You mean bookies and stuff? Just what I've seen in movies."

"Well, it's far more pervasive than most people realize, and it's not always as clear-cut as in the movies. Sometimes it presents like a casual wager between friends. No harm, no foul, right? But that's just the gateway into bigger things.

Cole met Gil. They share a love of sports statistics. And lacrosse. That led to a few illegal bets that seemed casual, at first."

"Who would bet on high school lacrosse?"

"Your brother, apparently. A surprising number of people bet on an astonishing number of things."

"This is about the money he needs, isn't it?" I stared down at my food. "He stole that money thinking he could double it or something by gambling. I should have known he would do something rash. I should have been there to stop him."

It was a tactical error, saying something so vulnerable to Sterling Lane. I'd set myself up for brutal recriminations. I closed my eyes, waiting for the onslaught, and in part craving it. As if Sterling Lane's verbal battery would absolve me of my failure to Cole.

"I don't think anyone could have seen this coming," Sterling said quietly. "Even Cole. I suspect he was in part swindled by our pal Gil. Guys like Gil zero in on desperation. Cole told me he borrowed the money from the team because he thought he could quadruple it and come through for the weight room. Twice Gilbert's advice had doubled Cole's money—but only small sums. My guess is Gilbert set Cole up—gave him some wins to lure him in, then when Cole was really backed into a corner, he lost the money. Bait and switch. He tempted Cole in deeper with a chance to get his money back, so after losing the money he'd stolen from the team, he bet again. On credit. He's in pretty far over his head, but only because a skilled manipulator led him down that path. Some people are born to be rule-breakers and some stumble into trouble by accident. Cole is the latter." He paused, that little grin reappearing. "Perceptive as you are, sweetheart, you can't blame yourself."

"Well, if that's the case, what Cole did doesn't seem that bad."

"I doubt the disciplinary committee will see it that way," Sterling replied. "I agree, from a personal morality perspective, what Cole did was well-intended. But it's still illegal on both counts. Trust me on this one, he'll be expelled. Your father will probably lock him up and throw away the key."

"Any evidence that Gilbert did this?"

"No." He looked up right then, spearing me with his eyes. "But we can't let that stop us, can we? Or at least you won't."

A slow flush crept up my cheeks. He was referring to the evidence I'd presented to Headmaster Lowell.

"I don't know what you're talking about." But I've always been a terrible liar, and we both knew the truth anyway. He'd already paid me back in Mini Coopers.

Sterling reached over and put his hand on my wrist. The warmth of his skin on mine startled me, but my hand refused to pull itself away.

"It's okay. Water under the bridge." He let the silence settle between us. "The question is, are you up for a repeat performance?" He leaned toward me. "This time, working together?"

"You've set this up quite nicely," I said. "You extracted a vague promise from me, and in exchange you get my help clearing your name as well as Cole's. Don't think I missed that part of our little arrangement."

"I didn't think you would. But if you recall, I'm entangled in this only because you turned me in for bailing your brother out. I'd say I'm being more than generous."

The waitress arrived with our bill and Sterling slipped her a credit card before I realized what was happening. I pulled a twenty out of my pocket, but Sterling waved it away.

"I insist," I said. "I don't want to owe you."

That's when the alligator smile returned, shattering the thin veneer of camaraderie that had settled over us during dinner.

"Too late," he said, rising. "And believe me, sweetheart, I'll cash that IOU."

"Stop calling me sweetheart," I said. "It's so condescending."

"A pleasure, as always," he replied. "It's a wonder you always dine alone."

"Shut up," I muttered as I scrambled to my feet and shoved my book into my bag. Only when I was standing over the table did I notice that my steak was still in front of his place, untouched. If I didn't know better, I'd almost think Sterling had switched plates to be nice.

"Did you know I'm vegetarian?"

"Rule 304." He turned to leave. "Forgot until I saw you picking around your plate."

I watched him strut toward the door, all long, lean limbs and broad shoulders, carrying himself like he thought the whole world should stop and admire the way he moved.

And I despised myself for doing just that.

I spent the whole night tossing and turning. No matter how I spun the situation in my mind, one thing was clear—we had to fight fire with fire. We had to play dirty. Fortunately, my partner in crime was an expert in that arena. I was so agitated and restless that at two in the morning, I climbed out of bed and Googled our pal Gilbert. Now that I had his name and place of employment, it was easy to run a background check, which led me straight to the real Gilbert—a retiree in Nevada. It seemed Cole's gambling buddy had a stolen car, a stolen plate, and a stolen identity. Armed with that information, I placed another call to the PI. This time it was worth my savings to have him dig a little deeper into Gilbert's true identity.

My neglected outlines were in arranged in stacks between our two beds—stacks that Kendall had knocked over three times that evening as she paraded around the room, trying to get me to vote on which shirt-sized dress she should wear on her date with Parker. Ever since

I'd helped get them back together, she was under the misguided notion that I was some sort of relationship guru, that my tell-it-like-it-is style was what was missing in her life. She'd even gone so far as to study with me—in public. And in an unplanned act of generosity, I'd let her borrow my outlines.

Kendall's room had been ready for days, but she had yet to mention moving out. And I was afraid to ask, because I both did and didn't want her to leave.

By the time Kendall's alarm went off, signifying the night was officially over, I was nearly caught up in all of my classes. While I'd worked, my subconscious had been busily whirring away, and a plan had coalesced in my mind—a simple plan to extract Gilbert's confession, but it required both Cole's and Sterling Lane's cooperation.

Kendall spent the entire morning in the art studio. I was so nervous for that night that I spent the morning baking a German chocolate cake so rich Kendall and I could barely put a dent in it, so we gave the rest to Cole and Parker and a group of the lacrosse guys. It was oddly gratifying, the way they dug right in and mumbled their thanks around mouthfuls.

Cole's bright smile was more than enough to make my work worthwhile.

Kendall and I spent the afternoon in the library, preparing for a calculus exam. A steady diet of caffeine held me together that day—that and the hope my plan had engendered.

After dinner, I walked across the quad to the boys' dorm, knowing that Cole would be at an extra calculus tutoring session and hoping Sterling hadn't gone, too. I came to a complete stop in the middle of the hallway to appreciate the odd enormity of the moment—I was actually seeking out Sterling Lane.

"*Entrez*." His voice stabbed my ears immediately after I knocked.

I dug my fingernails into my palm, willing myself to turn the door handle. It swung open slowly, allowing me to make a dramatic entrance into the room, which was promptly destroyed as I squinted into the darkness, searching for something the size and shape of a person.

The streetlamp shining in from the window silhouetted his armchair. He was almost completely concealed in darkness. The only giveaway was the curve of his disheveled head, tipped to the side against the wingback.

"Two nights in a row? You just can't get enough of me." I could hear the smile behind his words.

"Believe me, I'm not here for your company."

He reached up and switched on the bronze floor lamp hovering above his head. The warm light illuminated the planes of his face, casting shadows around his angular features. His nose. His cheekbones and forehead. Until he was striking and sinister all at once.

"You should sit down before you fall down," he said, rising and gesturing to his leather armchair. "You look terrible."

But I just stood there, my fingers fidgeting with the hem of my shirt. "I couldn't sleep last night. Worrying about Cole."

I set a plastic Tupperware container on his dresser. "Cupcakes. For your grandmother. If she doesn't like them, maybe the nurses will. I read somewhere that people actually receive better care if their families bribe the staff with food."

Sterling tipped his head to the side, studying me. I crossed my arms over my chest, wishing his gaze didn't make me feel like an exotic zoo animal. "Thank you," he said, but it sounded more like a question.

"I told you I couldn't sleep." I sounded far too defensive. The truth was, I'd always had a soft spot for grandmothers. I hated picturing her, confused and waiting for her prodigal grandson.

"I also got caught up in my classes," I added. "And I have a plan—for Cole, I mean."

Sterling strolled across the room, again gesturing me toward his chair. A small mirrored cabinet hung over the built-in drawers, and he reached inside and retrieved a silver flask. He opened his sock drawer and produced two crystal martini glasses, which he filled with clear liquid from the flask. He placed one hand on the corner of a squat bookshelf and tugged. A hidden door swung open, revealing that the books were in fact a false front, concealing a completely contraband mini-fridge. Inside, there was a dizzying array of glass jars and containers with fancy gourmet labels.

"This will help you sleep. After we discuss your plan, of course. Now, one olive or two?" He turned to look at me. "Sit, please. You're making me nervous with all that fidgeting."

"I don't drink," I told him, taking a deep breath and settling on Cole's wooden desk chair. Sitting in Sterling's brown leather chair seemed far too intimate.

"There's a first time for everything. You'll never have a better guide for exploring this new world of possibilities."

"Why are you so determined to make everyone bad?"

"I'm not," he replied, and for the first time, his smile didn't make me feel like he was dissecting me in his mind with a little scalpel. "I think you need to see the gray before you go around categorizing everything as black or white.

You're missing all of the nuance in life, and that's where the good stuff is. So I'll ask again: One olive or two?"

When I hesitated, because I truly had no idea how many olives I'd prefer, he tipped two into each glass. It was impressive that he crossed the room to me without spilling a drop, and even more impressive that he took a long sip without flinching. I couldn't help but respect that as I lifted my glass and took the tiniest of sips. After all, Rule 43 said it was okay to try new things as long as they were educational. And this truly was a novel experience.

I coughed. My entire throat was on fire. I jumped out of the chair, wondering if stop, drop, and roll would save me in this situation. I coughed again and Sterling thumped me gently on the back.

"You can do better than that." Sterling appraised the line of the liquid in my glass. "Remember I have Rules too, the most important of which is no wasting provisions. This particular treat isn't easy to find. I had to have it shipped from New York."

"How many Rules do you have?" I blurted out, disturbingly intrigued.

"Look at you all hot and bothered." He cracked a grin. My heart thumped a little faster. "I never bothered to count. I just call 'em as I see 'em. Unlike you, I keep things simple, straightforward. Then you're less likely to get tangled up in details."

"Then those aren't Rules at all," I said. "Rules are fixed. Unmoving."

"They don't have to be," he said, the teasing tone fading from his voice. "I've been thinking about what you told me—about your Rules and your mother. We're two sides of the same coin, limiting ourselves based on everyone else's expectations. For you, it's guilt over what was probably an offhand comment, and you've built your whole world around it. And for me, well, anything my dad wants me to do, I do the opposite. And I don't even really remember why. One day I just got fed up with all the pressure and expectations and *living up to the Lane name*." He deepened his voice, impersonating his father. "What does that even mean when you're five years old? If they're all so perfect, why try?"

"Sterling—" I wasn't sure what to say. I'd never seen him lose his characteristic cool. I wanted to reach out and touch him, comfort him. But I'd never dare. "You're actually pretty impressive on your own." A slow flush crept up my throat and the playful light returned to his eyes. "At school, I mean," I added. "When you try, that is."

"It's okay—I'm over it. But thank you for the caveated compliment. When it comes down to it, it's not like my dad was asking anything unreasonable. Sure, he'd love a Rhodes scholar, but he'd also be happy if I'd just try. Most parents just want us to do our best."

I swallowed hard. I wasn't sure I agreed with that last part—I didn't know what my mom would have wanted, and I'd been doing my best for years and Dad still preferred Cole.

"Here's to letting those expectations go and just being ourselves." His hand motioned to the drink in my hand. "Don't look so terrified, Harper. I'm not saying let's fail out of school. You're a good student—that's who you are. I'm just saying do it for *you*, not for *them*."

It made sense, it really did. I wanted to agree, but a little part of me held back. Even if the Rules were started by Mom, they were a part of me now.

"I'm passing all my classes," he said. "Better than passing in a few of them. I have you to thank for that." His glass clinked against mine. "Here's to hoping my transcript doesn't give the admiral a heart attack before he gets to gloat."

"That's wonderful, Sterling," I said. And I meant it. Who knew our little rivalry would *help* Sterling instead of getting us both expelled. "My dad can be — difficult, too. But ultimately, if we screw our lives up, we're the ones who have to live those lives, you know?"

"Funny thing is, I started trying at school to get back at you, and things with my dad have been better since then. You'd think I'd solved world hunger with a couple of Bs. And those Bs came hard. If your dad really doesn't get it, how hard you work to achieve what you've accomplished, then he needs his head screwed on straight."

The flush returned, creeping all the way across my cheeks. How had Sterling known exactly what I needed to hear?

We just stood there. I put my hands in my pockets. Then pulled them out and crossed my arms instead. There was no comfortable place to put them. No safe place for my eyes to land.

"Tell me about your plan," Sterling said, deftly changing the subject as he turned away.

I took a sip of my drink, using it to buy time to think. The fire from a moment before had been replaced with a soothing warmth. It felt good as it spread through my body. So I took another sip. Sure, I was underage, but maybe this wasn't such a bad thing. A giggle slipped out of me. "This must be what it feels like to be Kendall."

Sterling laughed and leaned back against the wall; his eyes never left mine until I was finally forced to look away. Heat crept up my neck — from the alcohol. Not from his razor-sharp scrutiny, tracking my every movement. He took the glass out of my hand and set it on his desk.

"Changed my mind," he murmured. "I think we should keep our heads clear."

"It was your idea in the first place," I snapped. "It's not like I showed up here looking to get wasted."

"Duly noted," he said. "Now if you're quite finished with this righteous indignation, I believe we had some business to discuss?"

"Right." I settled back into my chair. "We blackmail Gilbert right back. You say they're threatening Cole—trying to get him to throw a game or something. Well, we secretly record him, get a confession, and threaten to go to the police with it."

"That will get us halfway there," Sterling said. "But Cole's still on the hook with the disciplinary committee, or had you forgotten that little detail?"

"Well, that part—that part I might need your help on. I was thinking we spin it like Cole was trying to break up a gambling ring. Like he suspected this was going on and this was all part of his plan to bring an end to it, but it backfired a little."

"I like it." Sterling sat back in his chair. "Ruthless and clean. Leave the details of the last part to me. I may have an idea that bears exploring." His gaze met mine and lingered. I wanted to believe he was simply lost in thought, pondering my plan, but he looked far too focused on the present.

I was staring at the way his lips curled around the words and at the heavy-lidded look in his eyes despite the alertness I could sense in his body. He was aware of every movement I made. It sent a completely foreign, but not unwelcome, little shiver down my spine.

One remaining still-vigilant little brain cell politely

pointed out that now would be a good time to leave. We could make a plan to reconvene in the morning, someplace bright and brimming with other people. But another part of me, a part of me that was awake for the very first time, wouldn't let me move an inch.

"I should go." But neither of us believed me.

I rose from my chair and he did, too, which made me acutely aware of exactly how close we'd been sitting. His breath grazed my shoulder and for a moment, I thought his lips would follow. When they didn't, we stood like that, both of us waiting.

"Is that the only reason you came here tonight?" His voice was low and soothing. "To discuss Cole? You could have called or found me at lunch. Is there a reason you chose to come here alone, at night?"

There was. There wasn't. A million responses raced through my brain, but when I reached out to grab a hold of them, they slipped through my fingers like sand. Finally, my brain found its footing again, just as my heart threatened to hammer its way right out of my chest.

"Heaven forbid anyone see me fraternizing with you," I replied, stepping back, away. Anger was the answer, my lifeline back to the me I'd always been. "I'm only here to help Cole—and you're basically blackmailing me into working with you, anyway."

"Blackmail?" He took a step forward until his voice was a whisper in my ear, sliding right down my spine. "You do love to hurl those accusations around. Don't forget I bailed Cole out with that bookie."

"And you think I should be grateful?" I hated the fact that I still hadn't left.

Sterling leaned in so close I could taste the martini on his breath. It took me a moment to locate the thread of our conversation within the jumbled knot of my consciousness.

"No, I don't, since your form of gratitude involves breaking and entering so you can frame me for Cole's crime."

"Hypocrite! You broke into my room and tried to frame me for stealing a car."

He grinned. "That was quid pro quo. You want me to get your brother off the hook for a crime he most certainly committed. There's only one hypocrite here, sweetheart."

I stood up straight, like that would help overcome the height differential. "I did what I had to do to protect my family."

"I can tell you firsthand how well that excuse goes over with the disciplinary committee." He paused and dropped his voice into a low murmur. "You attack me for helping you and then hide behind your irrational value system. You can rationalize doing pretty much anything you want, including things you took the time to document as immoral on pastel index cards. You're a disaster. You fascinate me."

I turned his words over in my mind, untangling them. I wasn't really sure how offended I should be. Those last three words were stuck in my throat. "I'm flattered," I snapped. "It's an honor to entertain the poster child for jaded, spoiled rich boys."

"You always say whatever you want to anyone. No matter the consequences." He moved closer then, so close at first I thought he was trying to intimidate me. "That fascinates me, too." My stomach mounted a little roller coaster all by itself. Something was happening. Or was about to happen if I didn't turn and flee.

His fingers curled around my wrist when I took a halfhearted step away. My hand landed on his chest, acting fully of its own volition. Nothing good could come of this, but I still stood there, willing and wishing it to happen.

Then it did. His mouth slammed into mine, so sudden and fast that our front teeth clicked on impact. His hands cupped my cheeks, tipping my head to the side as his mouth collided with mine again. Even though I was hardly qualified to lead this dance of death, I certainly wasn't going to let Sterling be in charge, either. I wrapped my hands around the back of his neck, locking us together.

It was awkward, but only for the handful of seconds it took for us to fit together right, the way we were supposed to be. Because ultimately, kissing me was just one more thing Sterling Lane did far too well.

And all at once, as soon as our lips found their rhythm, he was everywhere.

Hands scrambled along the edges of my shirt, untucking it with nimble pickpocket fingers.

The same fingers slithered up my sides until they hit rib cage and kept on climbing, mapping each and every inch of me. It was the kind of touch I'd shamed myself out of craving. And now there was no containing it.

Worst of all, his hands were so confident, as if they'd long anticipated this open-door reception.

We fell backward into his chair. It was softer than I imagined, down-filled, smelling of leather oil and Sterling's citrusy cologne. Some other force within me had taken over, and it was like I was watching myself from the outside. Somehow I was on his lap, straddling him. Straddling Sterling Lane.

With one hand, he magically whipped my shirt up over my head. He hadn't undone one button, not even the tidy trademark French cuffs that accented all my school shirts.

My rational self came roaring back just as his Houdini hands slid up my back toward the clasp of my bra, trying to make the next piece of clothing disappear. I pushed back hard against his chest, which was now exposed underneath a half-unbuttoned shirt. Something I'd caused. Buttons I'd released from their shackles. My fingers itched with muscle memory as shame shot through me.

Each pulse, each beat of my heart, was a thunderclap in my ears. Blood cells raced through my veins like Formula One race cars.

My head was spinning, only it wasn't from the alcohol. The heady, cottony feeling was gone. It was just Sterling and me, alone in his bedroom, and I was completely out of control.

"Get off me," I said, pushing back.

He laughed. "Sweetheart, I'm under."

My hand shot out, reaching for the windowsill so I could hoist myself to my feet, away from him. But instead my desperate fingers found my martini glass, which I emptied right into his face.

He jumped, rubbing his eyes with one hand. "Do you have any idea how much that stings?" he demanded, raising his voice for possibly the first time ever. "And gin doesn't grow on trees."

But I didn't care. I was still struggling to extract myself. One leg was solidly wedged between his hip and the chair. So I kicked. Hard. Hoping I'd rupture his kidney as I dislodged myself from him and his stupid chair before they both sucked me down like quicksand.

The arm wrapped around me disappeared, leaving me even more strangely exposed. I was draped across him like an unwanted and unnecessary accessory. Then his hands came back, nudged under my elbows for a fraction of a second as I slid backward and found my feet.

I stood there shivering, arms folded across my chest,

like that covered anything. "Give me my shirt," I demanded. "I want to go home."

He rose and dropped a ball of crumpled white cotton into my outstretched hand.

"Why's it wet?" I snapped, even though I already knew it was my own fault. I didn't need to look at his face to see his grin. But when I glanced up, his expression was blank.

"It reeks of booze. You can't walk home like that." It was so matter-of-fact he could have been remarking on our physics homework rather than my state of undress.

He walked across the room, pulled open a dresser drawer, and tossed a sweatshirt at me. He was careful not to look directly at me, as if he hadn't already seen and touched everything I had on display.

"I'm not wearing a sweatshirt with your name on it. People will talk about me."

"They already do." He was pouring himself another drink. Three inches of a dark amber liquid tumbled into a carved crystal glass. He turned, and there was a flash of surprise before he dropped his gaze to his shoes. The tips of his ears turned red. I still just stood there, half naked and holding his shirt, and he was too ashamed of what we'd just done to even look at me.

"Besides," he said, missing only one or two beats, "I thought you didn't care what anyone thinks. Rule 56 is quite specific."

He walked across the room, studiously avoiding looking at me, as if I'd already left. He settled in his chair again, swirling the liquid in his glass. He left his shirt unbuttoned, his hair all rumpled like he'd just woken up from an impossibly active dream.

"You think you're so clever using my Rules against me." I hurled his sweatshirt back at him as I stormed across the room to Cole's closet. I dug out an old fleece he wouldn't miss and pulled it on over my head just in time.

The doorknob rattled once, weakly, before the door banged open and ricocheted against the wall. Cole paused at the threshold to let his eyes adjust to the relative darkness inside.

"Sterling?" he called out, looking around. "I'll never understand why you sit in the dark like this." There was something off about his voice, a slur.

Cole had been drinking. So much for his study group.

He flicked on the overhead light.

"Seems your coping strategy is rubbing off on my brother," I said.

Cole jumped and took a step toward me just as Sterling's voice drifted in between us. "Once again, we see exactly who's the hypocrite." He was so sure, so smug and self-righteous that I wanted to punch him right in his perfect nose.

"Is that my fleece?" Cole asked, tugging on the sleeve. "What happened?" His eyes flashed to the damp blouse tucked under my arm, then flew to Sterling, to the wet splash across the shoulder of his unbuttoned shirt, and the hair that would only stick up like that if someone had run their hands through it over and over again.

Paranoid nausea slammed into me as the gears between Cole's ears creaked into motion. I let my eyes follow his back to Sterling, to his exposed chest. It would take years of push-ups and a carefully regulated high-protein diet to get that kind of definition. Cole was staring at me while I watched Sterling. I flushed scarlet. But still Sterling wouldn't look at me, even after everything that had just happened.

"Are you okay?" Cole asked me. The worry lines on his

forehead disappeared when I nodded. "Why are you wet?"

"Harper spilled," Sterling replied mildly. There was an undeniable note of bitterness in his voice.

"On both of you?"

Sterling had carefully avoided my gaze until that moment. The expression on his face was like we'd traveled back in time to the day I'd lied to the headmaster and gotten him in trouble. The narrow-eyed gaze of a thwarted predator. "She was on my lap."

My stomach plunged to the center of the earth.

"Yeah, right. So she could get close enough to strangle you." Cole walked across the room. His shoes left clumps of dirt on the carpet. "What are you doing here, anyways?" Cole sprawled out on his bed and closed his eyes. "I won't cover for you if you murder my roommate."

"Not to worry, Cole," Sterling said. "Harper and I have come to an understanding. We're communicating better than ever."

"You're such a jerk," I snapped. "Cole's future is on the line and you're making snide little comments."

"Okay. You are obviously *not* okay." Cole opened his eyes and sat up. He took one look at me and frowned. "What the hell was going on in here?"

"Just a friendly meeting of the minds. But clearly, Harper and I still have some issues to resolve." Sterling took a healthy swallow of his drink. "But practice makes perfect."

I marched right over to his chair. "That won't ever happen again," I told him in a voice low enough that I hoped Cole didn't catch it.

Sterling tipped his head to the side and for a moment he was the vulnerable boy of moments ago, telling me about his father. Then the shrewd glint returned to his eyes. "Now, now, Harper," he said. "Don't sell yourself short. You're not *that* bad. One day some other guy will bite."

It was like he'd lit a firecracker right under my skin, the way those words exploded into me. I reached out and knocked his cocktail right up his nose. Even though I would have savored each moment of his suffering, I couldn't stick around to see how much it would sting.

I threw myself toward the door just as Cole pushed to his feet.

"What did you just say to her?" he asked Sterling. "I don't care what issues the two of you have. That's my sister you're messing with."

Sterling raised both hands, a gesture of surrender. "You're right. I'm sorry. I was out of line."

A lump rose in my throat. Either at Sterling's genuine-sounding apology or the fact that Cole was finally coming to my rescue, even if it was too little, too late. Then Cole was at my side, his hand curled around my wrist. "I'll walk you home," he said.

"No, I'm fine. Seriously, Cole. I'm just walking home across campus, like I do every night."

Cole tipped his head to the side, studying me. I forced my best smile—the only thing worse than my current walk of shame would be performing it with my brother.

"You'd tell me if something was wrong, right? Pinkie promise?"

"Pinkie promise," I told him, letting him link his little finger with mine. "The only thing wrong is your situation. I worry about you nonstop—about you getting expelled." I was anything but fine, but I had to get away from him before he figured it out. I had to be alone.

"I'll be okay," Cole said, releasing my wrist. "You worry about yourself."

I felt Cole's eyes on my back as I made my way down the hall toward the stairs. I forced myself to walk at a normal pace, but the second I was out of sight, I switched into a run—and didn't stop until I was outside gulping in the cool night air and calculating exactly how long I'd have to stand in the shower to wash Sterling's touch off my skin.

I loathed, despised, and was actively plotting the murder of Sterling Lane. He would die violently and painfully. I'd never forgive him for what had just happened, and for the casual way he could insult me moments later.

But most importantly, when I distilled my rage down to the kernel of emotion at its core, I hated how easily Sterling could flip a switch inside me. He made me feel alive. His touch transformed into pure energy. Every electron in my body was buzzing around in its valence shell, threatening to break free.

The devil on my shoulder would never let me forget what had happened that night, but there was no way I could ever let Sterling realize the power he held over me. Because if I did, he'd never let me forget it.

REASON 24:

IT WAS ONE TEENY-TINY LITTLE KISS—
IT MEANT ABSOLUTELY NOTHING.
ESPECIALLY TO ME.
AND FRANKLY, I'D RATHER DIE BEFORE
I'D EVEN CONSIDER DOING IT AGAIN.

ESPECIALLY WITH HIM.

ired as I was from a sleepless night, tumult raged through my mind that night, again keeping me awake until I decided the best course of action was to resume my usual routine. I erased the events of the previous evening from my mind, at least the ones that pertained to Sterling. Of course I'd still initiate my plan to blackmail Gilbert, but I could do that on my own. Sterling Lane could choke and die on his favor for all I cared.

On Monday, I arrived at history class a full twenty minutes early, silently chiding myself for succumbing to Sterling's destabilizing influence during the past few weeks. He'd thrown me completely off schedule. My outlines were screaming for attention, and I'd received a B on last week's calculus exam. Me. I needed a ninety-eight or higher on the next one to conserve my A average.

I'd grown weak, letting Sterling divide me from my Rules. They were my source of strength, like Samson's hair. I couldn't believe I'd let myself be severed from them so completely.

It was comforting to know that once I cut him completely out of my life, everything would settle back to normal.

The morning after the incident-that-shall-not-be-mentioned, Sterling slouched through the door on par with his habit of timing his entrée with the exact moment class officially began. He paused at my desk, and I sensed genuine hesitation in the way his knee bent before he straightened it fast. It was like he wanted to keep going but changed his mind. Anything less than 100 percent confidence was unusual in him, so I looked up. He was staring back at his former chair in the corner, the expression on his face theatrically wistful, like he was mourning his best friend. But the eyes that met mine were full of mischief. By even acknowledging him, I'd played right into his hand.

He turned and stalked around my desk in a slow circle before settling into the chair behind me.

I refused to look back at him. I sat there perfectly still, my eyes glued to the board. Skin not prickling in the least, definitely not with anticipation, when his chair creaked and he shifted forward in his seat. His breath skimmed my neck, then my cheek. All the places his lips had lingered the other night.

The warmth in my stomach was a purely caloric hunger, since I'd skipped breakfast in my eagerness to get to class.

"Cole was all mysterious this morning." He shifted closer and dropped his voice. "After a fifteen-minute whispered phone conversation conducted entirely in his closet."

I shook my head without turning around. I didn't dare. The whole world would know what had happened between us if I turned around. It would break me. I wasn't sure what I would do, just that it would probably be humiliating. The knowledge that he had run those long, tan fingers all over me would quite possibly make my head explode.

"You shouldn't be embarrassed," he said. "It's only a big deal if you make it one."

"I don't know what you're talking about," I told the whiteboard. I refused to turn, terrified those muddy brown eyes would slide all over me. Or that they wouldn't.

"Even the back of your neck is blushing right now, Harper," he whispered, still so close I could feel the heat radiating from his body. "Turn around and look at me, please. I'll provoke you into it if you don't." His voice was so soft and close that his mouth had to be mere inches away.

Something brushed my earlobe. It had to be my imagination; there was no way he'd let his lips actually brush my earlobe in public. We were in the front row. We had a live and very attentive audience for this little freak show. I scooted forward in my seat, as far away from him as I could get. Silence descended. I turned my face to the side, just enough to see that he'd settled back in his seat. The empty space behind me was worse than his looming proximity had been. Had he changed his mind? Or was this part of the promised provocation—pulling away to see if I'd follow? I couldn't give him the satisfaction of turning around, so I held perfectly still, waiting, as second after second ticked past.

I couldn't handle it—I had to know what he was doing—was he watching me? Had his focus already shifted to something else, because I mattered that little?

I tried counting backward from one hundred. I could feel him behind me, his presence pulling on me as if he had his own gravitational field. It tugged and tugged until I couldn't stand it any longer. I spun in my seat.

He was waiting, patient as a panther. His eyes tracked my every move.

"You know, you're hiding a fantastic little body under that pup tent." His words were low enough that only I could to hear.

"It's not a pup tent." My voice was shriller than I'd ever heard it. "It's a dress."

"A dress sized for a Sasquatch," he replied mildly. "And I, for one, am a feminist. Bra burning, and all that. Here to liberate you."

"Thank you for your concern, Sterling, but the women of my generation will craft our own model of feminism without input from self-centered, spoiled rich boys."

"I love it when you call me that." His chair creaked as he shifted closer, and I let myself lean closer, too. He wouldn't dare make a move in public—or would he?

"You're hiding one fantastic little body under that oversize inflated head of yours. Too bad I never want to see it again." In my panic to retort, I didn't pause to modulate my voice. The words flew out in a shriek.

Every eye in the classroom locked on me.

He cleared his throat and tipped his head toward the front of the room. Mrs. Stevens assumed her post, presiding over us, dry-erase marker in hand. She'd heard every word of what I'd just shrieked. I hung my head in shame, willing the moments to fly past as painlessly as possible, knowing that further humiliation waited mere inches behind me. And there he hovered for the rest of class, robbing me of every last drop of concentration.

When class finally ended, Sterling leaned forward in his seat. "There's no reason to be embarrassed," he said. "Look, I don't care that you steal your underwear from a nursing home. We've got bigger fish to fry. We need to talk."

My face burned hot enough to melt the ice caps.

The worst part was, I wasn't sure what bothered me

more—that he'd been thinking judgmental thoughts as we did all those things, while I'd been consumed with the disturbing reality of how very gorgeous he was, or that he'd chosen to share those thoughts with me in the middle of a crowded room.

My hands curled into fists, and my brain shut right down. Before I said something I'd definitely regret, I turned and walked away.

"Should I just shout the rest?" His words chased me into the hallway before soaring outward into the farthest reaches of the universe.

I froze.

"Thank you." He approached, dropping his voice into a whisper made just for me. "I have feelings, too, you know. It's common courtesy to at least hear me out before you storm away."

For once, I couldn't tell if he was teasing, and that made me more anxious than his constant barrage of banter.

"Neither of us is big on common courtesy," I said. "But you're absolutely inhuman if you can say those things to me after what happened."

His expression shifted into something approximating somber. "You're right," he said, looking me right in the eye. "I apologize."

The calm, open way he said it made me take a step back. Only Sterling Lane would be absolutely confident when admitting his mistakes.

"Will you walk with me, please?" He shoved his hands into his pockets and just stood there, waiting.

"Fine," I replied.

But as we started walking down the hall, Sterling didn't say a single thing. Instead he kept glancing sideways at me, until the silence stretched so thin I snapped.

"What did you want, Sterling?" I asked. "Don't you have some cheerleaders to chase?"

"My tastes have shifted these days," he replied, perking up. "You've raised the bar. If I don't get at least two drinks thrown in my face for my trouble, why bother?"

"Asshole."

"You're usually more creative," he said, visibly relaxing. "Guess I wore you out Saturday night—what with all the helping Cole, I mean."

"Get to the point," I said.

"Oh, the quills are extra sharp today," he said, finally sounding like himself again—all smug and self-satisfied. "Like I told you, Cole was on the phone. Right after I told him I'd be at some fake study group in the library, I overheard him making plans for this afternoon—meeting in our room. So I sneaked his phone out of his bag when he was in the shower. He'd called our old pal Gilbert."

"This is our chance," I said, excitement mingling with dread. "Do we tell Cole that we know? Get him to help us capture a confession?"

Sterling shook his head. "Cole isn't up for that kind of performance. We have to keep him in the dark. A grifter like Gilbert will smell play-acting a mile away. We just have to hope that whatever they discuss is incriminating." He glanced at his watch. "Meet me in my room at four."

"Your room?" I might have momentarily forgotten that I hated him, but I wasn't stupid enough to trust him. "Alone?"

"Cole's the one who chose our meeting place. That's where he's meeting Gil." He gave me a tight-lipped smile. "But if that brings back too many memories, you can always bring your best friend Kendall. We all know she's fantastic with secrets."

"Don't say that about Kendall." I scowled. Sure, I made fun of her, too, but at least I did it to her face. And most of the time she laughed and fired right back.

Regardless, Sterling was right; we couldn't risk bringing anyone else into this plan. The stakes were too high.

"This isn't a trick, is it? To get me into your room." My blush was likely visible from space. Not that we'd do *that* again, but the sheer humiliation of Cole walking in on us was more than enough to send shock waves of shame rippling through me.

"With what possible objective?" he asked, hands up in front of himself, all innocence.

"Never mind." I didn't trust myself to be alone with him. I took a step back, because we'd both let our personal space erode over the last few minutes.

"Don't worry, little Harper Campbell. This isn't some elaborate ruse to seduce you. Give me some credit. I know a girl like you would require a far more sophisticated approach."

"What is that supposed to mean?" A little part of me was flattered that he'd given it thought. Saturday night must have affected him, too—despite his ultracool and controlled exterior. But ultimately, it didn't matter. I couldn't afford to let myself give in to whatever was simmering between us.

"If only I knew." He looked me straight in the eye as he said it.

I had to get away from him and this confusing maze of a conversation. "There's something I forgot to tell you." I would never let Sterling have the upper hand. "I spent almost an entire night sifting through DMV records. It seems a car wasn't the only thing Gilbert has stolen."

Sterling tipped his head back, smiling.

"The real Gilbert is eighty-five and lives in Nevada."

"Then I'll bet our pasty little friend has much more to hide."

"Exactly," I said quietly. "I'm guessing you know a way to lift fingerprints? I grabbed Gilbert's pen that night at dinner. I found a service that'll run them for a fee if I can put them in this special kit."

"I'd say we're a pretty lethal combination." I could feel him watching my profile, but there was no way I was turning to acknowledge that playful smile.

"That's one way of putting it."

Sterling chuckled as he reached out and gave my shoulder a squeeze. "Four o'clock," he said as he turned and walked straight into the heart of the lacrosse clique, where he belonged.

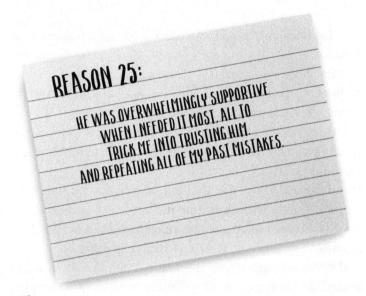

REASON 25:

HE WAS OVERWHELMINGLY SUPPORTIVE WHEN I NEEDED IT MOST. ALL TO TRICK ME INTO TRUSTING HIM. AND REPEATING ALL OF MY PAST MISTAKES.

I knocked on the door to Sterling and Cole's room at four o'clock sharp. Instead of calling out to me, this time Sterling went to the trouble of climbing out of his brown leather chair and opening the door. He looked disturbingly normal in his T-shirt and faded jeans, like any boy next door. I didn't think I'd ever seen him wearing anything other than tattered resort wear, so it took me a moment to process his attire. Just long enough that he cracked a grin.

"I can take my shirt off if it's getting in your way."

I blinked. "What?"

"I haven't been given such a thorough once-over since I took a modeling gig in eighth grade." Those teeth flashed. "Kinda nice to know I've still got it."

"If by *it*, you mean a massive ego, then yes," I replied.

"The way you're blushing confirms it's more than warranted." He slid his index finger down my wrist. I jerked my hand away, but not before his touch released an unwelcome little ripple of anticipation. He frowned, and for half an instant, I thought I saw uncertainty cross his face. Was it possible that painfully self-assured boy was upset I'd pulled away?

He shoved his hands into his pockets in an almost-shrug. As if hiding the offending appendages.

I opened my mouth to say something snappy, but nothing came out. I had no idea how to steer this interaction back into our familiar combative territory.

He strolled back toward his desk, leaving the door wide open. I took it as an invitation to follow, but I approached warily, careful to keep as much distance from his horrible leather chair as possible. Like it might jump up and grab me.

I glanced back at the hallway, wishing the dorm didn't feel so very deserted. I didn't want to be alone in a secluded place with him. Suddenly, I wasn't sure who I trusted less, Sterling or myself.

"You can leave the door open if that makes you more comfortable." Sterling glanced back at me with the oddest look in his eyes—guarded and unreadable. "But know that I *can* take a hint."

He turned back to whatever he was doing and I just stood there, unsure where to stand or what exactly I was doing there. Maybe I should leave the door open—maybe *he* would have preferred it that way. But I took a deep breath and pushed it closed behind me. Leaving the two of us alone. That tingling electric feeling in my limbs was back. For some perverse reason, I wanted it to continue.

"We've got about ten minutes," Sterling said. "Here." He handed me his phone and adjusted the screen of his laptop, all business. Apparently I was the only one whose thoughts kept drifting back to what happened the last time we were in this room together.

"The camera will send streaming video to my phone. I

told Cole I had a project due and I'd be at the library all evening. Let's hope he decides to stay here, but if not, you may have to run interference."

"Did you test this out?" I asked, turning the phone over in my hands. "What's the range?"

"Let's find out." He grabbed the phone and slipped out of the room into the hallway.

I stood there for an instant, examining his desk. In the middle was a photo of a pretty brown-haired girl set in a tarnished silver frame, resting on top of a stack of papers covered in Sterling's spidery scrawl. Last week's calculus exam half-concealed a bank statement with a mind-boggling balance. I scanned the exam. Even though the work was a messy tumble of misshapen numbers, he was far from stupid. I both hated and admired that about him.

I picked up the photo. There was a sweep of grassy lawn visible in the background and a blurry tree off in the distance.

"My sister," Sterling said, materializing behind me. "She's the only member of my family who isn't a complete asshole. Present company included."

"Actually, you're not entirely unpleasant," I said. "Except when you're trying to be."

I turned to face him. It brought us nearly chest to chest. And I let it. I had to know who'd step back first—whether he also felt a little lost at sea.

Of course it was Sterling who shifted, giving me far more personal space than I could ever need.

"High praise, coming from you," he said. The playful tone was back. He was watching me carefully, studying me, and suddenly I couldn't bring myself to look him in the face—which I'm sure he noted. I felt raw and exposed and completely confused by the way my pulse hammered every time he said or did anything. My face felt warm, like I was blushing. No doubt he noted that, too.

He turned his phone so I could see the screen, too. I had to lean my head in so close that my cheek brushed his shoulder. He stiffened, but this time he didn't retreat. Why was that suddenly a small victory to be celebrated?

There were no Rules to guide me now.

He played back a video of me reading his math exam, then scowling and staring at the picture of his sister for an uncomfortably long time. The image zoomed in and shifted, sweeping up over my body in a slow, dramatic arc, the way his hands had slid right over me the other day. I flushed again to think he'd examined me every bit as closely as I'd been examining him.

"I can manipulate the camera remotely." He was watching me from the corner of his eye, no doubt noting the impact his little film was having on me. It was just a test. It didn't mean anything.

"I feel guilty spying on Cole," I said to change the subject. "Maybe we just tell him what's going on? That we need him to get Gilbert's confession."

Sterling shook his head. "Like I said before, Cole isn't up to that kind of performance. What I just told you about my sister? Well, it's a problem."

I looked up at him, more curious than I cared to admit.

"She's too sweet. Trusts everyone. Assumes they've got the best of intentions, since she does. She's just like Cole. I think that's why I'm so dead set on helping him—at least it was that at first. She can't take care of herself, either, especially when she gets sucked into my world. I have to look out for her."

"What happened? At your last school, I mean," I said.

"When we first met, I acted like I knew why you were expelled, but I didn't. Not until Parker told me you lit someone's room on fire and it had something to do with your sister."

"I see," he replied. "I've got to say, the more I learn about you, the more I wondered about that comment. Because I'm guessing if you'd seen what happened, you'd have been the one to strike the match." He shook his head. "Worst part was, I'd been coasting all year. Smooth sailing. Contrary to what everyone assumes, I do care about my future. College, all that. But family is family. Found out her ex-boyfriend was pushing her around. He had a bit of a temper and hit her hard enough to leave a mark. You know the rest. But I guarantee he'll never hit a girl again. And if he does—well, I'm happy to arrange a repeat performance."

He met my gaze and held it steady. A firm and determined look settled over his sharp features, and I nodded. I understood. Sterling Lane had lit a guy's room on fire for abusing his sister, and in his shoes, I would have done the same.

I was staring again. That time it wasn't as awkward, since he was doing it, too. "You and me, Harper, we're tough," he said, finally turning away. "It's our job to look out for the little ones."

He was right. I hadn't realized exactly how similar the two of us were until that moment.

Sterling adjusted his camera so it had the broadest view possible. "Let's go," he said, moving toward the door. "We can watch from Parker's room. It's right next door." His smile was dagger-sharp. "But you already know that."

"I'm not going in there." Too many bizarre and unexpected things had happened to me in both that room and this one—I wasn't prepared for an awkward situation with Parker *and*

Sterling. What was with boys this spring, and why did they suddenly seem so acutely aware of my existence?

"He's not there." Sterling's voice almost sounded gentle. "Besides, I'll protect you."

"That's hardly reassuring."

"If you'd heard a word I'd just said, it would be." The intensity in his voice made me shiver.

"I can take care of myself, Sterling," I said. "If you think back over everything we've been through, I think I've more than proven I can handle you or any other boy who steps out of line."

"Touché," Sterling said. "But after everything we've been through, I also don't deserve to be lumped into that category. You might not need my help, but is it so horrible to know that if you ever need it, it's yours? I'd never let someone hurt you." His eyes searched mine before they cut away. "Parker is usually out until late. He won't even know we've been there." He glanced at his watch. "We don't have time to debate this."

"Fine." I followed him out into the hallway. He pulled something metal out of his pocket—definitely smaller than a key, but it popped the lock open just as easily.

"I'll pretend I didn't see that," I said.

"But you were curious, weren't you? About the tricks of my trade."

"Burglary? Not really. But I did wonder about the car. How you did it by yourself."

"Of course I didn't do it by myself," he said like I was an idiot. "But let's just say it was worth every penny. A considerable number of pennies."

I started to reply, but he looked at me sharply, a finger pressed against those sarcastic lips. He strode into the room and flicked off the desk lamp. It was pretty much the last thing in the world I wanted—to be alone in a darkened bedroom with Sterling Lane. Behind a closed door. There was nothing separating us but lengthening shadows and the pile of mildewing boy laundry on the floor. No one to see or interrupt whatever might happen next.

I did my best to banish the fluttering agitation in my chest. I took a deep breath and walked over to the window, always keeping out of the range of Sterling's sizable wingspan. Cole was approaching across the quad—I'd know that bouncy stride anywhere.

Sterling curled one hand around my elbow and pulled me away from the window. Instead of catching my balance right away, like I could have, I let myself fall back against him. I stayed there for a few heartbeats, pressed against his solid warmth.

I should have moved, but I didn't. Instead I turned, bringing us once again into dangerously close proximity— so close we might as well have been actually touching.

"I didn't mean to topple you," he murmured, looking down at me and never breaking eye contact. "But it won't help our cause if he sees us."

"I still feel bad about this," I said. "I mean, spying on Cole. It doesn't seem right."

I meant it—the guilt about Cole. But I also couldn't help noting that Sterling still hadn't moved away, and neither had I.

"We don't have any choice. Necessity is the mother of immorality."

"I think you mean the mother of invention."

"Do I?" He grinned. "If someone is starving to death, they don't invent a machine to suppress their appetite. They lie, cheat, or steal to get dinner."

"That's ridiculous," I said, but he pressed his index

finger against my lips, shushing me. I grabbed his hand away, because he didn't get to shush me, but once I clasped it, I didn't want to let it go.

"The only thing these walls keep out is light," he whispered, glancing down at our interlocked fingertips. "You wouldn't believe the things I've overheard from five feet that way." One eyebrow arched as he pointed toward his room. "Or that way." He shifted his gaze toward the door, making sure we both remembered the afternoon Parker tried to kiss me.

"Why do you keep bringing that up?" I hissed, "It wasn't my fault he tried to kiss me."

His eyebrow arched. "No, not at all your fault. But why else did you think a boy would lure you into his bedroom and close the door?"

"You're saying I was asking for it?" I was utterly shocked that anyone in this day and age could be so arcane.

"Of course not. Just letting you know something about guys. Use it how you will."

An awareness had stirred to life inside me after the incident on Sterling's armchair—the same awareness that lingered in Sterling's expression as he studied me. But I didn't know how to do it—how to communicate in this language I hadn't known existed until the other day.

There was a sharp knock on the door, and I jumped. But it wasn't us being summoned—it was Cole.

An instant later, low, muffled voices erupted from Cole and Sterling's room. Sterling stepped away, releasing me into the cold, lonely air. He settled on the floor, long legs stretched out in front of him, and pulled out his phone. He motioned me over, and I didn't have any choice but to join him. The screen was so small I had to lean in closer— close enough that my side was pressed against his. It sent another jolt of electric adrenaline shooting through me, so I shifted closer still, letting my arm settle along his thigh. There was really nowhere else to put it. He stilled, a stutter in his breath as he exhaled, long and slow.

Sterling had positioned his laptop perfectly so we had a view of the entire room. The moment Gilbert arrived, Cole paced around like he always did when he was nervous. Whereas Gilbert perched on Cole's desk chair, looking like a king on his throne.

"The game is this Friday, Cole," Gilbert said. "Enough stalling. You know this is the only way you'll be able to pay back what you owe."

"I only owe money because you screwed up," Cole replied. "It's awfully convenient we were winning so much when it was ten dollars here and there, but the minute it's real money, we lose." Cole tipped his head to the side, and I was so proud of my brother for standing up for himself, even as I was horrified at what he was confessing. "I'd hate to think you were setting me up."

I nudged Sterling with my elbow, surprised that I could do so while barely moving an inch. I'd subconsciously crept closer while watching Cole. "None of this is incriminating—they could be talking about anything."

"Shh," Sterling whispered. "Be patient."

I could smell his cologne, crisp and citrusy—a disturbingly alluring scent. I let my head settle against his shoulder. Again, he stilled and I reveled in this newfound power I had over him.

"I'm not throwing a game," Cole said, moving closer until he was firing the words right in Gilbert's face.

"I'm not asking you to," Gilbert said, an unmistakable flash of malice in his eyes. "I'm asking you to give up a few points here and there. You'll still win, just not by quite as much. It's no big deal. Pretend you're sick, not playing quite up to par. The team won't know the difference."

"But I will," Cole replied. "That's point-shaving. And I won't do it."

"Call it whatever you want, Cole. You don't have a choice."

"I might have been gullible enough to believe you were trying to help me before," Cole replied. "But I get what you're doing, trying to corner me. And this ends here. Today."

I squeezed Sterling's wrist in excitement. This was exactly the kind of footage we needed.

"Now we're getting somewhere," Sterling said. I looked up at him, and my gaze lingered. We were shoulder to shoulder on the rug. His arm was extended backward, behind me, supporting his weight but also curled around my back in something disturbingly similar to a half embrace. He glanced over and our eyes collided. That fluttery feeling in my insides was back, but this time it roared forward into a full-blown tremor as I leaned in close. His lips parted and his chest rose as he took a deep breath and let it out. Then he turned his face away, staring at his phone.

It seemed Sterling was true to his word—he wasn't going to push things. Sure, I was sending mixed signals, telling him to keep away while shifting closer myself. At that moment, though, I knew what I wanted, knew exactly how to tell him so he'd be sure to understand. But first, we had to handle this situation with Cole. I shifted so I could see the phone, careful to press every inch of my side against Sterling.

"You're in this up to your eyeballs," Gilbert told Cole. If there was any doubt in my mind he was a bad apple, it was erased by the threat in his tone. "These guys aren't joking around. This isn't some misunderstanding at the country club. They will seriously mess you up if you don't pay them back. This is the only way."

"And what about you, Gilbert?" Cole snapped back. "Why aren't they turning the screws on you, too?"

"Who's to say they aren't?" Gilbert pulled up his T-shirt, revealing a nasty purple bruise just below his rib cage, the size and shape of a human fist. I shuddered. I was pretty sure I'd murder anyone who inflicted that kind of harm on my brother. "I was told to deliver, and goddamn it, Cole, you'll deliver."

"I won't," Cole replied. "I'll find a way to get the rest of the money. I made a mistake betting on games and taking that money—actually believing it was that easy to just keep winning. I won't do this. I won't let my team down. I'd rather face my consequences now than get in deeper."

I was torn between utter horror at what Cole had just admitted and a deep, abiding pride that my brother was finally drawing a line.

"Get out," Cole said.

Gilbert hesitated, as if searching for one more thing that would bring Cole back in line. "You have until Friday to come to your senses." Then he left, slamming the door.

Cole walked across the room and flung himself down on his bed, covering his eyes with his forearm. My entire soul ached for my brother. I wanted nothing more than to rush in there and comfort him—and tell him that Sterling and I would find a way to fix everything. But if I had any hope of getting him out of this mess, we couldn't let him realize how much we knew.

"Well, that was a bigger success than I dared hope," Sterling whispered. "I thought it would take a few tries to catch all that."

The phone disappeared into his pocket, but I kept staring after it, wondering how on earth this could be considered a success.

"What were they talking about? Gil wants Cole to throw a game?"

"Not exactly," Sterling replied softly, turning his face toward mine. "Point-shaving means a leading athlete, like Cole, doesn't play up to par. Not so much that his team loses, but enough that they steer the final score toward a specific number. You get a much larger winning if you guess the correct score."

"Cole is in serious trouble." We had the footage we needed, evidence that Cole was being blackmailed. Agitated and relieved as I was at this discovery, all I could think about was steering the situation back to where we'd almost been a few minutes ago.

I shouldn't want this, but I did. I placed my palm flat on his chest, an undeniably deliberate action. Genuine surprise flashed in his eyes.

"We've got our work cut out for us," I added.

"But we'll get it done. Rome wasn't built in a day, sweetheart." He shifted closer, but there was a slow, measured quality to his movements. "Neither were those abs you keep staring at."

I should have smacked him for that, but I was too distracted by his proximity to process his words. His breath skimmed my jaw in a caress every bit as tangible as if he'd traced a line across my skin with his fingers.

We shifted closer, millimeter by agonizing millimeter.

"This time, tell me if it's too much." His lips brushed mine, then skimmed the line of my jaw before returning. A jolt of raw longing rocketed down my spine. An entire body's worth of sensation erupted from that one small point of contact.

I trembled—actually trembled—as his mouth settled on mine. He hesitated, moving oh-so-slowly as his lips parted mine. His hands, graspy and quick as they'd been last time, were notably absent. I craved them, ached for his fingers to slide across my skin like they had before. I leaned into him, pressing as close as I possibly could, praying he'd recognize the signal and give me what I needed.

But Sterling still just kissed me, long and languid, as if there were all the time in the world.

He had to know what he was doing—igniting a fire inside me but depriving it of the fuel it needed to burn.

I fisted the front of his shirt and yanked him closer. He made a sound deep in his throat, part growl, part groan. A sound that *I'd* inspired. I reveled in it—in knowing I'd made Sterling lose even the smallest shred of his signature self-control.

He pulled back. My eyes flew open, expecting to be greeted by his sarcastic grin. I was scared of how much I wanted him, of the power he could now wield over me. Yet vulnerable as I felt, I could handle whatever came next— whatever life or Sterling Lane threw at me.

But there was no pause, no sadistic smile. His eyes were closed, lips parted. He was utterly at my mercy. His hands finally joined the show, skimming up my back as he kissed me again, but this time at the feverish pace I needed.

I kicked my knee over his legs, rolling right up onto his lap. Straddling him for the second time. His chest rose and fell under my palm. A chuckle of surprise, or maybe delight—that I'd been the first to be consumed by the fire between us. But if I'd been first, he was only a half a second behind.

Hands cupped my hips. Quicksilver fingers untucked my shirt and slid underneath, inch by inch. It was terrifying, the way his touch left ripples of longing in its wake. Teeth grazed my earlobe. Lips traced a slow, languid line down my throat. I tipped my head back, praying for more. When he stopped, a mortifying little mewl slipped right out of me, the sound of a kitten left out in the rain.

He didn't pause to mock me or to celebrate the way he'd made me lose control. Instead his eyes locked on mine as his fingers slid my shirt up. I inhaled, exhaled in staccato bursts, trembling as his thumb traced my collarbone. He froze.

"Should I stop?" he whispered.

Yes. I should say it. I should push him away. I knew it from the way my Rules bayed like banshees. But I couldn't make myself do it, couldn't make myself care about Rules or consequences.

I shook my head over and over again.

I slid my hands up under his shirt, skimming along his back until I could feel every twitch of muscle as he moved. And it still wasn't enough. I bunched up his T-shirt and tugged it over his head. We paused just long enough for him to shrug right out of it.

Then his lips were on my collarbone and I thought I might actually die. I'd taken charge of this situation only to lose it again, surrendering completely under the experienced touch of my mortal enemy. I couldn't let Sterling Lane win. His breath hitched; I had power over him, too.

I pushed his chest hard, forcing him down, pressing him into the carpet with my body. I kissed his throat, sliding my fingers up his stomach, mimicking what he'd done just moments ago. I felt him tremble just like I had, felt his heart hammering underneath my fingertips. I gloried in the power, in the confusing ripples of pleasure and aggression that shot through me as his hand curled around my neck, locking my mouth against his. I was out of control—*we* were out of control. We'd boarded a runaway train, and I wouldn't have had it any other way.

Light flooded the room, but my body begged me to ignore it. This feeling could never end—I wouldn't let it. Voices echoed through the room from the open bedroom door.

I bolted upright, right on Sterling's stomach. I grabbed my shirt, fumbling to pull it over my head while Sterling rolled lazily up on one elbow and helped, tugging it down just in time. The door swung open the rest of the way. Parker was talking to someone in the hallway, so it took a moment before he turned his eyes toward the inside of the room and saw us.

Eyebrows shot up. Lips curled down at the corners.

"What the hell?" Parker demanded.

"Sterling fell," I said. "I was helping him."

"Helping him what? Stay down?"

Parker had a point, so I pulled myself to my feet, brushing off my jeans. Fibers from the ancient rug coated every inch of my clothing. I looked at Sterling for help, but he just flashed a cruel little smile and motioned with one hand for me to continue.

"We were studying."

"In the dark?" Parker scoffed. "In my room?"

"It was a science experiment," I said, an explanation forming in my mind.

"What kind of experiment?" Parker asked skeptically.

"Human anatomy," Sterling interjected, looking me right in the eye.

I flinched. "I was going to say something about electricity," I hissed at him.

"Yes, there was that, too," he said in a voice that made my knees go wobbly.

"I thought you took physics?" Parker's forehead creased, and I was painfully embarrassed for all of us when the meaning behind Sterling's words finally settled in.

Sterling's smile widened. He was an alligator that wouldn't bother to bite before swallowing me whole.

Parker took a step into the room. His hunkering posture was vaguely threatening. "Yeah, well, whatever you're doing, do it in your own room. I don't even want to know how you got in here."

"We needed privacy," Sterling said. "And, well, Cole is in there. That could be a little awkward."

"Shut up, Sterling," I snapped. "You are so obnoxious."

"And you love that about me." He sat up all the way and reached for his wallet. "Hundred bucks if you clear out for an hour," he said to Parker.

"Hundred bucks?" Parker was actually considering the offer.

"Well, I hope you're buying solitude," I growled at Sterling, "because I'm leaving."

"Of course. But I suggest you adjust yourself first." His eyes were leveled at my chest. I looked down at half a shirt's worth of buttons dangling limp and alone, wrenched loose from their better halves.

"Thanks," I said. "Thanks so much to both of you for not telling me sooner. And for letting me make a complete fool of myself."

Parker smiled awkwardly and looked away.

"That's hardly what I'd call it," Sterling replied quietly before his voice sharpened. "And Parker, you should watch where you're looking. Some people—Kendall, perhaps—might get jealous. And she's not the only one." Sterling inclined his head toward me. "Stay away from this one."

Parker's hands curled into fists, and as much as I'd have loved to stay for that macho showdown, I was dizzy. Confused. Shocked at what had happened, at what my treacherous hormones had nearly led me to do. My pending shower would drain the local reservoir, trying to wash all that shame away.

I started for the door, but Sterling was up in an instant. "You're not going out like that." He caught my hand and turned me, fastening the buttons himself with his impossibly nimble fingers.

"Guess what, Sterling? I don't care anymore. Let the entire campus get a good eyeful of what your influence will get them."

"No. I don't like to share." Sterling's voice chased me out the door as I pushed past Parker. "And Rule 364 stipulates that provocative clothing is inappropriate in every context, but most especially at school."

I ignored him, just like I tried to ignore Cole when his head popped out his door, curious about the shouting.

"Are you and Sterling going at it again?" he called after me, exasperated.

"You have no idea," I shot back. I wasn't sure if Cole noticed my state of disarray, but I didn't care. Maybe it would be good for him to know that he wasn't the only one with secrets. I was beginning to realize the danger of repressed feelings, of holding yourself back and denying who you were. You could only keep it up for so long before you exploded all over the place—whether that meant gambling or stealing or rolling around on the floor with a wickedly beautiful boy, the results were the same.

Utter chaos. A level of madness that not even externally imposed discipline could contain. Not 537 Rules. Not the law or the disciplinary committee. It was time to let myself emerge from behind the shadow of my Rules. They were no longer enough; perhaps they'd never been.

The worst part of this whole fiasco was how feverishly I wanted to go back to Parker's room and do it all over again. It was as if Sterling Lane had left an indelible imprint. His touch was tattooed onto my skin, an ever-present echo that I knew would never entirely fade away.

But that didn't mean I was giving in to Sterling, or that I'd been corrupted by his insidious influence. I already knew he was no good for a girl like me. But that didn't mean another boy couldn't be. Maybe Kendall and all those other girls I'd mocked weren't so ridiculous after all. That kiss had turned my universe upside down. I'd thrown out everything—even my Rules—in the heat of that moment, which is exactly why I could never let it happen again. Not like that. Not in the out-of-control collision course that Sterling seemed to inspire.

And that's when it happened. I released my confusing knot of conflicting emotions for Sterling, let it float away into the evening sky as I walked away, across the quad to my dorm. After all, I had to thank him for opening my eyes, not just to boys and taking risks and making friends like Kendall. He made me realize how much Cole truly mattered to me. Now I'd be there when Cole needed me most, no matter what.

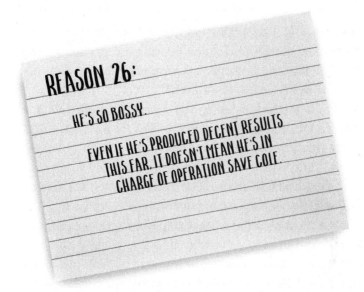

REASON 26:

HE'S SO BOSSY.

EVEN IF HE'S PRODUCED DECENT RESULTS THIS FAR, IT DOESN'T MEAN HE'S IN CHARGE OF OPERATION SAVE COLE.

*U*pon further reflection and after a decent night's sleep, I managed to push Sterling Lane from my mind. The storm had passed. Even if they weren't entirely gone, all thoughts of kissing him had been recategorized as memories. They were part of my past and had no place in my future. Still, I decided it wouldn't be a bad idea to avoid being alone with him—particularly after he slipped me a note in history ordering me to meet him in the basement of the library during lunch. I'd heard stories about what went on down there in the stacks that no one ever visited. He was insane if he thought he could trick me so easily.

Halfway through lunch, he dropped a massive dusty book next to my lunch tray. The impact tipped my water all over my tray and Sterling made no move to clean it up.

"Not accustomed to being stood up," he said. He leaned in close, almost as close as he'd been the two times we'd kissed. "Then it hit me—you don't trust yourself to be alone with me. Can't keep your hands to yourself."

"I think you'll find that's no longer a problem," I said, keeping my tone professional. Firm but friendly. "But thank you for being so understanding."

He tipped his head to the side, eyeing me like I had a knife hidden behind my back. "Where are the quills?"

"I don't know what you're talking about." I forced a smile. "Did you have something you needed to discuss?"

"Yes," he said, the suspicion in his eyes so overblown we could have been starring in a vintage detective show. You could almost hear the dramatic musical montage as his eyes bored into mine, eyebrow arched theatrically. "Cole and I received official notification from the headmaster that the disciplinary committee is hearing our case tomorrow. Your father is driving up for the occasion, and I'm hoping thanks to his travel schedule my father is still in the dark. Can you meet me before dinner?"

I was glad I'd already eaten enough of my lunch to sustain me through the afternoon, because my appetite officially vanished. "What are we gonna do?"

"Have a little chat with Gil."

"You can do that alone."

"And just the other day you were chomping at the bit, refusing to take a backseat. This is for Cole, remember?"

"Well, I think you can tackle this part by yourself. Remember my little problem with inconvenient outbursts?"

"Of course, I'm happy to be your errand boy," he said drily. "But it'll cost you."

"How much?"

"Another favor. And this time, no special parameters. Anything I want."

"Nice try," I snapped, "Mr. Manipulator. It hasn't escaped my notice that this little rendezvous benefits you, too."

His eyes lit up, like he'd just been reunited with a long-lost friend.

"Fine. You were right—I don't want to be alone with you. Things keep happening."

My favorite of his many smiles flashed across his face, straight white teeth and all. "Yes, they do. Things worth repeating."

At that, my body went all wobbly. There was no way he missed the color rising in my cheeks.

"I know you're the kind of girl who never backs down. So I know you won't let whatever this is distract you from helping Cole. Six o'clock sharp. Parking lot."

He started to rise, and as he did, he reached over and picked a carrot off my plate. It crunched between his shiny white incisors, and I wondered if he was doing that just to draw attention to his lips. Or maybe his jaw, which led me down to his neck and shoulders until I flushed at the memory of what they'd felt like under my fingertips. My hands tingled, an achingly perfect balance of revulsion and longing.

"It looks nice," he said. "Mascara, new shirt." He gestured vaguely in my direction.

"It's not new." I hated him for noticing, but flat-out despised myself for the satisfied warmth that flooded my chest when he did. "I just haven't had occasion to wear it yet."

"Flattered you want to catch my eye," he said, winking. "It worked."

I started to object, tell him it had nothing to do with him, but I bit back those words. Rule 12 had already skipped to my frontal lobe, reminding me we don't lie. At least, not anymore. So I just got quiet and looked down at my plate, hoping he'd leave before I broke another one of the promises I'd made to myself that morning.

When I looked up, he was already halfway across the dining hall, headed straight for the lacrosse team's table. He looked back just once and grinned when he saw I was watching.

That afternoon, I decided to finish making my physics flash cards underneath a tree near the parking lot. The repetitive nature of the task would help me mentally prepare for the upcoming encounter with Sterling Lane. There was nothing more relaxing than flash card creation. The steady movement of my pen against the index card reminded me of the happy days when my Rules prevailed, before Sterling Lane exposed me to the many holes in their armor.

Sterling arrived five minutes early. And he wasn't alone—a group of sophomore girls was giggling along beside him, hanging on his every word while he blazed ahead, talking and pointing like a tour guide.

He came to a stop in front of me, and once again, I pretended I hadn't noticed he was there, that my pile of index cards was completely engrossing.

He cleared his throat. I looked up, and our eyes locked. In the periphery, I could see the girls glancing back and forth between us, like they were watching a tennis match.

"Ladies," he said. "This is where I leave you. Harper and I have plans."

"What kind of plans?" one of the girls asked.

"Wouldn't you like to know?" Sterling dropped his voice to a salacious whisper. "But I'm afraid Harper wouldn't want this sort of thing publicized."

"Leave it to you to make it sound like we're having a sordid affair," I snapped. "Mind in the gutter."

"And leave it you to jump in right after me. I'm sure

everyone knows we'd never do anything like that, would we?" The sarcasm was impossible to miss. I hurled my pen at him, but he caught it easily and slid it into his front pocket. "And you'd better be careful—you're skating dangerously close to violating Rules 12 and 16."

Lying? Hardly. Our little romps were over. They ended last night when Parker flicked on the lights.

"You draw a very convenient distinction between omissions and lying," I shot back.

"Of course. But I count on you to be the higher moral authority."

I glared at him, just as an auburn-haired girl said, "What's Rule 12? And 15?"

"Never do business with the big bad wolf," I replied. "Now scurry along before he blows your house down."

Auburn girl stared at me, aghast and more than a little puzzled, while her friends shifted nervously.

"She's calling me the big bad wolf," Sterling said, shooting me a conspiratorial look. "No insult to you was intended."

In their eyes, he could do no wrong. Auburn girl shot him a wistful parting smile before wandering off with her friends. A slow simmer of jealousy burned in my gut, and that just made my frustration swell.

Instead of leaving, the girls loitered on the grass, close enough to spy on us. I swallowed hard, realizing how very little I wanted the whole school to find out about our outing. Sterling seemed determined to write it across the sky.

He pulled a vibrating cell phone out of his pocket. "Just in time."

There was a taxi idling on the curb. I hadn't even known Cedar Creek had a taxi company, but Sterling Lane was a master of the unexpected and improbable.

"Why do we need a cab?" I asked.

"*Someone* accused me of stealing, and even though I specifically asked him not to, Headmaster Lowell mentioned it to the admiral, who decided to wait a few weeks before shipping down my car. Make sure I wasn't expelled before it got here."

"You have an amazing knack for hurling my errors back at me when I least expect it."

"I have an amazing knack for a great many things," he said, paralyzing me with his smile. He reached up, skimming my chin with his thumb. Warmth flooded my face.

"On second thought, I'll walk and meet you there," I said quickly, backing away. The interior of the cab would be small and cozy. In those close confines, I could already imagine how his long limbs would accidentally brush mine. The way my body would likely betray me, trembling at the contact.

I didn't think I could just sit there making small talk, but I also couldn't endure to ride in a fully loaded silence.

"It's ten miles, Harper," Sterling said, using that condescending voice. "Get in. Hands to myself. Promise." He made a ridiculous show of shoving his hands into his pockets. When he climbed in and noted the driver's baseball cap, he launched into a protracted conversation about baseball. He tried to engage me in their little chat, but I vacillated between irritation that he wasn't talking to me and anxiety about old patterns when he was.

It was a fifteen-minute drive to Gilbert's address, and given the creepy farm road we rumbled down, I was glad Sterling had planned ahead for transportation. Finally, we came to a stop in front of a run-down apartment building next to a gas station. It was in the middle of nowhere. White paint flaked off the siding in shavings the size of notebook paper. A rusted-out gray sedan basked in the sun, one wheel-free axle resting on a cinder block. The car had been there long enough that weeds were poking through the rust holes on the door.

The building was two stories of doors that all opened to the outside, like a roadside motel, with a blue metal railing clinging to the upper level, promising to tumble to the ground at the slightest breeze.

Sterling handed the driver a stack of bills. "Wait here. We'll be less than ten minutes."

Once we stepped outside, out of earshot of the very curious cab driver, Sterling turned to me.

"This is where he lives?" I asked. Gil. The boy who was blackmailing my brother. I felt bad for all my hate-filled thoughts of him when I saw it. But then I remembered that Gil wasn't his real name at all, just a moniker to hide whatever crimes he'd committed before dragging Cole down, too.

As if he could hear my thoughts, Sterling looked at me, squinting in the sun. "Before you feel bad for him, know that it's only because he's on the run. You can lease here without a background check. I don't think Cole is the first one he's swindled."

Without even hesitating, he walked right up to unit number two and rapped loudly on the door.

There was a long pause before Gilbert cracked the door open, and when he finally did, water from his wet hair dripped onto his shoulders. We'd caught him in the middle of a shower and he'd crammed himself into a pair of khaki cotton shorts to answer the door. The top of his boxers peeked up above the belt line.

"What do *you* want?" Gilbert braced one arm across the doorway, like we'd barge right in with the SWAT team at our heels. My muscles tensed as I thought back to Victor. We could be walking into a seriously dangerous situation, but Sterling rocked back on his heels and smiled without a care in the world.

"Just some friendly conversation," Sterling said. "And I think it would be best for everyone if we did it inside." He pulled out his cell phone and tapped the screen. Gilbert's voice drifted out of the speaker.

I'm not asking you to. I'm asking you to give up a few points here and there. You'll still win, just not by quite as much. It's no big deal. Pretend you're sick, not playing quite up to par. The team won't know the difference.

Gilbert stepped away from the open door. It was the closest thing we'd get to an engraved invitation, so I walked inside, hoping against hope that there weren't thugs loitering inside, waiting to break us in two.

The interior was every bit as grimy as the peeled-paint exterior—it was one room with a kitchenette in the corner. The floor was covered in stained gray carpet, all except for the glaringly new yellow linoleum underneath the kitchenette in the corner. The only decoration adorning the wall was a watermark the size of a Volkswagen.

"Waiting tables doesn't pay as well as trust funds." Gilbert glared at Sterling, who did a slow circuit around the room before coming to a stop.

"Little does," Sterling replied. "I came to terms with my privilege years ago."

"Came to terms with it?" I said. "We'd all love to hear how the spoiled rich boy has coped with his wealth."

Sterling shot a pointed glance in my direction, as if asking whose side I was on.

"Excuse my word choice," he said. "I recognize that I have more than most. And I'm truly sorry that circumstances have brought you to this point, Gil. But your choices have made things complicated for the two of us. And for Cole. You are going to create a video confession that we'll distribute to the police, claiming responsibility for stealing the money from the coach's office, and you're going to disappear. You're going to pay whatever remaining money is owed—I suspect Cole has already paid in full, factoring in the times you defrauded him. You're going to leave and forget all about Cole."

"Why should I?" Gilbert asked, his lips twisting into a surprisingly sinister smile.

"Yes, Sterling, why?" I added, annoyed at his bossiness and that what he was saying wasn't all that different from my planned direction of attack.

Sterling reached over and gave my hand a bone-crushing squeeze.

"Patience," Sterling murmured in my direction. "You recall Harper's charming little story about the ants? Let's just say this recording is all the attorney general would need to take action."

Gilbert paled and took a step back. "It wasn't my idea."

"I imagine that's true. Let me guess, some middling bookie sends you in to get kids like Cole into gambling debt, and you convince them to point-shave to pay their way back. And you turn a tidy little profit at their expense. The minute they go along with the plan, they're ensnared, aren't they? You can threaten to tell their team or the league unless they do whatever you ask. This is your chance to get ahead of the storm, Gilbert."

"I'd stop and listen, Gilbert," I said. Sterling squeezed my hand again, but I wasn't about to let him take over this show so completely. "I did some research—this could put you behind bars for years, especially if they find out what you did in Arkansas."

Gilbert's skin went from pale to gray. Sterling shot me a sideways glance. I'd kept that little gem for myself, something I'd unearthed through obsessive cyberstalking once his prints led us to his real name. It seemed this was hardly Gilbert's first time at the rodeo. There was no way I'd let Sterling steal all the glory.

We watched Gilbert pack, and when he was done, Sterling very politely invited him to share our taxi into town. Gilbert refused.

We rode back to school in silence, but for once it wasn't loaded. We were companionably quiet, and I spent the time wallowing in relief that this ordeal with Cole was nearly over.

When the taxi deposited us back at school, I assumed we'd part ways until the disciplinary hearing. But Sterling stopped in the middle of the sidewalk, and suddenly his hands were under my elbows, pulling me closer.

"Not in public," I growled.

"I like the sound of that."

"We haven't gotten Cole off the hook yet," I reminded him. "And no matter what, I'm not thanking you like that."

"Like what?"

"I'm not fooling around with you out of some misguided sense of obligation—"

He interrupted, talking right over me. "So you're doing it because you want to?"

My ears were hotter than the sun. "That's not what I meant. I meant in the future."

"Outstanding. You'll be doing it because you want me against your better judgment—which, frankly, is pretty hot. The other night? Reset my standards."

"I didn't mean for any of that to happen," I said.

"Could have fooled me," he said, lips curling into a smile. "Even right now, when you're pretending to push me away, you've got me in a vise grip."

I looked down. Entirely of their own accord, my clenched fists were desperately clutching his shirt, knuckles pressing into the sculpted muscles hiding beneath.

"Enough," I said, pushing him away for real this time. "This isn't about us. There *is* no us. I even made a new Rule about it—no kissing you."

He glowed like someone just handed him the sun. "A new Rule? About me?"

"I shouldn't have told you that," I said, backing away.

"No kissing? At least that leaves the door wide open." He shot me a filthy little smile.

"I hate you."

"I know. And doesn't that make things much more fun?" He pushed up his sleeve, showing me his biceps. "How would five thirty-eight look tattooed right here?"

I wasn't quick enough to dodge away. His hands found my waist and he spun me back until we were chest to chest.

"Stop it," I hissed. I took a deep breath, struggling against the overwhelming urge to just melt right into him. It was so much easier than fighting both Sterling and my own base instincts. Once again, my rebellious little fingers made their way to his stomach, savoring the solid feel of him. I mentally ran through my list of all the things he'd done to infuriate me. That was what it took to find the strength to break out of his arms. "What is your problem, Sterling? I said *not in public*."

"Maybe I shouldn't be so flattered," he continued, like I hadn't said a word. "Given that most of your Rules are ridiculous. I mean, I'm hardly in elite company when Rule 202 is about the proper way to fold socks."

"Enough," I said, raising my voice and immediately wishing I hadn't. Somehow, I managed to disentangle from his arms, but not before we'd collected dozens of curious stares.

"Point taken. There will be time for that later. We'll need to be on our toes tomorrow. Sleep well, sweetheart." He leaned in and kissed my cheek before breaking away, heading in the direction of his dorm. "I know I will. Rule 538's jurisdiction doesn't extend to your dreams."

REASON 27:

AFTER EVERYTHING WE'D BEEN THROUGH, AND ALL THE TRUST I'D PLACED IN HIM, WHEN THE CHIPS WERE ON THE TABLE, HE TOOK OUR GAME WAY TOO FAR.

The disciplinary committee meeting was scheduled to begin at one, but Sterling and I had no intention of letting that body convene.

The butterflies in my stomach were performing F-16-caliber maneuvers as I scarfed down my breakfast, studiously ignoring Sterling when he settled in the seat opposite me.

"Do you always eat your egg like that?" he finally asked.

His grin made me instantly wary. "Like what?"

"You cut it into eight equally sized, perfectly symmetrical pieces before you took one bite. I swear if we had a scale and calipers, we could prove they're exactly the same."

"Of course they are," I said.

"The eggs didn't get their own Rule, though. I must be a serious liability." He paused. "But come to think of it, why didn't they?"

"Because the number of bites changes depending on the size of the egg. And it's a purely subjective calculation."

"Fascinating," he said, burying the sarcasm so deep it almost sounded sincere. "I was thinking last night about how much time we've spent together. And you still don't bore me."

I narrowed my eyes, waiting for the punch line. But it never came. It was a strange moment, sitting there with Sterling, united by a common purpose that was drawing to its conclusion, for better or worse. That afternoon, Cole and Sterling could be expelled. We were hanging together, teetering over the edge of anything.

So it seemed only natural to add my own confession to the mix, since this could very well be the last time I saw him. "You're the first boy I've ever kissed. I mean, other than that misunderstanding with Parker."

"Really? I couldn't tell." The wicked quirk in his smile was back. "Plus, you're so approachable. And sweet."

I picked up one of my perfectly measured pieces of egg and threw it at him. He snatched it out of the air, laughing. And just like that, my nerves disappeared. There was no way Headmaster Lowell or anyone else would defeat us. Just like my Rules, the two of us were invincible.

*H*eadmaster Lowell was sitting in his office with the door open, flipping through the same stack of papers over and over again. He was trying to look important, like he figured the head of a school should. It was ridiculous that his secretary made us wait in the hard plastic chairs outside when he was obviously just wasting time.

Finally he looked up, as if he'd just realized we were there, even though we were sitting a mere five feet from his desk.

"Sterling, Harper, thank you so much for waiting. Come in, please."

As I settled in the chair nearest his desk, I glanced at the papers strewn across its surface—brochures for golf resorts. It took every ounce of my self-control to keep from pointing out his obvious disregard for his students' needs.

I glanced at my watch. We'd told Cole to meet us here, and he was late. We needed to stall, which wasn't exactly an optimal start to our plan. Just as I launched into a rambling explanation of why we were here, Cole walked in—followed by our father.

That was an unexpected development, but not necessarily an unwelcome one. With my father there, the headmaster would have to take our evidence more seriously.

Dad looked from me to Sterling before his eyes narrowed.

"What's going on?" He frowned at Sterling like he somehow knew all about the things we'd been up to behind closed bedroom doors. "Cole said you were meeting here."

"We have something important to discuss, Dad," I said. "This is Cole's roommate, Sterling Lane."

At that, Dad's frown transformed into the confident, deal-making smile that mortified me. In his mind he was reaching out and shaking hands with Admiral Lane himself. The ability to rub elbows with kids like Sterling was the whole reason Dad had sent us off to boarding school in the first place—and he rarely let us forget it.

Sterling nodded. "Pleasure to meet you, sir."

Somewhere along the way, I'd stopped noticing Sterling's polished East Coast diction, the way he exuded confidence from every pore. A firm handshake and a direct, honest smile were encoded in his DNA.

Sterling Lane was the culmination of all the things my father aspired for us to achieve, but I didn't resent him for it. I had to fight back a smile at the contrast between this version of Sterling and the boy who'd deposited a Mini Cooper in my dorm room.

"Dad, I'm glad you came early," I said as he pulled an extra chair from the waiting room into the office. "Sterling and I could use a little support. We can prove Cole is innocent."

"Prove definitively?" Headmaster Lowell asked.

Sterling set our manila folder of documents on the headmaster's desk. "Exhibit one," he said. "One Thomas Janssen, aka Gilbert James."

Out of the corner of my eye, I watched Cole's reaction. His hands were folded on his lap, but they tightened into fists at the sight of Gilbert's photo.

"He's wanted in Arkansas for an assortment of felony misdemeanors. He obtained a fake identity when he took up residency in Cedar Creek."

"What does this have to do with anything?" Headmaster Lowell said.

"He's been threatening Cole," I said. "Blackmailing him."

"Is this true?" Dad asked, putting a hand on Cole's shoulder.

Cole nodded. He opened his mouth to say something, but I shook my head ever so slightly. The last thing we needed was Cole confessing to more than we'd care to have him admit.

My father sighed. "Dare I ask what dirt this guy had on you?"

Cole's eyes pivoted to me. He was letting us take full control of the situation, just like I'd hoped he would.

"Gilbert associates with an illegal gambling ring. Cole was aware that high school betting was within their purview and had reason to suspect someone within Sablebrook was participating in this ring. Particularly when money mysteriously disappeared."

"That would be troubling indeed. But we need proof of something more than a fake identity," Headmaster Lowell said, flipping through the documentation we'd printed off the internet—the newspaper article about Gilbert's arrest in Arkansas for illegal gambling, and a photo of the real Gilbert James's driver's license.

Sterling set his cell phone on the desk. "We obtained a confession." He pressed play.

I watched a few games and realized Cole was the type of player who set the pace for the whole team. So when I saw him alone in town I waited for a chance to strike up a conversation. About lacrosse. I dabble in side bets. At first, Cole really wasn't into it. But I've done this a dozen times. Found a way to hook him in, so that he owed money and was on the ropes. Then he got into a little financial trouble of his own, so I added a little heat to keep him coming back.

"Harper and I deduced that Cole was in some sort of trouble—and I mean outside of the missing money. So we did a little investigating of our own."

"So Cole, you admit you did take the money?" Headmaster Lowell asked. "Gambling aside, that alone is grounds for expulsion."

I hadn't factored Headmaster Lowell's taking such a hard line on the money. I'd thought we could dance a gambling scandal in front of him and tear the focus away.

Sterling cleared his throat, ready to defend them both, but I couldn't take the chance that his dramatic edge would blow this.

"No," I said. "Gilbert did." It wasn't altogether untrue—he simply swindled the money from Cole once Cole lifted it from the lockbox.

I could feel both Sterling and Cole staring at me, shocked. I hoped against hope that I hadn't just taken too hard a left into utter fiction.

"Gilbert took the money to try to frame and blackmail Cole into point-shaving. But Cole went to Sterling and borrowed enough money to replace the missing cash, hence Sterling's large withdrawal. Granted, we all took too much upon ourselves, not telling the administration what was going on—but we were all in over our heads trying to keep this gambling ring from putting Cole in concrete shoes."

Cole's eyes widened. Perhaps I'd gone a little far.

Sterling was watching me with an expression I'd never seen on him before—a sort of bemused irritation. I wondered what he was thinking. Most likely he was outraged that I was breaking my Rules again, lying, bending and rearranging my moral code at my own convenience. We both knew my brother had done more than a few things worthy of serious consequences. He'd gambled, stolen, and lied to cover his tracks. Sterling wasn't one to overlook the irony of our situation.

"Well, that does raise an interesting point, doesn't it?" Headmaster Lowell said. "How do we know Cole didn't just make up this story after the fact to cover his actions?"

"Wait just a minute," my father interrupted. "You heard that confession tape. Cole refused to cooperate with this point-shaving business. I'm proud of my son for standing his ground."

"Given all the secrets swirling around this event, Cal, I'm not sure what to believe. I'd like to hear what Gilbert has to say about the matter."

"You can't," Sterling said. "He left town."

"Isn't that convenient," the headmaster said drily. "You've muddied the water considerably with these gambling issues—which, I assure you, I'll be investigating separately. But while you've demonstrated Gilbert is guilty of coercing Cole, I'm afraid you've far from proven Cole's and Sterling's innocence."

"And I'm afraid, Headmaster, you've got that backward," my father said, clearing his throat. "According to my lawyer and the United States federal government, these boys are innocent until proven guilty. You're the one who needs to produce evidence of their guilt, not the other way around."

"That might be true in a court of law, Cal," Headmaster Lowell said, straightening in his chair but still failing to look headmasterly. "But this is a school, and my powers are considerably broader. Cole sat in this office and didn't say one word about what was going on. How do I know this isn't just an excuse to cover up your crimes after the fact?"

The situation was slipping out of control. I looked at Cole, then at Sterling, and back to Cole. Sterling was perfectly poised; he had expulsion down to an art form.

But Cole was ashen, like his life was flashing before his eyes. Sure, he'd never starve. He could always work for Dad. But I knew he wanted more than that—he wanted a life of his own. And I'd make sure he got it, whatever it took. I could outsmart Headmaster Lowell and bring a definitive end to this debacle, all before second period.

"Headmaster, I have something to say." My voice cracked, lending credibility to my lie. I sounded legitimately terrified. "I know you want to get to the bottom of this— know the absolute truth. I want to tell it to you, but first, I need to know that you'll overlook lesser transgressions that might have occurred that night. Things that fall within the purview of the five least significant school rules. If I tell you the truth about this horrible crime, it will unearth another, very minor transgression done for the greater good of the school."

Sterling fidgeted in his seat, visibly irritated that I was deviating from our plan, but really, I had no choice.

"Well, I can't promise anything until I understand what happened."

"It was a violation of one of the rules cited in section four of the student handbook. I can't be any more specific than that while trying to protect the not-so-innocent."

I was shocked when the headmaster reached for a copy of the student handbook. As headmaster, he should have its rules committed to memory.

"Let's see, section four." He thumbed through the book, then wasted forty-five seconds perusing the passage in question.

"I think I can swing this, Harper. Nothing here is all that serious. What did you want to say?"

"I know Cole and Sterling were in their room the night the money went missing because I was there, too. Cole and Sterling were there all night."

The room went deathly silent, and I held my chin up, defying them to challenge my story.

It was against school rules to be out of my dorm at night, and against a second school rule that I was in the boys' dorm. I hoped it would be my saving grace that Cole was my brother.

"Why?" my father asked. He wasn't mad, just mystified.

I'd reached a crossroads in my story. Should I lie and tell him I needed Cole's support—like I did when we were little when I had a nightmare and would curl up and sleep on Cole's floor? Or should I embrace this crazy mess with Sterling Lane and blend enough fact with fiction to confound everyone?

"Sterling and I fought a lot when we first met, but then things changed." My face was burning. I couldn't look at him. "Sterling and I have had kind of a thing going on. In secret."

Sterling reached over and twined his fingers through mine. The back of his hand was resting on my thigh. Even in front of the headmaster and most of my family, his touch made every nerve ending in my body fire all at once. He cleared his throat. "It's true. But I'd say these days it's something pretty serious?"

I could feel Sterling looking at me for confirmation, but I couldn't do it—couldn't look at his face and see the mischief dancing in his brown eyes.

Cole's eyes were so wide you could have projected an IMAX film onto the whites. I hoped to God he'd just keep his mouth shut. And he did.

"Harper Eloise Campbell." My father sounded more shocked than anything. He was shocked someone would want me, and that that someone would be the gorgeous and disgusting boy sitting next to me.

Sterling cradled my hand like it was a tiny, fragile bird. I was grateful and furious at how masterfully he took this charade to the next level. Once again, we were in the headmaster's office explaining our relationship. I could barely sort through my feelings myself, yet here I was, poised to defend them to my red-faced father.

Headmaster Lowell shook his head. "I know there's been some sort of situation with you two," he said, clearing his throat. "But this is unexpected. Normally, I'm not sure I'd take a student's word so seriously. But you, Harper, have always been disturbingly honest—often far transcending the realm of what the listener appreciates hearing."

Headmaster Lowell stared at me like he'd see through my skin to the lies etched into my soul. Only the steady pressure of Sterling's fingers against mine kept my whole body from shaking like an earthquake at what a horrible liar I was.

"The combined weight of this evidence—an alibi plus a confession…" Headmaster Lowell steepled his fingers in front of him and leaned back in his chair. I was sure he practiced this pose in the mirror along with the feigned professorial throat-clearing. "I'm canceling the meeting this afternoon. It seems to me that Cole had his heart in the right place and fell into a few bad decisions."

It was eerie how when presented with a pile of erroneous information, Headmaster Lowell somehow managed to arrive at the same conclusion I had. It only took about a zillion falsehoods to get him there.

"He wasn't the only one." Dad was glaring at Sterling. "I don't care who your father is. Harper has never stepped one toe out of line, and suddenly she's sneaking into your dorm." He leaned forward in his chair. "I know your story and your type, Sterling. Harper, you are forbidden from associating with him—Headmaster, I want Cole switched to a more suitable rooming situation."

My head started to spin. I'd hoped and prayed for this a few weeks ago, but now that it was finally coming true, it was a disaster.

"Really, sir," Sterling said. "It's not like it sounds." He flashed his Rulebreaking grin, and I braced myself for impact. "But in my former life it probably would have been."

"Dammit, Sterling." I buried my face in my hands,

unable to look at a single person in that room. I could picture too perfectly Cole's wide-eyed shock, my father's purple-faced outrage.

"I thought you'd appreciate honesty, sir. Because if I were you, my first thought would be 'why should I believe *him*, the kid who's been expelled so many times his grandmother loses track of where to send holiday cards?' But I've changed. Harper changed me. I've earned her trust, and I'll do whatever it takes to earn yours."

My father's eyes narrowed. "I'd say we're pretty far past that possibility."

"Believe me, I understand. I have a sister I'd do anything to protect. And Cole is the same way. Do you really think he'd let his roommate harm his sister?"

Dad crossed his arms and shook his head. I couldn't believe it—Sterling was actually softening him.

"I've made a lot of mistakes in my life, but now, finally, I'm doing something right. This isn't exactly how I imagined this going down, but I've got some pretty serious feelings for Harper. And I'm not willing to let her go." He squeezed my hand—either for show or as an actual act of solidarity. Because I'd been diligently studying my cuticles the entire time he spoke.

The room got so quiet I wondered if Sterling had given the rest of them simultaneous heart attacks.

I had to look up and face the consequences.

"It's really not a big deal, Dad," I said, careful to avoid looking at Sterling. "Nothing that I wouldn't have told you about when I got the chance. I was in their room that night just talking. Cole was there, too. It got late and I knew I'd get in even bigger trouble if I got caught wandering around the school at night, so Cole gave me his bed and slept on the floor."

My father leaned back in his chair. "I'm not through with you." He pointed at Sterling. "We'll have a little chat when we're done here." The red splotches on his face started to disband. "Harper and Cole, I'm extremely disappointed in you both."

Cole nodded without lifting his eyes from my face. He was staring at me in utter disbelief, like I'd just flown down from Mars for the weekend. My father's face held the same sentiment. Headmaster Lowell narrowed his eyes when he looked at me, as if trying to imagine what Sterling could see in Harper the Hag.

But no one in that room was as stunned as me. Sterling Lane had carried our little farce far past the limits of sanity. He'd have to endure a lecture from my father and awkward questions from my brother, all for a situation that could easily have been remedied by my tidy little lie.

He'd said his feelings were serious—that he wasn't going to let me go. Did he mean it? He couldn't. Was it all part of the game, designed to torment me while casting a smoke screen wide enough to hide the truth forever? My gaze cut to Sterling and the way he leaned back in his chair, poised and in command, while I felt like my internal organs were on display.

Whatever Sterling was up to, however this moment fit into his master plan, I would find a way to face it and still live up to my own standards.

REASON 28:

AFTER JUST A FEW SHORT WEEKS, HE KNEW MY BROTHER BETTER THAN I DID.

BUT WORST OF ALL, HE'D BEEN RIGHT ABOUT PRETTY MUCH EVERYTHING.

I avoided both Cole and Sterling for the rest of the day. I couldn't bear to look Sterling in the face. Not after the things he'd said—in front of my father, no less.

I knew he was mortified by the horrifying explanation he'd had to craft on the fly to cover up for my incompetent lies. Worst of all, my father had dragged Sterling away when we'd all parted, no doubt to have the awkward, overprotective chat—the kind of thing that should only happen in the Middle Ages when girls weren't deemed capable of defending themselves. And I was even better able to do that than Cole, whose dates would never get a series of stern warnings from Dad.

Sterling made no attempt to approach me, so I kept to myself as well, watching him from the corner of my eye during lunch. He sat alone, which was out of character. Part of me burned to speak to him, to ask him what on earth he'd been thinking, just as part of me was terrified of what he'd say. The possibilities made me nauseous, which didn't help me sort out my own feelings one bit.

It wasn't until the end of classes that Cole finally sought me out. He didn't say anything at all, just pulled me into a hug.

"I can't believe you did that—you lied for me." His voice was wobbly with emotion.

"Don't ever say that out loud again," I said, glancing around. Fortunately, no one was close enough to overhear. "It's imprudent. Besides, I'd probably kill for you, Cole Campbell. But I'd rather you didn't make me. It's against Rules 13 and 132."

"I've missed you. And your Rules, weirdo." He smiled. "Forgive me?"

"For what?"

"For being stupid." He looked down at his shoes. "And an asshole. I was just under so much pressure, and—"

"You know you're neither of those things. Seriously, Cole, the only thing I'm mad about is that you didn't tell me. You know I could've helped."

"It wasn't like that," he said. "I just got in over my head and I was ashamed. Sterling—he found out by accident. Not much gets past him." He glanced at me from the corner of his eye. "I don't know what I would have done without that loan."

"It's over now."

"Yes," Cole said. "Thanks to you and Sterling."

We walked across the quad in silence. I was surprised when he nudged me with his elbow, playfully.

"Is there really something between you two? Or was that just one more story to get us off the hook? I assumed it was a fib until I saw the look on your face."

"I hardly see how that matters."

"Holy shit," Cole said. "I assumed he'd be working his

way through Kendall's crowd. You know, brainless seems more his type."

"Girl is Sterling's type," I replied. "And don't knock Kendall. That girl's got more brains than you sometimes. And after a month of living together in my monastery, we've come to an understanding of each other."

Cole smiled at me. "See, I knew you could convert an acquaintance into a friend. And look at you, going for a double-header, all on your first go-around. Sterling might be unpredictable, but he's no idiot. He knows a good thing when he sees one."

"Well, it was all just a big mistake." I shook my head even as Cole's words sent a little ripple of anxiety through me. Did I actually *care* what Sterling and Kendall thought of me? Would I miss Kendall when she moved out—and miss Sterling when our tentative truce expired?

"It doesn't matter," I said, more to myself than to him.

"Yeah, right. My sister lied to the headmaster. That's major. Here you were worried Sterling would get his claws into me when you're the one he was after."

I scowled at him, so he added, "I mean that in a good way. Relax. Serious feelings for you—who would have seen that coming after how you two fought?"

"He wasn't after me. That was just a side effect of being thrown together all the time." But even as the words left my mouth, I knew the connection between Sterling and me was more than that. I just wasn't ready to define what, exactly. "No more ridiculous scrapes, please. I don't know that I have the moral fortitude to endure this again."

We said goodbye at the front door of Cole's dorm. I refused to go inside, just in case Sterling was there—settled in his armchair, martini in hand. But as I walked away, I saw Sterling sitting underneath a tree with his head tipped back against the trunk. His aviator shades were perched in place on that aristocratic nose. He was out of place there in the windswept greenery. Once again, I could picture him in a chaise at the end of a pier, soaking in the sun, maintaining that even golden glow that contrasted so starkly against the pallor of my own skin.

I couldn't tell if Sterling saw me. Knowing him, he was probably fast asleep and dreaming of all the trouble he'd cause now that he'd been exonerated. It wasn't a good idea to stick around long enough to find out. I squared my shoulders and trudged back toward my dorm.

I opened the door to my room, braced for Kendall's half to be empty. Her room was repaired and the excitement of my prank war with Sterling had faded, so it was only a matter of days before she'd disappear back into her clique of beautiful people. I would be alone again, just the way I liked it.

So I was surprised to find her sitting on her bed, shoes planted squarely on the floor for once. My history outline was spread open on her bed, and to my astonishment, she appeared to be drafting an outline of her own. Ordinarily such blatant plagiarism would have made my head spin full circle, but Kendall worked hard. She wasn't expecting a free ride, just finding the most efficient way to study. And really, there was nothing wrong with that.

"I need to talk to you." She was bouncing a little at my arrival, like a golden retriever. "My old room has been fixed for a while."

"I heard." I'd known this goodbye was coming, but I still needed a moment to prepare myself. I closed my eyes and added, "I can't believe I'm saying this, but I think I'll miss you. Thank you for everything you did for me."

A smile spread across her face, the one she knew no one could deny. Instantly, I realized I'd made a misstep. The last time I'd seen her smile that way, Parker spent an entire Saturday assembling shelves for her shoe collection. And here I'd actually hoped for a moment of honesty.

"I was thinking…"

"A dangerous activity."

"I like you." Her grin never faltered. "Even now, when you're Sarcastic Harper."

"What are you buttering me up for?" I demanded. "Just out with it, already. I've had a really long day."

"So I heard." She wiggled an eyebrow. It seemed Kendall knew something I didn't—a landmark event. "But that's the thing. See, I can move back in with Celia, but every time I picture myself back there, I just—I don't know. I like it better here with you. I always know where I stand with you—where everything stands with you. I think that's kinda rare in my life."

Of all the things I'd heard that day, this was by far the most unexpected. The glamorous Kendall Frank wanted to live with Harper the Hag. A little firecracker of joy exploded somewhere inside me. I was smiling. I *liked* living with Kendall—I just hadn't let myself truly feel it until I knew it was something I would get to keep.

Kendall started bouncing again, grinning back at me. "So can I stay, roomie?" she asked. "We can get my TV out of storage. And I have every shade of nail polish."

"You can stay." I sighed like it was a huge inconvenience. In a way, it was. I hadn't counted on caring about Kendall or what she thought of me, but I did. "But keep your nail polish to yourself."

"You sure? Because I have a feeling you'll be needing it, and possibly this divine little dress I just bought. It's too small for me, you know, until I drop a few pounds. But it'll fit you perfectly."

"Why would I need that?" I demanded.

She lifted an envelope from the bed at her side and held it out to me. It was gold, embossed with a large black L on the flap. My heart started to tap-dance around my rib cage.

"What is it?"

She shrugged and looked down, making a big show of examining her cuticles while I opened it.

I call upon you, Harper Campbell, to perform one favor:
Friday, 6:00 p.m., Saint James Hotel
Cocktail attire
And that twisty thing you've been doing with your hair
Plus the mascara

It didn't need to be signed. It was scrawled all over Sterling Lane's monogrammed stationery.

My stomach pole-vaulted over my large intestine.

When I'd done all those bad things over the last few weeks, I'd known one day I would account for all of my Rulebreaking, all of my sins and undeniable transgressions. But this Friday seemed a little soon for that day of reckoning.

Because nothing good would come from this date with the devil, particularly considering his Rules on the matter.

*H*ow do you prepare for a summons like this? How do you arm for war on uncertain terrain against an enemy you wish you didn't have to fight?

I spent at least an hour staring at my closet, wondering which of my turtleneck sweaters made me look the most severe and was therefore least appropriate for a night out with an obnoxiously attractive boy. I'd settled on a black ensemble—a baggy black turtleneck paired with slacks I was pretty sure I'd inherited from my grandmother.

Unfortunately, Kendall intervened. She walked into our room with her phone pressed against her ear, nodding so vigorously I thought her head might pop right off.

"You are so lucky you called me," she said into the receiver, eyeing me up and down. "Sister Harper couldn't be showing less skin if she was wearing two habits."

My temper flared. I held out my hand. "Give me the phone, Kendall."

She reluctantly complied.

"This is absurd, Sterling. I'm not doing this."

"Remember our deal," he said. "Tonight, you have to listen to me, and I'm extending that authority to Kendall for the next ten minutes. Let her help you."

"Help me with what, exactly?" But I knew the answer as I saw Kendall pull a dress out of her closet. To her credit, it was something I might have picked out if I wore cocktail dresses—a simple black sheath dress, not too short, but not exactly long, either. I shook my head, momentarily forgetting that Sterling wouldn't be able to see my refusal. "Absolutely not," I told her. "I'm not wearing that."

"A promise is a promise," he said. "Don't forget I made one, too. And I'll make another one: I promise you'll enjoy it." There was a *click* on the line. He was gone. I handed the phone to Kendall, then snatched it back and hit the redial button. It went straight to Sterling's voicemail.

It. What did he mean by *it*?

There was only one reason a boy lured you into his bedroom and closed the door. Sterling's own words.

"What's he up to?" I asked as Kendall thrust the dress at me. It really wasn't that bad; it was just the principle of the matter.

"Honestly? I don't know. But I don't think I'd tell you if I did. It's so romantic."

"That's exactly what I'm afraid of." I plopped down on my bed and buried my face in my hands. "And what about coercion is romantic?"

"It's not coercion, silly. You can say no. But—and I can say this because I'm with Parker now, but back when I was interested in Sterling—" She lowered her voice and I looked up, more curious than I'd care to admit. "I gave up because he just wasn't like this. You know, his second-date rule. I mean, Parker was scared to commit, too, but that was all a misunderstanding. Most people don't put it all out there in the open so you know where you stand, like Sterling does. Trust me on that one." There was a shimmer of moisture in her eyes, so I awkwardly patted her hand. "Parker and I wasted months with our stupid games."

I couldn't really argue with her, and not just because of my lack of experience in this arena. I'd seen it happen around me enough times to know the truth. And I knew I could wear my turtleneck. Or I could move out of my comfort zone a little and try something new. "If you're trying to make me feel better, it's not working. There are plenty of nice guys in the world. Guys who don't play these demented games. Why would I want to go on a date with a boy like him?"

She tugged on my turtleneck, so I finally cooperated and pulled it up over my head, dismissing my own mortification at changing in front of her because I was fully unwilling to interrupt this conversation.

"Because you've already done it a zillion times," she said, talking to me like I was slow. The same way I'd always talked to her. "You are so blind. You're the only person he sits with for all of lunch. He always sits near you in class. He's already broken his rules just like he made you break a bunch of yours. The two of you are just—bizarrely, diametrically opposite, but that makes you fit together somehow."

It was an uncomfortable feeling, sitting there realizing Kendall had a point. Perhaps all along Sterling had been toying with me, or maybe the two of us had unwittingly fallen into this disaster together. I was so taken aback that I didn't fight her as she slid the dress over my head.

"How did you know about my Rules?" I asked, a little stunned.

"I have ears, you know." She looked me up and down. "I'm not pulling your pants off. There are limits to friendship, Harper."

It was a foreign word. Foreign concept. I just obeyed. Even though I hadn't touched them since my grandmother's funeral, I obediently accepted the black heels she dug out of the back of my closet. I put on sensible shoes, though, and slid the heels into my bag. It was large enough to hold the shoes as well as two books. In case I got bored.

"You look really pretty," Kendall said, smiling as she surveyed the fruits of her labor. "He won't know what hit him. Use that to your advantage, since you're walking into unknown terrain. Now, do you know where you're supposed to go?"

I shook my head.

She slipped Sterling's note back into my hand. The Saint James Hotel downtown—the fancy place all the über-rich parents stayed when they were in town. *Room 804* was scrawled across the bottom in Sterling's lazy, boyish handwriting.

The blood in my veins froze in place. My heart had been replaced with a solid block of ice.

"I'm not going to a hotel room."

"Yes. You. Are." Kendall pushed me toward the door, leaning into it with all her might. Finally, I took a step forward, throwing her so off-balance on her ridiculous platforms that she almost tumbled forward onto the floor.

"I promised him a favor," I said. "This is too much."

"One hell of a favor," she said, grinning. "You used to be so difficult, Harper. Well, you still are, but in a new and improved way. He isn't playing games with you this time. This is it—the big gesture. And before you jump to conclusions—this isn't like that. He spent way too much time chipping away at your defenses just to try to seduce you in a hotel room. Live a little. See what happens."

"I'll tell you what's gonna happen," I told her. "I'm gonna rip his head off. I can't believe he'd ruin everything like this."

At that, Kendall gave me a sympathetic smile. "Give him a chance," she said. "I'll bet he comes through."

I slung my bag up over my shoulder and started walking, but with every step, my thoughts cycled back to the basic insult in what Sterling had done. I couldn't be ordered up like a pizza—to a hotel room, no less. Of all the disrespectful, condescending little Sterling games, this was far and away the most despicable. His curt summons cheapened what we'd had—the times we'd been alone together behind closed doors. In the headmaster's office, he'd professed to care about me. I'd let myself believe, in a remote corner of my brain, that he meant it—that he viewed me as a person deserving of his care and respect. But now that tentative hope was shattered. Underneath all of my justifiable outrage, the truth of our situation was what hurt most of all.

If I ever spent a night with him—or with anyone—it would be a decision arrived at together. Discussed and weighed and measured, with defined parameters and commitments. Never like this—at the whim of that spoiled, gorgeous boy who thought that his dazzling smile and a few mumbled words of affection addressed to my father would be enough to win me. The mere idea of it made my blood boil.

That little bit of rage was all it took to switch me into overdrive. I was going to tell Sterling Lane exactly what I thought of him and his sadistic games. I hurtled out the door of my dorm, walking at a pace that would smoke most professional speed walkers. As I went, I rehearsed my speech in my mind, the scathing way I'd rebuke him for even conceiving of this favor in return for his paltry aid. He'd done nothing I couldn't have done myself.

It was a ten-block walk to the hotel, and I flew across town in less than fifteen minutes—including brief pauses at two traffic lights.

A bellhop held the door open as I approached. I poured right in, charging through the baroque, overdecorated lobby, brimming with spindly antique chairs and even more brittle patrons.

I pressed the elevator button.

While I waited for the elevator, I slid the heels out of my bag and put them on. I would look dignified, if nothing else, while I made Sterling Lane regret the day he assumed too much. Sure, those two times we'd kissed had been incredible, and the second time, I'd been the one to ratchet it all into overdrive. Perhaps that was why he thought I would be receptive to this. Ultimately, there were probably worse things in the world than an evening with Sterling Lane. In the attraction category, at least, it would be hard to do better. It wasn't like I was religious or had some other reason to wait. And I was curious—in a purely academic way, of course.

But never under the auspices of this favor—that was coercion. Never under his thumb. Never. Never. Never. I would be his openly acknowledged equal or I wouldn't play this game at all.

I stood there for a moment, weighted down by my oversize bag and fully disgusted by the turn my thoughts were taking. What if I was wrong? What if this was some grand gesture, like Kendall suggested? The thought set my nerve endings on fire. No matter what happened in the next five minutes, there was a very good chance I'd spontaneously combust.

The elevator doors opened, but I let them close again. I watched my reflection in the shiny copper doors. I ran my fingers through my hair and adjusted the neckline of the dress. No matter what Sterling threw at me, I was ready to face it. He was the one who should be on his guard, not me. I'd more than demonstrated that I would retaliate tenfold for any wrongs committed against me.

I pressed the button again, took a deep breath, and stepped inside. The antique machinery climbed so slowly I could have pulled myself up faster with a pulley and a hand crank. My shoes pinched. The dress was too loose. And too tight. In all the least appropriate places. I should have put on less makeup. It looked like I was trying too hard, thanks to Kendall.

Room 804 was all the way at the end of the hallway, marked with a shiny gold plaque. It must have had some view of the river and the hills beyond. It was the only door at that end of the building, so either there was a storage closet sucking up space or it was a massive suite of rooms. Only Sterling would book something so ridiculous.

I knocked on the door and it opened immediately.

Sterling Lane was standing there. Hair trimmed, shirt starched, slacks pressed. Tie front and center, straight in a Windsor knot.

"You got dressed up for nothing," I told him. "You have grievously misjudged this situation. Meeting in a hotel room? Let's get one thing straight, Mr. Manipulator. I'm not sleeping with you. I don't care what you say about me."

I could tell he was surprised by the way his hand flew to the knot of his tie, adjusting it like it could get any tighter.

"Blackmailing dates?" a deep voice murmured. "A new low, even for you."

I jumped, and Sterling grinned a crocodile smile.

"Hardly," he replied. "She's elevated me to new heights." He took a step back, grabbing my hand.

"You never fail to entertain, sweetheart," he whispered as he towed me into the room.

It was a living room—two uptight little white couches surrounded a narrow coffee table. In the corner, an older man in a crisp business suit was sitting at a table typing on a laptop. I'd stumbled into an entirely different scenario than I'd been envisioning.

The man looked up, his gaze traveling down to our clasped hands. He was way too interested in us for my comfort.

"Well, well, could it be it has a heart?" the man shot back.

"Grew one just last week, in fact. Maybe there's hope for you, too." Sterling pulled me forward. "Harper, the shark in the suit is Uncle Howard. Don't let his smile fool you—anything you say can and will be used against any future transgressions."

"You're still mad about that?" Uncle Howard replied mildly. "Next time you lie about stealing your mother's car, don't leave your wallet in the backseat." His focus shifted to me. "Oh, the stories I could tell, Harper."

My eyes cut to Sterling in time to see his ears turn pink. It seemed his car prank was in part inspired by his own past.

"Uncle Howard, the New York attorney general?" I asked. My heart started to pound. This couldn't be happening— good things like that didn't happen to *Harper the Hag*. "It's so nice to meet you. When Sterling told me about you, I looked you up. Your handling of the Landsberg case was nothing short of brilliant."

"Thought you'd like to meet him. Although when you hear his five-hour replay of that Landsberg case, you might change your mind. Who knew embezzling could be so boring?"

The man rolled his eyes, but with affection rather than true irritation.

"That was so rude," I whispered.

"Fine," Sterling said, squeezing my fingers. "I apologize."

As he said it, the double doors across the room opened and a man strolled through. He was taller than Sterling, but had the same chiseled features and razor-sharp brown eyes. The same wavy brown hair, even if it was speckled with gray. Like Sterling, he clearly missed nothing, and it took a fraction of an instant for his gaze to zero in on me.

"I must be hearing things," the man said. "Sterling didn't apologize when he deposited his mother's car in the Hudson. Either the hotel is incinerating around us or the rehabilitation continues." He flashed a huge handsome grin that was alarmingly identical to Sterling's, except lacking the self-satisfied little curl in the corners. "Is this really her? I've been looking forward to this, Harper. Can't believe the changes in him. He's passing all his classes— even talking about majoring in history. Any other tricks up your sleeve—raise the dead? Levitate?"

I was queasy as all three men turned and looked at me. And I was oh-so-glad I'd worn heels. I felt minuscule standing there with the two of them, and I couldn't fathom why Sterling had brought me here to play conquering hero when I'd done nothing to rehabilitate Sterling Lane except fight back.

"I'm afraid Sterling drained me of all my powers," I said, willing my voice not to shake. "I'm fresh out of miracles."

A cell phone pinged and Admiral Lane glanced at the display. "I need to take this one. I apologize for the interruption. I'll only be a moment." He winked at me and

I was astounded by the similarity between father and son. "Now that he finally cares what someone thinks, I look forward to watching him squirm. The stories I have to tell. Prepare yourself for seventeen years' worth of pent-up parental frustration."

"I look forward to it, sir," I said. And I meant it.

"I think I'll sit this one out," Sterling muttered. "Let the three of you amuse yourselves while I hit the bar."

I didn't think his father heard the last part, but I couldn't quite be sure. His father disappeared through the double doors, his posture every bit as crisp as the khaki slacks and white button-down shirt he was wearing.

"I like your dad."

"Good," he said. "He likes you, too. I knew he would."

"Care to tell me what this is all about?" I asked. "Don't get me wrong, I'm looking forward to making fun of you at dinner. But you've been a little light on the details of exactly what this favor is."

"Figured I'd just steamroll you into going along with it." He hadn't loosened his grip on my hand, and now he towed me across the room, toward a closed door.

Uncle Howard glanced up from his laptop screen. "Where are you going?"

"The bathroom," Sterling replied, pushing me through the open door.

"You're going together?" Uncle Howard was laughing now. And my face went bright red.

"Yep," Sterling said. "She has aquaphobia."

Whatever Uncle Howard said in response was muffled by the *click* of the bathroom door as it slid into place.

Sterling moved closer, and his chest brushed mine. Then he put his hands on my hips, lifting me up onto the vanity. He stood there, right in front of me, planting his hands on either side of me.

He leaned in to kiss me but I turned my face away. "You're not as hot as you seem to think," I lied. "You can't distract me. You have to explain first."

"How about after?" His lips grazed my neck, and I was about to relent—because honestly, Sterling Lane was inconveniently good at a great number of things. This most of all.

"After what, exactly? Because after that summons, I was pretty sure you expected a lot more than I'm prepared to give right now."

"I would never do that." He sounded so shocked as he pulled back and cupped my face in both hands. "Never. My father wanted to meet you. I told him everything about us. How you changed me—changed everything." He paused. "Sure, it started off as a rivalry thing—God, you pissed me off—but then it changed. I had to show you I could keep up. It wasn't enough to just know it myself. You were—are— the first big crush of my life." Sterling looked me straight in the eye as he said it. So confident, so unafraid to just put it all out there, like Kendall had said. "So when I told the admiral, he wanted to meet you. Tonight we have dinner with him and Uncle Howard. My grandmother, too. But I figured next Friday it could be just us. Then we'll, you know, see where it goes." He shrugged.

My head was spinning. Sure, I'd known it was a possibility he'd meant what he said in the headmaster's office. But this was over and above what I'd ever imagined. He'd even invited the attorney general here to meet me. Me. It was the most thoughtful gesture I could ever imagine. My hands pressed themselves flat against his chest, then clutched the fabric of his shirt, wrinkling the freshly pressed cotton. There was a pretty good chance I was never letting go.

"What about no second dates?" I asked.

"You broke your Rules," he said with a self-satisfied smirk. "And look how great it worked out. You get all this." He motioned to himself with one hand. "Figured I'd give it a shot."

"I broke some of them, and only because it was an emergency," I told him. "I'm still the same. You haven't changed me. You realize that, right? We're still a disaster, and I'm pretty sure I still hate you." But as I said it, my hand broke rank and slid around his neck, guiding his face to mine. "I'm still the same," I repeated. "I haven't changed."

"I'm counting on it," he said. "All uptight and erratic. Anything less than full-blown Harper and I'm likely to get bored. Let's say we agree to disagree? All the time, but with a few notable exceptions. Like, say, in bathrooms. Or Parker's bedroom."

Those memories were about all I could take. I grabbed his tie, right by that trim little Windsor knot, and yanked him forward. A jolt of adrenaline shot through me when his eyes widened in surprise.

Nothing was as exhilarating as catching Sterling Lane off guard.

I kissed him, curling my hands into his hair until there was no way he was ever getting away. His hands slid around my waist, holding me so close I could barely breathe.

"I'm counting on you for some discreetly dismissed felony charges in the future," I said. "And some horribly smug little smiles."

"They're all yours," he murmured.

My eyes were closed, but I could still feel his smile as his lips found mine again.

Even though it might seem like I'd given in, that I'd let that lazy, spoiled boy corrupt me, ruin me, I hadn't. I knew it in my heart. In the way the Rules were back, arranging themselves in balcony seats to watch the remainder of the show.

All but one. Rule 538 was conspicuously absent, and I knew it would stay that way.

Because at the end of the day, changing my mind wasn't against the Rules. Neither was dating, or being locked in a bathroom at the Saint James Hotel kissing a boy with liquid trouble coursing through his veins. I could still be me, and he could still be him, and we'd figure out what we'd be together.

And I would know.

Because I loathe Sterling Lane.

Every bone in that perfect body.

ACKNOWLEDGMENTS

This book would not exist without the support of my amazing critique group. Martha, Heidi, Whitney, and Veronica, thank you for pulling me through and making me laugh when I need it most. I am eternally grateful to the Entangled team for taking a chance on *Sterling*. The amazing Kate Brauning, who has tirelessly read and commented, and her guidance has taken this project to the next level. I was no longer alone in Harper's head! Last but not least, thank you to my husband and children for putting up with me when I'm living inside a book for weeks at a time. I couldn't chase this dream without your sacrifices and support.

GRAB THE ENTANGLED TEEN RELEASES READERS ARE TALKING ABOUT!

OFF THE ICE
BY JULIE CROSS

All is fair in love and hockey…

Claire O'Connor is back in Juniper Falls, but that doesn't mean she wants to be. One semester off, that's what she promised herself. Just long enough to take care of her father and keep the family business—a hockey bar beside the ice rink—afloat. After that, she's getting the hell out. Again.

Enter Tate Tanley. What happened between them the night before she left town resurfaces the second they lay eyes on each other. But the guy she remembers has been replaced by a total hottie. When Tate is unexpectedly called in to take over for the hockey team's star goalie, suddenly he's in the spotlight and on his way to becoming just another egotistical varsity hockey player. And Claire's sworn off Juniper Falls hockey players for good.

It's the absolute worst time to fall in love.

For Tate and Claire, hockey isn't just a game. And they both might not survive a body check to the heart.

REMEMBER ME FOREVER
BY SARA WOLF

Isis Blake hasn't fallen in love in three years, forty-three weeks, and two days. Or so she thinks. The boy she maybe-sort-of-definitely loved and sort-of-maybe-definitely hated has dropped off the face of the planet, leaving a Jack Hunter–shaped hole. Determined to be happy, Isis fills it in with lies and puts on a brave smile for her new life at Ohio State University. But the smile lasts only until he shows up. The threat from her past, her darkest moment…Nameless, attending OSU right alongside her. Whispering that he has something Isis wants—something she needs to see to move forward. To move on.

Isis is good at pretending everything is okay, at putting herself back together. But Jack Hunter is better.

OTHER BREAKABLE THINGS
BY KELLEY YORK AND ROWAN ALTWOOD

Luc Argent has always been intimately acquainted with death. After a car crash got him a second chance at life—via someone else's transplanted heart—he tried to embrace it. He truly did. But he always knew death could be right around the corner again. And now it is. Luc is ready to let his failing heart give out, ready to give up. A road trip to Oregon—where death with dignity is legal—is his answer. But along for the ride is his best friend, Evelyn. And she's not giving up so easily.

SECRETS OF A RELUCTANT PRINCESS
BY CASEY GRIFFIN

At Beverly Hills High, you have to be ruthless to survive…

Adrianna Bottom always wanted to be liked. But this wasn't *exactly* what she had in mind. Now, she's in the spotlight…and out of her geeky comfort zone. She'll do whatever it takes to turn the rumor mill in her favor—even if it means keeping secrets. So far, it's working.

Wear the right clothes. Say the right things. Be seen with the right people.

Kevin, the adorable sketch artist who shares her love of all things nerd, isn't *exactly* the right people. But that doesn't stop Adrianna from crushing on him. The only way she can spend time with him is in disguise, as Princess Andy, the masked girl he's been LARPing with. If he found out who she really was, though, he'd hate her.

The rules have been set. The teams have their players. Game on.

Violet Grenade
by Victoria Scott

DOMINO (def.): A girl with blue hair and a demon in her mind.

CAIN (def.): A stone giant on the brink of exploding.

MADAM KARINA (def.): A woman who demands obedience.

WILSON (def.): The one who will destroy them all.

When Madam Karina discovers Domino in an alleyway, she offers her a position inside her home for entertainers in secluded West Texas. Left with few alternatives and an agenda of her own, Domino accepts. It isn't long before she is fighting her way up the ranks to gain the madam's approval. But after suffering weeks of bullying and unearthing the madam's secrets, Domino decides to leave. It'll be harder than she thinks, though, because the madam doesn't like to lose inventory. But then, Madam Karina doesn't know about the person living inside Domino's mind. Madam Karina doesn't know about Wilson.

Lost Girls
by Merrie Destefano

Yesterday, Rachel went to sleep curled up in her grammy's quilt, worrying about geometry. Today, she woke up in a ditch, bloodied, bruised, and missing a year of her life. She's not the only girl to go missing within the last year...but she's the only girl to come back. And as much as her dark, dangerous new life scares her, it calls to her. Seductively. But wherever she's been—whomever she's been with—isn't done with her yet...